A Fine Target

Also by Margaret Duffy

Brass Eagle
Dressed To Kill
Gallows Bird
Prospect of Death

A Fine Target

Margaret Duffy

PIATKUS

First published in Great Britain in 1998 by
Judy Piatkus (Publishers) Ltd of
5 Windmill Street, London W1

This edition published 1998

*A catalogue record for this book
is available from the British Library*

ISBN 0 7499 0446 1

Phototypeset in Times by Intype London Ltd

Printed and bound in Great Britain by
Butler & Tanner Ltd, Frome and London

Prologue

The big, dark blue BMW had remained in the car park on the shores of Chew Valley Lake, near Bristol, for two days and, except for a woman living alone in a nearby cottage, no one had noticed. Fishermen, yachtsmen and bird-watchers had come and gone and not one of these people, seemingly, had spared a glance for the car that, as it were, waited for someone to come and drive it away. The woman had ventured up to it once and perceived that the alarm was set – that's if the little flashing red light on the dash *was* the alarm indicator – and that was the only outward sign that the vehicle had not been stolen; for surely no thief abandoning his booty would do such a thing. There was no apparent damage and nothing seemed to be missing.

As for the car itself: had it been a sentient being, and not merely 1,500 kilograms of machinery, it would have told a tale of violence and death. But a car is, after all, just a tool in the hands of its owner and when that person has departed nothing remains to tell of the manner of their going. Except for clues discernible only to a forensic scientist.

The woman in the cottage, a kindly, worrying soul, was closing her curtains on the second evening – and by this time she was not sure whether she was worrying about the car or whoever normally drove it – when she realised that she was being rather stupid in not telephoning the police. She went to the phone, hesitated momentarily when it occurred to her that the vehicle might belong to visitors staying farther along the shore at the house where the people lived like hermits and spoke to no one, shrugged to

1

herself and dialled. No, she told herself sternly, the time for timidity was past.

Even though it was a little after ten at night it was still very warm, the mid-summer day having been sultry and cloudless. Out on the lake small ducks dipped and dived and a family of swans glided hopefully and regally in the direction of a group of late walkers. The lightest of breezes ruffled the water and caused the reeds to stir with a dry rustling sound. It would have taken a very keen-sighted person to notice the human hand in the clump of reeds nearest to the shore.

It was a man's hand, the fingers long and delicate-looking, unadorned by rings. The rest of the body, waterlogged, was still settling slowly among the submerged stems of the reeds. The water was shallow here and the corpse was almost at the end of its journey. Already, tiny creatures, dragonfly larvae and sticklebacks, were exploring this surprising new world that had suddenly been made available to them. They swam through and around the locks of black, greying hair that moved this way and that with the currents of the water. The eyes, closed peacefully as if in sleep, were also grey and in life had mirrored a lively and keen intellect. But this had not been a peaceful death: the bullet hole in the left temple was neat enough but the exit wound was still clouding the water with red, attracting yet more small fish and water creatures.

Chapter 1

Chief Inspector James Carrick parked his car at the rear of Bath's Manvers Street police station and ran the fifty yards or so to the back door of the building. His haste was due to the fact that it was teeming with rain and he had forgotten to bring a coat. He had his own reserved space at the front but this was at present occupied by another vehicle, an ancient and rusting Mini.

This was the culmination of a very bad morning – he had had a couple of calls to make on his way to the station – that had started with the onset of a thunderstorm, still ongoing, at two a.m. and progressed after several sleepless hours to the discovery that his alarm clock was unaccountably three-quarters of an hour slow. After a few minor domestic disasters – the toaster incinerating his breakfast and refusing to yield the blackened remains, realising he was wearing yesterday's shirt – he had gone out to his car to see that he had a puncture in his near-side front tyre. Most of these things would not have happened if his wife, Joanna, had been at home. Perhaps he now relied on her too much to organise him in the mornings.

Scattering drops of water as he shook it from his fair hair, he strode through the door intent on spreading a little mild terror. It must be said in his defence that Carrick was normally a man very slow to anger.

Sergeant Woods, on duty at the desk, was taking details from a woman about her noisy neighbours. When she saw that they were about to be interrupted she gave Carrick a withering look.

'Who owns that filthy rust-bucket out the front?' he demanded to know.

Woods, a diplomat to the last breath and having no idea to what Carrick was referring, smiled bravely and calmly. 'I'll find out for you, sir.'

'I want it *moved*.'

'Yes, sir.'

'This is a nick, not a scrapyard.'

He accidentally timed his eruption into the main office with a simultaneous crack of thunder right overhead and was greeted by the sight of Detective Sergeant Bob Ingrams spilling coffee all over himself.

'God, sir, you gave me a shock,' said Ingrams, mopping frantically with a none-too-clean handkerchief.

Lightning zipped seemingly right past the window, there was a huge bang and all the lights went out.

'Anything I ought to know about?' Carrick asked in the ensuing gloom, peering into the loaded in-tray on his sergeant's desk.

'Another couple of tourists were mugged last night – Americans.'

'Where, exactly?'

'Ryan's Walk – down by the river near Pulteney Bridge.'

Carrick frowned. 'How many's that since this time last week?'

'Six, sir.'

'Were they hurt?'

'The man was knocked to the ground when he initially refused to hand over his wallet. They got that, his video camera and his wife's watch and rings which she threw at them in case they decided to do anything else to her husband.'

'Any descriptions?'

'It sounds like the same pair that committed all the others. Both in their twenties, white, one with earrings, the other a skinhead type with leathers and chains.'

'Where are the Americans staying?'

'At the Royalty in North Parade. Their name's Hausner.'

'I'll go and see them. I want you to drop everything else and make this a number one priority. Find out from Bristol

4

if they've been given any similar descriptions of muggers recently. These young thugs might be transferring their attentions here looking for richer, easier prey. Let me know if you need help and I'll organise something.' He grinned wolfishly. 'Who knows? The Royalty might have some real coffee that's still hot.'

Ingrams cleared his throat, aware that the information he was about to impart would really ruin Carrick's morning. 'Inspector Hobbs is here.'

'Here?' whispered Carrick, a forefinger pointing floorwards.

'In your office.'

'We *are* talking about Crispin Hobbs?'

Ingrams nodded.

Still speaking quietly Carrick said, 'And what does the grapevine tell us about the purpose of his visit?'

'It seems he's been posted here to be your right-hand man.'

Carrick groaned. 'What the hell's my right hand done to deserve that?'

Hobbs had been thumbing through a file on the desk but dropped it, jumping like a shot stag when the door of the room detonated inwards and Carrick entered. They had met already, before Carrick had been promoted, and on that occasion the blood on the carpet – dangerously close to fact rather than being a figure of speech – had been Hobbs's.

For several seconds there was absolute silence.

'I've an idea the Super didn't tell you,' Hobbs observed, adding 'sir' just a little too late.

'He's in California playing golf,' Carrick said. 'Do I take it that you're temporarily filling our vacancy?'

'It's permanent. At least – so far as these things can be.'

Carrick surveyed the man he had once threatened with violence. 'You'd better sit down.'

Hobbs drew up a chair. General opinion of the repeatable kind on his previous visit was that he resembled a tailor's dummy modelling designer clothing and had about as much flair and imagination. This was indeed fair comment as he had a pasty, somewhat bland face, neatly combed straight, mouse-coloured hair and a thin, almost non-existent mous-

5

tache. There had been a few complaints from the victims of crime that he had walked into their misery and destitution with a designer sneer on his face.

After another short silence Carrick said, 'You once accused me of lurking in the wings playing bloody Macbeth. I've no objection to carrying on in that vein if you continue to be a flippant, offensive smart-arse.'

Hobbs shook his head. 'I treat situations as I think fit. But don't let it worry you, the situation's different now. And insubordination's not one of my failings.'

Quite. He was also a toady.

'I prefer a good working relationship with my staff,' Carrick said.

'Time will tell,' Hobbs said with a thin smile, 'sir.'

Carrick ignored the remark. 'I have to go out. I'd like you to start collating all the evidence we have on a robbery at a computer store in the city centre two days ago. A security guard was clubbed to the ground and is in hospital with a fractured skull. Sergeant Ingrams has all the details.'

Carrick left Hobbs sitting there and, borrowing a Mounted Branch waterproof that had been hanging in a locker room for weeks waiting for someone to claim it, went out into the rain. He left in his wake a very faint aroma of horse.

Ingrams watched him leaving for a moment and then turned away with a shrug. Carrick's promotion had left the position of DI vacant and there was no one at Manvers Street with sufficient seniority – nay, ability, Ingrams was forced to admit – to fill it. That meant a newcomer. There had been some temporary assistance from Headquarters over the months but then while Carrick had been on leave recently a rumour started as to who might fill the vacant post. Most people had hoped that the rumour was wrong. Clearly, it had not been.

And now, of course, Carrick had remarried. His first wife had died from a rare form of bone cancer several years previously. Ingrams kept well clear of the new bride, Joanna, Carrick's one-time sergeant, mainly for the reason that the lady had a devastating right hook. This fact he had learned painfully after making an unwise comment at their last

6

meeting. No, he had discovered, you do not make leery sexual remarks to today's newly independent women.

Woods arrived with several buff-coloured files under one arm and dropped three of them on Ingrams's desk. 'The last time that little toad showed his face in here we were almost on a war footing in a week.'

Ingrams scooped up the files and hurled them into a tray on the next, unoccupied, desk giving Woods a dirty look as he did so.

'Oh, and the coffee machine's broken down,' Woods added.

'That's because there's a power cut,' Ingrams pointed out heavily.

'Funny, it doesn't usually leak water all over the floor when it's turned off,' was Woods's parting shot.

Hobbs wandered in. 'I don't seem to have a desk,' he said. His gaze came to rest on the one next to Ingrams's.

'That's Gascon's, sir,' he said hurriedly. 'He's out on a job.'

'Perhaps you could fix me up with something then,' Hobbs said. 'Someone said that Carrick's old office is being used as a store. I'd like the stuff all shifted out so I can use the room.'

'You'll have to see Admin about that, sir,' Ingrams told him. 'It's being used for some of the records as the records office is full to bursting. When they build the new extension next year we'll have more space.'

Hobbs shrugged. 'It's not my worry. I'll just use Carrick's room until something's organised. Well, don't stand there like a moron, man – find me the stuff on the computer store robbery.'

Outside, a youth who had been buying a new pair of windscreen wipers for his Mini from the car parts dealer opposite got into it and drove away. The silencer fell off as a rear wheel bumped down the kerb and the vehicle roared off, audible above the next rumble of thunder.

The Royalty was not a large hotel but very popular with visitors to the city as it overlooked Parade Gardens and had a French restaurant that was reputed to be the finest in

7

the West Country. Carrick spared a regretful glance for the magnificent scarlet pelargoniums in stone urns to either side of the entrance, being pounded to pieces by the rain – the pavement scattered with petals like spots of blood – then plunged indoors.

'They're at breakfast,' the receptionist, a middle-aged woman, reported after he had told her the purpose of his visit and shown her his warrant card. 'In the Beaufort Room. Shall I tell them you're here?'

Carrick could smell fresh coffee. And grilled bacon and kippers and . . . 'I don't want to intrude on their meal. Perhaps I could wait here?' He indicated a chair in the foyer.

'Is it about the mugging?'

'Yes.'

'I'm sure they'll be *delighted* to see you. Such a pleasant couple. It always seems to be nice people who have dreadful things happen to them, doesn't it? I'll check with them.' She went away but returned almost immediately, beckoning to Carrick. In the doorway she said, 'I do hope you catch these crooks. A man travelling alone who stayed here was robbed last week. Bath will get a bad reputation.'

'We have good descriptions,' Carrick told her.

The Hausners, both of generous build, were tucking into a large English breakfast, giving every impression that their ordeal of the previous night had not spoiled their appetites.

'Siddown, Chief!' boomed the robbery victim. 'Herbert and Connie Hausner at your service. Call me Herbie. Everyone does.'

'I kinda hope, Herbie,' his wife ventured, 'that he's at ours.' She gazed somewhat nervously up at Carrick. 'Yes, please sit down. Would you like some coffee? There's a power cut but the kitchen here has gas stoves.' She flinched as there was a loud rumble of thunder. 'Do excuse me. I'm all jumpy this morning.'

Carrick gladly accepted the offer and had time to assess the Hausners while another cup and saucer and a further pot of coffee were brought by the waiting staff. The pair were probably in their late-fifties, not powerfully rich, he felt, but enjoying the fruits of an industrious life. They were

8

both fair-haired, Herbie's thin and greying, and had the kind of outdoor complexions and faded blue eyes that Carrick had come across before with friends who sailed a lot. He wondered if the Hausners had a boat at home.

'They were just kids really,' Herbie said. 'The young unmentionables who attacked us. If I'd been younger and on my own I'd have kicked their asses. But I didn't dare risk Connie getting hurt.'

'I let them have my mother's ring,' she mourned softly. 'Such a pity with her dead all these years.'

'You've given a full description of the items stolen last night,' Carrick said. 'Have you remembered anything else that might be useful to us?'

They both thought for a moment and then Herbie said, 'I'd know them again, that's for sure. They didn't have masks on or anything. Must have been damned sure of themselves.'

'Or just plain stupid,' Carrick observed.

He was given long thoughtful looks.

'That too,' Connie agreed. 'The one with no hair didn't exactly look as though he'd fetched his brain out of the closet that morning. It was lucky for us that we'd left most of our travellers' cheques in our room here. Plus Mother's pearls and the diamond bracelet that Aunt Augusta gave me last fall for my birthday. She's a really old lady now – must be in her late-nineties though I daren't ask. She's—'

'Now don't go gossipin' on, honey,' Herbie admonished fondly through a mouthful of bacon. He waved his fork in their visitor's direction. 'The Chief here hasn't come to gossip. Have you?' he shot at Carrick.

Carrick grinned at him, genuinely amused. 'I came to make sure that you weren't hurt. And, as I said—'

It was his turn to be interrupted. 'The other fella, the little one with rings in his ears . . . Lord, he really looked as though he needed a wash.'

'You noticed that even though it was dark?'

'Yup. There was a street light not too far away. That's how we saw the way they were dressed. Perhaps the guy's a garage mechanic or whatever. It looked like oil on his face. Are there any coal mines around here?'

'Not any longer,' Carrick replied. 'You said in your state-

9

ment last night that they were both wearing jeans, one had on a tee shirt and the other a leather jacket with chains.'

'And trainers,' Herbie added.

'No, honey, the big one was wearing boots,' Connie said. 'Long ones that sort of went with his jacket. Perhaps he had a motor bike.'

'Did you hear a bike?' Carrick asked.

Neither of them had, Herbie commenting that he was too busy picking himself up off the sidewalk to hear anything.

'He had a lisp,' Connie said decidedly. 'It might have been because of his teeth.'

'Teeth?' Carrick queried, getting out his notebook.

'Yeah. Perhaps we forgot to say. The little one, the dirty one who did all the talking, had gaps in his front teeth. Been fighting, I should guess.'

'How long are you in the city?' Carrick asked, making a note of this.

'It depends,' Herbie said. 'We're not on a package tour if that's what you mean – just going where the fancy takes us.'

'Would you be prepared to attend an identity parade?'

'What, pick those hoodlums out from a line of other guys? Sure, why not?'

'I'm not so sure,' Connie said. 'I mean, what if they turn mean on us or it's the wrong ones?'

'Honey, they'll be in custody, for God's sake,' said Herbie with some asperity. 'And if it's the wrong ones the Chief here'll know it's the wrong ones.'

Well, yes, sort of, Carrick thought. The trouble was he had enough material from local known talent for several identity parades, missing teeth included. 'We're giving this priority,' he assured them. 'Meanwhile I suggest you go for your walks by the river during the day and not late at night, and leave as many of your valuables as possible in the hotel safe. If we make any arrests and recover stolen property I'll be in touch with you immediately. Please let me know when you intend to leave Bath or if you happen to spot these people loafing around. Don't under any circumstances approach them yourselves.' He wrote down his phone number on a slip of paper torn from his notebook and gave it to them, then he finished his coffee and left.

10

Herbie shook his head, smiling. 'These English cops. I wonder what sort of results he gets being all quiet and polite like that. I've never seen a cop like him at home – like as not we'd have been bawled out for taking risks back in Gaynesville.'

'He's as tough as hell,' Connie declared. 'You weren't looking into the man's eyes.'

'I was,' Herbie argued petulantly. 'They were blue.'

'And as bleak as the Appalachians in winter,' his spouse told him. 'He gets results all right.'

'With the ladies?' Herbie teased.

'You didn't notice his wedding ring either,' she said triumphantly.

The rain had not abated when Carrick paused in the hotel entrance, having collected his still-dripping coat. Now he had Hobbs to contend with. No doubt the man was using his, Carrick's, office as there was nowhere else for him to work at the moment.

'I shall find a space for him,' he promised the cascading heavens. 'Even if it means turning the whole bloody nick upside down to do it.'

The moment when he had lost his temper at their previous spell of duty together had been a bad mistake. Nothing had actually happened, he had merely found himself closing in on the man with malice aforethought after Hobbs had provoked him too far. The speed with which Hobbs had bolted through the door had not gone unnoticed, however, and all kinds of lurid rumours had circulated for a while, not least that Carrick had thrown his skene dhu in the general direction of a certain delicate part of that gentleman's anatomy. Now, a *sgian dubh* is not a throwing knife, Carrick found himself thinking furiously as he quickmarched through the rain. You keep them in your hand and slit people from stem to stern with them.

His pager bleeped and it was quicker to break into a run than find a phone, his own mobile having been left at home, another of the morning's mishaps. Unusually, it was Woods and not a member of his CID team who wanted to speak to him.

11

'This might be absolutely nothing to worry about, sir, at least as far as you're concerned, but last night a woman – a Mrs Adams – reported that a car had been left at Chew Valley Lake for a couple of days and no one had been to collect it. It's rather a good motor and she was worried that someone might steal it. We've checked on the owner and made enquiries about him but no one seems to know exactly where he is.'

'What has this to do with me?' Carrick asked.

'That's what I was just coming, to' said Woods, who hated being rushed to the point. 'I believe you know the man and I'm pretty sure I've seen a car of the description, a dark blue BMW, parked outside the nick last year when he was involved in a case you were investigating. Gillard, sir. Patrick Gillard. The address is Bracken Ridge, Lydtor, Devon.'

For a moment Carrick was bereft of speech. Then he said, 'I take it the car hasn't already been reported stolen?'

'No, sir. And the vehicle's alarm's set. A phone call was made to the registered address and it appears that only a nanny is there looking after the two children. Gillard's wife is a writer and is in the States in connection with a book launch. The nanny wouldn't give any information about Gillard's whereabouts over the phone, saying only that he is on leave.'

'He works for MI5,' Carrick said.

Woods smiled deferentially. 'Yes, it was guessed that he was involved with something along those lines from the way she worded her reply. Someone from the Devon and Cornwall Force was asked to speak to her. They confirmed in a fax what you've just said, sir. But she genuinely doesn't know where he is – only that he left home last week, Wednesday morning, and said he'd be away for a few days.'

Carrick was feeling distinctly shaken by all this. He said, 'He's in love with that car of his. Positively the last thing he'd do under normal circumstances would be to leave it in a public car park and go off somewhere else without telling anyone.'

'It needn't mean anything sinister's happened though, sir.'

'We're talking about someone on several terrorist hit-lists.'

'Do you know any reason why he should be in the Bristol area?'

'No, I don't. His parents live at Hinton Littlemoor but that's only a few miles from here and in the opposite direction. Did the nanny know exactly where his wife, Ingrid, is?'

'New York, sir.'

'Well, we can't leave the car where it is, that's for sure. I'll arrange to have it moved to the pound. But before we go anywhere near it I want someone from Bomb Squad to give it a once over.'

Woods's eyes widened.

'The car's a replacement for one that was destroyed in a bomb attack a couple of years ago,' Carrick said. 'I'm damned if I'm taking any chances.'

'I hope he doesn't turn up while it's being lifted onto the lorry,' the Sergeant observed dryly.

'I shall give him hell if he does,' Carrick said over his shoulder as he went out.

He supposed he ought to take Bob Ingrams with him, he usually did. But the muggings investigation was more important right now than a Lieutenant-colonel leaving his car lying around in the English countryside. Carrick was praying that there was nothing more sinister to it than that.

13

Chapter 2

Chew Valley Lake was situated to the south of Bristol and supplied that city with water. Fed by numerous small streams that ran off the Mendip Hills, the lake was several square miles in extent. Rightly so, it was a favourite beauty spot. On the eastern shore, near the hamlet of Little Hollow, was a car park. There were only three vehicles in total when Carrick arrived; a much-travelled Land Rover with canoes on a roof-rack, a Volvo estate hitched to a caravan, and the BMW. Thankfully, it had almost stopped raining.

Carrick parked some distance away and approached Patrick Gillard's car on foot. There was a folded newspaper on the front passenger seat, the *Guardian*, the date not visible, a green waterproof jacket and a well-thumbed road atlas in the back. The jacket was not new either and had patches of dried mud on it. Carrick stared at it in surprise. Patrick was not the kind of man to put such a grubby garment on his leather seats and he possessed, to Carrick's certain knowledge, a blue Barbour that was normally kept in the boot.

It was the kind of alarm that would go off if he so much as tried a door handle. Carrick wandered around the vehicle, desperate for clues. At any moment he expected the familiar figure to appear; a tall, slim man with waving black hair, now greying, and a sombre air that was utterly banished when he smiled. Yes, a man of mercurial and contrasting moods; warm and yet keeping those around him at a distance, humorous and yet prone to moments of chilling reserve. Ingrid had once remarked to Carrick, smiling wryly,

14

that she sometimes wondered if Patrick acted a rôle all the time and she had never in fact discovered what he was really like. Afterwards, Carrick had perceived that the remark held a peculiar horror.

He made himself concentrate on the job in hand. It was perfectly possible, of course, that the car had developed some kind of fault and before Gillard could arrange repairs he had been summoned by his superiors to London, even though he was on leave. A request to a garage to collect the vehicle might have gone awry. But surely if his plans had changed he would have sent a message home?

Carrick radioed his contact in Bomb Squad.

The woman who had reported the car's presence lived in the only house in sight, a cottage that could have come straight from a children's storybook. There was a slight dip in the thatched roof and the windows, upstairs and down, peeped through creepers and rambler roses. Hollyhocks brushed the low eaves and more roses lined the black-and-white-tiled path to the front door. Through a side gate neat rows of runner beans with scarlet flowers could be glimpsed and there was one, quite sensational, sunflower.

Mrs Adams, who had observed his arrival and opened the door before he knocked, was in her seventies. Although her face was lined and her hair snow white she possessed a wiry, active frame that spoke of long hours looking after her immaculate garden.

'I hope I haven't wasted police time,' she said shyly when Carrick had introduced himself.

She reminded him of his mother and it was easy to smile reassuringly. 'Mrs Adams, if all citizens were as sharp-eyed and caring the police would have half the work they do now.'

She asked him in and folded away some embroidery from the settee by the window so he could sit down. The window was open and the garden seemed to be gaining entry through it, the ledge crammed with flowering plants in pots. On a chintz cushion set upon a wooden chair a tortoiseshell cat regarded him loftily with her orange eyes for a few seconds and then settled down for further sleep. An old clock ticked on the wall.

15

'Did you see the person who parked the car?' was Carrick's opening question.

Mrs Adams perched on the edge of an armchair opposite. 'No. There are a lot of comings and goings here on nice days as I'm sure you realise. I suppose I should have reported it when it was left for the first night but cars do get parked until very late some nights and I'd hate to get a reputation for being nosy. There's nothing worse than the curtain-twitching brigade.'

'Besides which, you're far too busy with your garden to have time to sit and watch what everyone's doing.'

'Yes, I am,' she agreed, making herself more comfortable. 'I didn't see whoever it was.' She paused. 'I'm not psychic either but the whole thing makes me feel uncomfortable. I hope he's all right. It must be a man surely – it's a man's car.'

'Have you ever noticed it here before?'

'No.'

'Have you any idea *when* it was parked here?'

'I think it might have been on Saturday evening but I've no real way of knowing. It was there when I first looked out on Sunday morning. That was quite early – I get up early in the summer and do some gardening before it gets too hot.'

'Around seven-thirty then?'

She smiled self-consciously. 'No, it was actually just after six. Samantha's always on the prowl for breakfast at around that time too.'

'And you think the car might have been there all night?'

'Just a feeling, that's all.'

'Did you hear anything in the night that might have been connected with the vehicle's arrival?'

'No, my room's at the back. I can't even hear the passing traffic.'

'Did you approach the car at all?'

'Oh, yes. Of course. I was worried that the driver might have been taken ill or something. Or be drunk or asleep on the back seat. I did that on the Sunday. There didn't seem to be anything amiss. At least ...'

'Yes?' Carrick encouraged.

16

'No, nothing,' Mrs Adams said with an emphatic shake of her head.

'Even the smallest details can be of vital importance.'

'No, nothing like clues of any kind. Just feelings. Policemen don't work on the feelings of old women.'

'You said you weren't psychic.'

'No, I'm not.'

'But you have a feeling about this car?'

After a longish pause, during which Carrick waited patiently, Mrs Adams said, speaking a trifle sharply, 'I sometimes have dreams, that's all. My mother used to say that I had an over-active imagination. I had a dream on Saturday night.'

'Tell me about it.'

'I'd rather not. If you act on it and it comes to nothing I shall have cost the police a lot of money and never be able to live it down.'

'Then let me be the judge and I shall take responsibility.'

After another silence she said, 'I've had dreams before and sometimes they come true. Not exactly though – there's usually a twist to them. I once dreamt that a tree fell on this house during a gale. But there are no large trees nearby. And then a friend wrote from Kent to tell me that an elm had been blown down and wrecked their garage. It seems as though I dream about me and mine and then something happens to someone else. It's not always bad things. Earlier this year I had a dream about my husband – he's been dead for over thirty years – and soon afterwards I was contacted by a friend of his who had emigrated to Canada. But the nightmare I had on Saturday night – and even to think about it makes me feel quite shaky – was that a man had dragged me down towards the lake, shot me and dumped my body in the water. I was dead but I could feel the stems of the reeds in my hands and the mud on my face. Then I woke up.'

Carrick suddenly felt stifled and took a deep, careful breath.

'Whereabouts in the lake?' he asked softly.

'In that clump of reeds closest to the bank. I think the man must have waded out with me but I wasn't aware of

17

anything like that.' She clasped her hands tightly together for a moment. 'I felt quite odd when I went up to the car on Sunday but it wasn't in my dream ... I'm so sorry, I should have asked you if you'd like some tea.'

Carrick accepted, realising that a hot drink would do her good. Then he said, 'The man in your dream – what was he like?'

'I couldn't see his face. He was wearing one of those dreadful balaclava things over his head. And his gun had a silencer on it.'

'It would've had to. Otherwise you would have heard the shot.'

Mrs Adams had paused on her way to the kitchen in order to answer his question. 'Now you're not talking about my dream.'

'No.'

A little later Carrick left the cottage, having learned nothing else of interest. The sun was hazy through thin cloud and the afternoon was already hot; the previous night's storm did not seem to have cleared the air at all. The road steamed and, over the expanse of water, a faint mist had formed.

Nothing untoward could be glimpsed in the nearest clump of reeds.

A patrol car drew up just then and two uniformed constables got out. One opened a rear door and another man emerged. Carrick did not recognise anyone so introduced himself and learned that the two constables were stationed in Bristol.

'This is Mr Grantly, sir,' one of them said, indicating the man with them. 'He's the service manager from the BMW main dealer in the city centre. He has the keys.'

'You're a genius!' Carrick exclaimed. 'How did this come about?'

The man smiled his pleasure. 'Well, we thought it would have to be moved fairly soon, sir,' he began, glancing in his colleague's direction to include him in the praise. 'And we had an idea that CID might be interested as the owner's involved with the security services. We were passing the dealership and popped in to see if there were skeleton keys or whatever.'

'They hit the jackpot,' Grantly said. 'We had the vehicle in last week to do some work on it.'

'So how come you still have a set of keys?' Carrick enquired.

Grantly was short, fat and genial. 'I'll tell you the full story. It was brought in on Thursday morning with a leaking radiator. As it was still under warranty we fitted it with a new one free of charge. There was some urgency – the owner doesn't live in the area – and we did the job in twenty-four hours. But it wasn't actually collected until Saturday morning. For some reason there were two sets of keys and the mechanic put one set in my office while the other was put with the paperwork at reception. I wasn't there when the vehicle was handed back and the keys in the office were overlooked. I discovered them on Monday morning, yesterday. It's just a question of putting them in an envelope and posting them back.'

'You say it was brought in on Thursday. Just out of the blue?'

'No, there had been a phone call on Wednesday afternoon.'

'Did you see the owner when the car was brought in?'

'No, my office doesn't overlook the reception desk.'

'Presumably the car wasn't bought from you?'

'That's correct – it was purchased from our outlet in Plymouth.'

'I shall need to talk to members of your staff who were on duty when the car was brought in and collected. Are you aware of any comments the driver made? Did he mention a destination?'

'Not to my knowledge, Chief Inspector.'

Carrick asked for, and was given, the keys. Then he said, 'We'll wait until someone comes to check it over before we do anything else. Mr Grantly, perhaps you wouldn't mind waiting in the car – someone will run you back shortly.' Speaking to the others he said, 'I think it's time we cordoned off the whole area. No more cars are to be parked here and anyone who returns to the vehicles already here is to be

19

asked to leave immediately. Perhaps you'd check that no one's asleep in the caravan.'

'Foul play?' Grantly whispered.

'I don't know yet,' Carrick replied. 'Did you let him have a courtesy car while this one was being repaired?'

'We would have done if he'd asked,' said Grantly, resentment in his tone as though he felt he was being blamed for some, as yet unspecified, misdemeanour.

No, Carrick thought, Gillard would not have mentioned destinations or his plans. Those who work for the security services never discuss their movements, not even when they are on holiday. But what had he used for transport in the interim?

During the next half hour a member of the Bomb Squad arrived and declared the vehicle free from dangerous devices. Shortly after his arrival a police recovery vehicle drew up and preparations were made to lift the BMW onto it. But first, Carrick donned gloves, deactivated the alarm and unlocked it.

There was a slight but pleasant smell inside; aftershave perhaps, and leather. Carrick picked up the waterproof jacket and examined it. There was no clue as to ownership and the pockets were empty but for three wrappers from sweets, mints of some kind. The newspaper was dated the previous Saturday and judging by the crumpled state of it had been well-read. The road atlas yielded no information either.

Suppose the car had been left at Hinton Littlemoor where Gillard's parents lived – his father was rector there – and *had* subsequently been stolen but no one had yet realised it was missing? Perhaps the couple were themselves away. It was a long shot but worth investigating.

'No luck, sir?' asked one of the constables.

'Not really,' Carrick said. 'But none of the stuff in the car reflects the man I know to be the owner. For example, I've only ever seen him with *The Times* or *Telegraph*. Have the vehicle taken to the pound and take Mr Grantly back to Bristol. Talk to the people who checked the car in and out and get a description of the driver. Perhaps you'll get back to me later.'

He glanced at the clump of reeds as he drove away. Hopefully, an old lady's nightmares played no part in this puzzle.

Even after the night's heavy rain Hinton Littlemoor was a picture-postcard village; the winding street lined with thatched cottages, the tiny village green, the quaint Ring O'Bells pub next to the church of St Michael. The rectory was reached down a drive to one side of the church boundary wall with a much larger house to the rear, The Grange. But Carrick was not beguiled by thatch and whimsy on this occasion. His sense of unease had increased with each mile of his journey.

He saw with a sinking heart that the Gillards were at home. In fact, they were both in the garden having what appeared to be a discussion about the roses. The rector's wife had a trug filled with spent blooms at her feet and was wielding a pair of secateurs with aplomb. They both approached the car that had entered their drive.

There could be no doubt as to their identities even though Carrick had never met them before. This couple were not house-sitters. The rector was tall, dark and slim like his son, his wife elegant even in old gardening clothes. Any lingering doubt Carrick might have been experiencing was immediately dispelled when he got out of the car and found himself gazing into her eyes. They were grey with the same vibrant glitter he remembered so well.

Carrick introduced himself, adding, 'I'm a friend of Patrick's.' It sounded so banal.

'John Gillard,' said the rector as they shook hands. 'This is my wife, Elspeth. I hope that nothing's wrong?'

Carrick said, 'Is there any reason, to your knowledge, why Patrick's car should have been left at Chew Valley Lake – possibly on Saturday night?'

'Left there?' Elspeth said. 'No, of course not. *Left* there?'

'I think you'd better come in,' John said and led the way indoors. His wife fell into step beside Carrick.

'Patrick has spoken about you,' she confided. 'You're not really worried about him, are you? It really *is* his car?'

She was the kind of woman to expect honest answers.

'Yes, to both questions,' Carrick said.

She frowned. 'We've been away for a few days to stay

21

with friends on Sark. They used to live next door. May I call you James? I feel as though I've known you for ages.'

Carrick smiled his permission.

She nodded briskly. 'Well, James, I've had some really bad scares with Patrick. *Really* bad scares. When he came back from the Falklands he was not only horribly injured but his mental state was a bit scary too. And then there was the business of him getting shot in Canada. *Then* he went and turned himself into a Hell's Angel for another assignment and I thought his father would never speak to him again. There have been all kinds of trouble and carpetings for him, and I've had armed police in the onion bed and heaven knows what else! And now you say he's left his car at Chew Valley Lake and hasn't been back to collect it? The last time I spoke to him on the phone he said he was going on leave.'

'When was this?' Carrick asked.

'Just before we went away. Let me see . . .'

'The Sunday,' her husband said over his shoulder.

'Yes, of course. I phoned when we got back from the mid-morning Communion Service. Ingrid was flying out to the States later in the day and I wanted to wish her *bon voyage*.'

'Had he planned to do anything in particular, do you know?' Carrick asked.

'Well, as you might expect, Patrick doesn't usually *say*. Not even to us. He has to be very careful, especially over an open line. Sometimes he goes with Ingrid, but not this time. I rather think he was going to stay at home and potter. He really doesn't have much of a chance to do that as he's away such a lot in connection with his job. And, naturally, he loves being with the children.'

'Have you heard from him or seen him since?'

'No.'

They had reached the back door and Carrick waited until Elspeth had removed her gardening shoes. 'And yet he appears to have left home last Wednesday. The BMW dealer in Bristol was contacted that afternoon as the car had a leaking radiator. It was taken in the following morning and collected early on Saturday. That night, or possibly on Sunday morning, it was parked by the lake.'

22

Elspeth ushered him into a bright, lofty living room. 'I wonder if he was recalled to London and someone else picked it up from the garage for him? That must have been what happened. Patrick wouldn't go and look at a lake – lakes aren't his kind of thing at all. Do sit down and make yourself comfortable and I'll make some tea. We're gasping for a cup and I'm sure you are.' She went out.

Normally it was Carrick's practice to note carefully his surroundings but, this time, other than an awareness that the room was sunny yet cool, it remained a blank to him.

'Have you contacted Patrick's superiors?' John enquired. 'They're the people to know where he is.'

'I was hoping you could give me a name and a phone number,' Carrick told him. 'Trying to trace someone who knows about someone else in MI5 is not easy – even for a policeman.'

'I keep an emergency number noted down in my wallet,' John said, and also left the room. At that moment Carrick's pager bleeped.

'May I use your phone?' he called down the hall in the direction of the kitchen.

'On the table to the left of the door,' Elspeth informed him.

Carrick was on the phone for perhaps five minutes and when he got back to the sitting room the rector had returned and handed him a slip of paper. Carrick sat down but did not look at it.

'You've had bad news,' Elspeth said, entering carrying a tray. 'John, give him a nip of whisky. He looks quite ill.'

'No, but thank you,' Carrick managed to say. 'I've just been speaking to one of the men I left by the lake. Shortly after I departed some people arrived by car and parked farther along the shore – we had the car park cordoned off. They let several dogs out of the car for a run. One of them, a spaniel, went for a swim. It was splashing about in a clump of reeds close to the shore when it started barking. The owners could not get it to return to them and approached the patrolmen as they were sure something was amiss. A man with a canoe was persuaded to paddle out to where

23

the dog was. There's a body – just visible beneath the surface of the water.'

The silence seemed to go on for ever, as if time itself was frozen.

'You'll want someone to identify it,' Elspeth said huskily.

'It might not be . . .' John began.

'Who else?' his wife whispered.

'My dear, there's no need for you to—'

'I've dreaded this day,' she interrupted quietly. 'But I've prepared myself for it. *I* shall come with you, James. John, your immediate responsibilities lie with your parishioners. There's a funeral later this afternoon.'

Carrick said, 'I've alerted the relevant people. By the time we get there they will probably have brought the body to the shore.'

'I prided myself,' John said, almost inaudibly, 'that when the time came – and he's lived life extremely dangerously – that I'd somehow *know*.' He looked up and there were tears in his eyes. 'But that's the thing about pride, isn't it? It's always wrong.' Quickly, he left them and they heard his study door close.

'Soldiers,' Elspeth sighed, going over to stand by the window, her back to the room. 'Sometimes they're brought home on their shields.' She spun round and Carrick was taken aback by her blazing anger. 'But this wasn't war, was it? Someone has murdered my son and foully disposed of his body.'

Carrick stood up. 'The sooner . . .'

'Yes, you're right,' she said, her shoulders drooping. 'I must try to behave as Patrick would have done in similar circumstances.'

You already are, Carrick thought.

Afterwards he could remember no details of the drive back to the lake or even whether he and his passenger exchanged a word of conversation. He thought not.

A full murder investigation was in operation by the time they arrived; several police vehicles and an ambulance parked in the cordoned-off area, this now enlarged to encompass part of the shore. Radios chattered and, by a Range Rover inside which several dogs were barking, a

24

couple were giving details to a policewoman. Bob Ingrams had just arrived – Carrick had called in and asked him to be there.

'Would you mind staying in the car while I find out what's going on?' Carrick said to Elspeth.

It had been unnecessary to call in the services of a frogman as the body had been lying in such shallow water. A small rowing boat had been requisitioned and, with difficulty, the corpse had been brought ashore. Someone had placed a sheet of plastic over it while a small crowd that had gathered had been moved farther away.

Most of the police personnel were from Bristol. Carrick went up to the burly detective who appeared to be in charge and said, tersely, 'DCI Carrick. This might be a friend of mine.'

The top of the plastic was turned back.

'Yes?' said the man from Bristol, DCI Hall.

Carrick stared down into that quiet, dead face. Perhaps the body had been in the water for longer than the car's movements suggested. 'Yes,' he said.

'No chance with a head shot like that,' Hall commented.

'I have his mother in the car. She'll insist on making an identification now.'

'It would be better if the mortuary people tidied him up a bit first.'

'I know.'

Elspeth Gillard did not have to ask. She knew the answer already from the expression on Carrick's face.

'One thing . . .' he said, detaining her from leaving the car with a hand on her arm. 'He's been shot in the head. It's not pleasant.'

'He once sewed up a cut on my hand,' she murmured. 'He was very good at first aid and stitches, you know. We both managed not to flinch too much. Thank you, James, but it's the least I can do for him now.'

A path was cleared for them as they went down the slight slope to where the body lay.

'Yes, thank you, I'm all right,' Elspeth said in response to Hall's queries. She swayed a little when the plastic sheet was again lifted and Carrick gently steadied her.

25

A breeze sighed through the reeds with a dry, dead whisper, the only sound for a few seconds, even the dogs and the radios falling silent.

'No,' Elspeth said in an undertone. Moments later she looked up and saw that everyone was still waiting. 'No,' she repeated, a little louder.

'No!' Carrick exclaimed. 'It's not Patrick? But—'

'This is my other son, Lawrence.'

Chapter 3

Carrick refrained from bombarding her with questions just then or mentioning that he had thought the features a little different from those he remembered. He had put that down to the changes that had taken place after death.

'Perhaps it could be confirmed by removing the shoe and sock from his right foot,' Elspeth was saying with a practicality that was breathtaking. 'Not that Patrick ever wears red socks,' she continued when the whole of the body – dressed in pale blue slacks and white tee shirt – was visible. 'Nor such down-at-heel shoes. He lost the lower part of his right leg following injuries he received during the Falklands War,' she went on, addressing no one in particular as Hall bent down to attend to the request. 'Yes, there you are, he has his own foot.' She took a deep, deep breath. 'Poor Lawrence. He never could live up to his brother and now it looks as though he might have died instead of him.' The tears came then, taking her completely by surprise, and Carrick put an arm around her and led her away.

By the car Elspeth recovered her composure. In a low voice she said, 'He has – had – two lovely children. I must concentrate on them and plan for the future. Lawrence was divorced. His wife Shirley took to the bottle, left them, and the last I heard was in a clinic in connection with her problem. She can't be expected to help and I don't want her to. James, I know this is a first reaction and it hasn't really sunk in yet but if I start even to hint at how relieved I am that it isn't Patrick, you'll think me a very wicked and hard-hearted woman.'

27

Carrick himself was trying to suppress relief at the revelation that this was not Patrick's body. 'Where are the children now?' he asked.

'With my sister and her husband at our holiday cottage in Wales. It meant taking them out of school but was a last-minute arrangement. The cottage is booked solid for the school holidays. Do you think the children ought to return immediately?'

'I shall have to have a quiet chat with them. How old are they?'

'Matthew's eleven, Katie nine.'

'I suggest you do as you think fit but there's no urgency for them to return as far as I'm concerned. They might be better where they are for a few days.'

'Yes, I agree. Thank you.'

'So where *is* Patrick?'

'I've simply no idea. I suggest you ring the number John gave you. Obviously, we shall have to try to get hold of him too.'

Gazing at her steadily Carrick said, 'You're not a hard-hearted woman at all, are you?'

Eyes brimming, she shook her head. 'No. I've lost my ordinary, patient, home-spun, *cuddly* son, a man who would burst into my kitchen on Mothers' Day wearing odd socks and a huge smile on his face and carrying a bunch of flowers that looked as though it had lost an argument with a combine harvester.' She wept afresh.

There was no suspicion of suicide even discounting the business of the body having subsequently been moved to the reed bed. The shot had been fired from an estimated distance of three feet. The PM further revealed that Lawrence Gillard had been comparatively fit and healthy for a man of his age, forty-one, that he had not consumed any alcohol on the day of his death and that shortly before he had died he had eaten fish and chips. In the view of the pathologist the shot had killed him instantly and he had been dead when placed in the water. It was impossible to tell how much time had elapsed between these occurrences. Also open to question was whether the murder victim had arrived alone

28

or with his killer even though, oddly, only Lawrence Gillard's fingerprints were found on the interior and exterior of the vehicle. This was soon found to have a simple explanation; the mechanic who had worked on the car had diligently cleaned the wheel and controls to remove any marks he might have made and had then handed it over to be valeted.

Neither the bullet nor the weapon that had fired it had been found despite divers being called in to search a fifty-yard stretch of the lake. Carrick, who had asked for and received permission to handle the case, immediately ordered that the search be widened. He had already been told that the heavy rain had obliterated all footprints or other wheel-tracks that might have been made.

Photographs of the dead man had been shown to the staff of the garage where the BMW had been repaired, and also – Carrick was careful – a couple of his brother. Those of Lawrence, whose face was slightly fleshier, were picked out as being the nearest likeness to the man who had both brought in and collected the car.

The first action Carrick had taken had been to dial the number given to him by John Gillard. A woman had answered and upon being requested to connect Carrick with the person in charge, had asked him to wait.

'How can I help you, Chief Inspector?' a clipped, military sort of voice, awash with authority, eventually enquired.

'The Reverend John Gillard gave me this number,' Carrick had replied, unaware that his Scottish accent was always strongly apparent when he was under stress. 'His son Lawrence has been shot dead. The body was then dumped in a lake.'

'When?' the man demanded to know.

'There's no firm evidence as yet but it might have been late last Saturday night. Forensic evidence suggests that the body was immersed for between two and three days so that's about right. May I know to whom I'm speaking?'

After a short silence the man had said, 'Why not? The era of openness and accountability is upon us. Discreet of the Gillards not to tell you. The name's Daws – Richard Daws. So there's no question of it's not being foul play?'

'It's worse than that. He was driving his brother's car. We have to bear in mind that someone might have thought he was Patrick. There was quite a close physical resemblance, even though Lawrence wasn't so tall.'

'And you're concerned that this someone's after the Lieutenant-colonel? I think I can put your mind at rest there – we look after our own.'

'I was rather hoping you could tell me where he is,' Carrick had gone on to say, trying not to sound as angry as he felt. 'For one thing he almost certainly doesn't know that his brother's dead, and for another he's likely to be an important witness in a murder inquiry.'

'I can only tell you that he's on leave for a fortnight and isn't due back here until next Monday morning,' Daws had calmly responded.

'Doesn't he have a mobile phone?'

'Er – yes, but I'm afraid it's classified information so I can't give you the number.'

'That isn't good enough,' Carrick had snapped.

'I'm sorry, Chief Inspector, but I simply can't reveal the information you want over an open line. But I will try to contact him personally and tell him to get in touch with you.'

'You might ask him to contact his parents first.' Carrick had banged down the phone.

Then he had rung Elspeth.

'Yes, we used to know his mobile phone number,' she had said. 'But then it was changed and they got all security conscious so even we weren't allowed to know what it was. It's crazy, isn't it? Patrick didn't dare give it to us on the quiet either because calls go through a switchboard, so they can check.'

Carrick and Ingrams had gone to the deceased's home, a first-floor flat in the Brandon Hill area of Bristol. Subsequent to his divorce, Elspeth had said, Lawrence – known to almost everyone as Larry – had gone to live with a friend, Lorna Templeton, at her cottage. But they had broken up a few months previously and he had rented the flat. It was not far from the school where he taught English and Social Studies.

Carrick was very much aware that he must not automatically assume that Larry had not been the intended target. With this in mind he had taken a quick look around the victim's incredibly untidy home and had then called in the scene-of-crime team to conduct a full search. Nothing of real interest had been found.

And now, a full week since Patrick Gillard had left home for destination unknown, the local papers briefly covered the story of a man's body having been found at Chew Valley Lake and noted that the police were treating the death as suspicious. The identity of the victim had not been revealed, the reason for this being that Daws had quickly contacted Carrick again and had asked that no details be released at present. Carrick, realising that he might have to go to the faceless MI5 man for help, had decided to co-operate. Only Daws and those with whom Gillard worked would know the identities of his enemies.

First of all, though, Carrick had to make quite sure that the wrong man had been killed.

Late the previous afternoon he had called in at the school, Haswell Comprehensive, where Larry had taught and given the bad news to the headmaster. This morning he had an interview with Lorna Templeton, Larry's ex-girlfriend, a meeting that had been arranged for one of her free periods. She was waiting for him in a room set aside for interviews with parents.

It was a petite, dark-haired woman who rose from her chair as Carrick entered. Obviously she had taken the news of Larry's death very badly.

'No, please don't get up,' he said, drawing up a chair of his own. 'I feel I must apologise to you for not telling you about this personally yesterday. Mrs Gillard told me of your friendship with Lawrence but it must have slipped her mind to add that you taught at the same school. I learned that from the headmaster when I rang this morning to ask him if anyone here had known Larry really well.'

Lorna Templeton was fighting back tears. 'I'm sure that poor Elspeth has quite enough on her mind without remembering everything about me.'

31

'I hope you won't mind if I ask when you and he split up?'

'About four months ago. Things hadn't been going very well for a while. And it's always more difficult when there are children involved.'

'Was that the real reason for the break-up?'

'No, by no means. The kids are super. A little awkward at times but that's to be expected when there's been a family split. Divorce shatters their world, you know. If only people would think of them a bit more when they decide to part . . . I realise it wasn't Larry's fault. Shirley left him and from what I've heard about her it was just as well she did. No, Larry and I broke up just because of us. I was beginning to feel overwhelmed by the situation. I didn't seem to have any space to myself anymore. I know that sounds terribly selfish but you'd have had to live in the same house as the man to know what I mean.

'We were all crammed into my tiny two-bedroomed cottage at Priston and all the time, every day, the place was seemingly knee-deep in someone else's belongings. Don't misunderstand me, I really loved him. I'd have married him if he'd asked me. We could have moved to somewhere larger. But he didn't want any more commitments and that was that. In the end I felt just like his landlady with not a square inch of my home that I could call my own. He'd come in and dump everything he was carrying in the kitchen, go upstairs, get undressed and leave all his clothes on the floor, have a shower and drop the wet towels in the bath.'

Having said that Lorna burst into noisy tears, blurting something that Carrick just caught as: 'And now he's dead and I'm a real cow for talking about him like this.'

There is nothing a policeman can do in these circumstances but wait politely and, if necessary, offer a clean handkerchief.

'Sorry,' Miss Templeton mumbled a little later, blowing her nose.

'Is there anyone, to your knowledge, with whom he had a serious argument or who's been threatening him?'

She shook her head. 'No. Larry wasn't the kind of man

anyone *hated*. Except Shirley perhaps. He was just infuriating sometimes.'

'There's usually a reason why wives start drinking and leave their husbands,' Carrick prompted gently.

'I never asked him about that. I only met her once and took an instant dislike to her. She's a big woman with a red face and a loud voice. Larry did say once that she used to taunt him about his low pay and how he couldn't get a better teaching post.'

'Was he in any kind of trouble?'

'Nothing that I know of. I mean, he was just an ordinary bloke. He didn't smoke or gamble and just drank the occasional beer at weekends. He lived for his children – was always taking them to theme parks and museums and things like that. We all used to go. It was fun but he always made sure the kids learned something as well. He doted on his mum and dad too.'

'And his brother? Did he dote on him?'

'Patrick? Well, they'd had their differences in the past but they got on all right as far as I know. We used to call in and see them when we were in Devon on holiday. Larry really loved Justin and little Victoria, Patrick and Ingrid's children. Mind you, Justin can be a real handful sometimes. Elspeth says he's just like his father used to be. I wouldn't know, I don't know Patrick very well.'

None of this was at all fruitful.

Diffidently, Lorna said, 'I take it from what you've said that Larry was murdered somehow. *How* did he die?'

The papers had only mentioned that a body had been found. 'He was shot,' Carrick told her.

Her face hardened. 'Larry had been shot before.'

'When?'

'A couple of years ago, just before Shirley left him. He was running adventure weekends for the kids here and on one trip someone took a pot shot at him.'

'Was he injured?'

'Not then. There had been other happenings too. Ropes had been cut and the climbing kit tampered with. Larry asked Patrick for help and they staged a re-run, only just with adults. Larry was shot then.'

33

'What the hell happened?'

'I don't know the full story but I don't see how there could be any connection with what's happened now. Those people were caught. It was something to do with someone not wanting tourists in the area.'

'Which was?'

'The Brecon Beacons.'

'Whoever it is might be out of prison and wanting to settle old scores,' Carrick pointed out. 'Who else knows about this?'

'Well, Patrick and Ingrid do, obviously. And we met a colleague of his at their place and they were talking about it in a guarded sort of way. His name's Terry. He married the Gillards' previous nanny.'

'Have you any idea if this Terry was involved with sorting out the problem?'

'Oh, yes, that's what I meant. As I said, they were talking about it.'

Carrick raised his eyebrows enquiringly.

'I know I wasn't supposed to be listening,' Lorna went on, thus encouraged, with a slight flush on her pale cheeks. 'It was after dinner and I was helping Ingrid clear away. I sort of paused while I was putting away the cutlery in the next room. They referred to what happened as Operation Rookshoot.'

Sometimes, for no apparent reason when he was interviewing people, a tingle would slowly travel down Carrick's spine. It did so now.

'I didn't ask about it,' she continued. 'I knew that I wasn't supposed to know. All that affected Larry and me was that the children's expeditions could continue.'

'He fully recovered?'

'Oh, yes. It was only a flesh wound. Larry always healed beautifully – he didn't even have a scar.' A few tears escaped but she dashed them away with an impatient gesture.

'And you're quite sure that there have been no repercussions from this? No strange phone calls or letters that he didn't want to talk about?'

'No. Nothing like that at all, to my knowledge.'

'Did the brothers speak of it ever in your company?'

'No, it was never mentioned.'

Interesting, Carrick thought. Normally something like that would have been yarned about for years.

'Do you have any maps or other info concerning these trips that I could look at?'

'I've got everything. Larry left it behind – it's all in my loft. But if you don't mind my suggesting it, it would be a lot quicker to ask Patrick.'

'When I find him,' Carrick commented a trifle sourly. 'He seems to be on some kind of secret mission. Presumably you saw Larry most days?'

'Yes. But he'd been off sick. Then he rang me last Saturday morning to ask if I wanted to go for a run in a really posh car. His words. But I'd already promised a friend I'd go round the shops with her as she's getting married soon and looking for a wedding dress. We'd planned to have a meal out and make a day out of it. I was just going out of the door so might have been a bit off-hand. That's one of the reasons I feel so dreadful – it was the last time I heard his voice.'

'Did he explain about the car?'

'No. I thought it was a joke. His car's a battered old Escort. He used to refer to it as his Roller. I thought he meant that.'

'Where did he keep it?'

'Just parked outside in the road.'

There had been no elderly Escorts parked at the front of the terrace where Lawrence Gillard had lived.

Carrick said, 'I'm really glad you didn't go for that car ride, Miss Templeton.'

He drove the short distance to the row of sandstone houses where Lawrence Gillard's flat was and parked, with difficulty, between dustbins awaiting emptying and an overflowing rubbish skip. The tree nearest to the entrance to the flat had had all the bark peeled off it by vandals and was dead. Carrick wondered what the two children had thought of being removed from a cottage in the country and then brought to this place. And what would happen to them now? Surely they would not be sent to their alcoholic mother.

The keys to the front door and also the set he had used for his brother's car had been found in the dead man's pocket. Strangely, he had been carrying no money nor means of identification and Carrick's first reaction on being told this was to believe that the killer had stolen his wallet. But it had been found on a hall table at the flat together with the morning's post, unopened, and sundry other items.

Larry had phoned Lorna Templeton on Saturday morning, presumably just after he had collected the car from the garage. Had his invitation to her stemmed from a wish to renew their relationship? Perhaps he had hoped they could have a day out together. Her refusal – and Carrick could easily picture the scene – might have sent Larry slamming out of the flat later that day, forgetting to pick up his wallet, after many hours of lonely brooding. He had been all alone; the children were at the cottage in Wales. He had probably taken the car out from a sense of duty, to make sure that all was now well with it.

Someone with the time to lock a car and pocket the keys is, surely, not aware of any danger. So unless his killer carried out those actions after the shot was fired it had to be assumed that whoever pulled the trigger had stalked his victim or else had lain in wait. The latter had to be discounted unless Larry had arranged to meet whoever had killed him. In which case no mistake had been made and the intended victim had been killed.

But if someone had been tailing Patrick . . .

Carrick paused on the stairs up to the first floor and thought about it. Anyone watching Patrick would have seen him enter this building. This was working on the assumption that when his car had given trouble he had called in to see his brother, aware that he was not at work due to illness. If he had asked to borrow the Escort for the remainder of his journey and requested that Larry take the BMW to be repaired then it fitted the evidence already to hand. And the someone outside might have discounted a man who emerged from the building – there were literally dozens of flats – got into a car that had been parked in the street

36

already and driven off. It was possible that Patrick had changed his clothes, put on a coat, anything like that.

Carrick carried on ascending. He must not allow himself to drift off into flights of fancy.

But the theory fitted everything he knew about the man. Patrick Gillard tended to blend into the scenery when off duty. He was very careful about things like that as his life could depend on it. He was the man in the old jeans and ill-favoured sweater. Unconsciously, perhaps, he might have adopted his brother's walk and manner. It was second nature to him. It also amused him, when he did think about it; he had said as much to Carrick.

Only this time it might have resulted in his brother's death.

Carrick let himself into the flat and left the front door wide open. Outwardly similar in appearance the brothers might have been but that was where the similarity had ended. Lawrence had slummed it. Even though the linen on the children's beds was clean there was dust everywhere and belongings strewn on the floors and on every piece of furniture. Wardrobes were crammed with clothes, the doors not able to be closed properly. One set of shelves in the living room, cheap DIY ones that did not look as though they had been erected properly, were on the point of collapse under the weight of books, folders and magazines heaped upon them.

All this SOCO had examined very thoroughly; every cupboard, drawer and shelf. Every letter, bill, receipt and holiday postcard had been carefully perused. In the end all that had been taken back to Manvers Street were a few audio tapes which were unlabelled. A couple sampled on the late tenant's music system appeared to be of recordings of conversation interspersed with snatches of music.

One grabbed at straws in such enquiries.

Carrick wandered through into the kitchen. The view from the window was of the backs of the houses in the next road and the gardens, yards really, in between. Like the rest of the flat this room had the same sad air of neglect; the emulsion paint peeling from the walls, the worktops slightly sticky to the touch.

'I need to talk to Joanna,' Carrick said out loud. She of the razor sharp intellect, wonderful red hair, magical green eyes and breasts like . . .

He groaned and went down into the fresh air, delving in his pocket for his mobile phone. No, he couldn't talk to Joanna, she was at her university summer school several hundred miles away.

'I'm glad you rang, James,' Elspeth said matter-of-factly. 'I've remembered something. It's not much, I'm afraid, and I might be right off-beam but it could explain Patrick's apparent disappearance.'

'First, though, how are you?'

'Oh, managing. John's very supportive and I've discovered that being bereaved is terribly tiring. It's a real surprise to get a good night's sleep. If I get my eight hours I can cope with all sorts of things.

'Now, I remember Patrick saying to me a while ago that he had to go for his annual assessment in June – this month. It's a terrible bore as they make him go on route marches with full pack and rifle – or sometimes allow him to prove his fitness on an exercise bike. It depends which medic's in charge. There's rifle and pistol shooting only it's not as simple as that, not on a range. There's a special building, a warehouse containing rooms like film sets, and they get put into all sorts of nasty scenarios and have to get to the end of a course without losing points. He's always utterly worn out when he returns home and Ingrid gets furious because she says it's so unfair on account of his leg. Especially so as apparently he trained most of the instructors and they constantly try to outwit him.

'I can imagine that if he had a choice of dates for this he might have deliberately gone while Ingrid is away. When she gets angry, you see, it puts her off writing, and if Ingrid can't write the atmosphere at home is dreadful.'

'Do you know where this is held? Can you contact him there?'

'No, that's the trouble, we don't. More silly secrecy. They're allowed no contact with the outside world at all while they're there. I believe they get put under a lot of psychological pressure and that's part of it. All I can tell you is that it usually starts and ends mid-week. Sometimes he pops in here on the way home to unwind a bit. I shouldn't think it's too far from Bath, actually.'

'Please let me know as soon as he makes contact with you.'

'Of course. Did you want to ask me something?'

'Only about Larry's car. Did he still own the old Escort?'

'Yes. At least, I *think* he would have mentioned it to us if he'd got rid of it. He wasn't at all interested in cars really and as it was so reliable . . . Why? Has it gone?'

'Yes.'

'Perhaps he lent it to Patrick.'

'That crossed my mind too.'

'He wouldn't have been very pleased. Patrick, I mean. Larry never cleaned it and the inside's indescribable. James, I know you're a very busy man but you will come over and see us, won't you? Especially if you find out anything.'

'Yes, of course I will,' he promised.

'I was wondering when we could have Larry's body.'

'I see no reason why you shouldn't have it tomorrow. All the formalities so far as we're concerned have been attended to. I'll see to it as soon as I get back to the office.'

Carrick knew, somehow, that she was was in tears before she replaced the receiver.

Smacking the aerial back into his phone he went indoors and back up the stairs. He wanted to have another look through the bookshelves in case there were diaries which related to the years when Larry had run the adventure weekends.

The door was still open – as he had left it – and he went quickly in the direction of the living room, mulling over the possibilities of lunch at a small café he knew of where the sandwiches were much better than average. He cannoned into someone in the narrow hallway. There was no time to react before something crashed into his temple and he fell into a yawning blackness.

The phone was ringing.

'For God's sake, answer the bloody thing,' Carrick muttered.

No one did.

He then realised he was lying on the floor. The phone was still ringing. No, not his mobile, the one on the low table. He crawled over to it, the entire universe going round and round in the most sickening fashion.

'Hello,' he said thickly when he had knocked the whole thing on to the floor in order to speak.

'Sorry if you were in the john,' said a cheerful but very fuzzy-sounding voice.

'I wasn't,' Carrick said, puzzled. This wasn't his flat. Or was it?

'Larry?'

'No, it's James.' The words had tripped off his tongue but he was not sure if it was the truth. Darkness still seemed to be hovering around him. It was coming closer.

'Is Larry there?' asked the man very fuzzily indeed.

'No, he's dead. I'm sorry but I can hardly hear you. All I know is that I'm a policeman and someone's hit me on the head. Please could you . . .'

Then darkness descended and took him away again.

Chapter 4

Waking up and returning to reality was a painful and unpleasant business – he threw up a bitter-tasting fluid in the ambulance that he thought for a moment was blood. The wail of the siren was agony.

'Is your wife at home?' was one of the interminable questions he was asked after a journey on a trolley to the X-ray Department.

Carrick's head was pounding like a foundry hammer. 'No, she's doing a summer school for her degree course. I'm all right and I'll phone her this evening.'

He would have to stay in overnight, he was told, for observation. There might be a skull fracture and he certainly had concussion. And after more questions and people shining lights in his eyes he was taken to a ward, the only good news being that nothing was cracked or broken. He was wondering how he could get himself discharged when he fell very suddenly asleep and did not wake up until the following morning.

Bob Ingrams was seated by the bed. 'Are you okay, sir?' he asked solicitously.

'Starving,' Carrick told him. Moving his head, he soon discovered, was not a good idea.

'How long are they keeping you here?'

'They're not. I'm leaving just as soon as I can get someone to sign me off.'

'The Super's back. He wants to know what happened.' Ingrams took out his notebook and looked expectant.

'A cup of tea,' Carrick said. 'Some toast and marmalade and then more tea.' He closed his eyes. 'Write that down.'

'Hobbs has arrested Lieutenant-colonel Gillard for his brother's murder.'

'*What*?' Carrick gasped.

'Last night at his parents' house. There's evidence to support it. You remember we took some of the dead man's tapes back to the nick? Hobbs played them through. They're mostly of kids playing recorders and rehearsals of school plays and stuff like that. But on an otherwise blank tape there's a spoken message – threats. It's Patrick Gillard's voice. The gist of it is that he's going to do all kinds of unpleasant things to his brother. It's revolting, it really takes your breath away.'

'You're *sure* it's Patrick's voice?'

'It sounds like him. I was there when Hobbs brought him in. Not that Gillard's speaking to him.'

Carrick could imagine the situation. Could imagine the resultant row when Daws had made a complaint and his, Carrick's, head was on the block.

Ingrams said, 'It starts off, "This is the brother you've always loathed". It's his voice all right but there's a sort of madness that comes through. Makes your hair stand on end. Oh, and Hobbs asked him to unlock the briefcase that he had with him. It contained a hand gun, a Smith and Wesson. According to Forensic it's been fired recently.'

Carrick got out of bed and sat on the edge of it until the dizziness abated. 'Would you close the curtains so I can get dressed?' he requested. 'I'm coming with you. Where is Gillard now?'

'He refused to talk so Hobbs had him put in a cell for the night. He didn't ask for a solicitor or anything.'

'I'll shove the little toad up his own backside!'

Ingrams surveyed him stolidly with his small dark eyes. 'Just because Gillard's a senior army bod it doesn't mean he didn't shoot his brother.'

'What was Gillard's reaction to the tape?'

'As I said, he's not speaking to Hobbs.' Ingrams was having trouble with the curtains; the fittings had jammed on the track. 'He did ask me how you were, though.'

'How did he know? Did you tell him?'

'No. Perhaps it was him who hit you.'

'Look, Bob. This man is a friend of mine. He's hardly likely to—'

Unusually for him, Ingrams interrupted. 'So it's really important to be even-handed, isn't it? Perhaps Inspector Hobbs should handle the case and then you wouldn't be personally involved.'

Carrick stared at him. Ingrams was looking distinctly mulish. So it had started already, had it? On Hobbs's previous visit he had immediately commenced to undermine Carrick's authority and ingratiate himself with those of higher rank. What exactly was he up to now?

Having got dressed – he had discovered his clothes in the bedside cupboard – Carrick made his intentions plain to the nursing staff. He signed a form as he was discharging himself – the doctor not yet due to make his rounds – and ten minutes later he was in Ingrams's car being driven in the direction of the city centre. It was a little after eight-thirty.

Sergeant Woods, on duty at the desk, had been mentally bracing himself for this moment and actually had the keys to cell number two ready to hand. He held them out when he saw Carrick approaching and then, against his better judgement, offered a little advice. He was, after all, old enough to be the superior officer's father.

'Do take care, sir,' he said quietly as the keys were passed across.

Carrick's gaze and mind seemed to clear and he saw a thousand and one stark warnings in the sombre brown eyes regarding him.

'Thank you, Derek,' he said softly. 'I will.'

The cells were only around a right-angled corner and some fifteen seconds later Carrick had unlocked the door and walked over to the wide wooden shelf with a thin mattress that passed muster for a bunk. The prisoner was lying there with his hands behind his head and seemed perfectly relaxed.

'I had an idea you'd be here soon,' Gillard said. He gave

43

Carrick a keen stare. 'You look as though you were pistol-whipped. Have you come straight from hospital?'

'Yes,' he replied. 'I'm very sorry about your brother.'

'He was a great guy. James, for God's sake, go home and have a shower and shave, two painkillers, forty winks and some breakfast. You'll feel much better then. Don't worry, I won't go away.'

It came as an odd shock, seeing Patrick in such circumstances, his face so similar to that of the corpse. And there had been no humour in that last remark, none at all. The man could get himself out of custody, one way or another, in five minutes flat. By producing his MI5 ID card, for example.

Carrick left the cell without saying another word, returned the key to Woods – who breathed out carefully, aware that Hobbs was in Carrick's office – and went home. An hour later he was back, minus the forty winks but nevertheless feeling a little better.

Hobbs was still in his office, reading through a file. He gave Carrick a dismissive glance and said, 'Did you see enough of the person who assaulted you to be able to give a useful description?'

'No,' Carrick said. He went away for a few minutes and then returned to say, 'I've just had a word with Bob. There's a spare desk in the store room and it's just a question of shifting a few filing cabinets to make room for it in the main office.' For a fleeting moment that remained etched into his memory for the rest of his life he yearned to go over to Hobbs, yank him out of the chair and hurl him through the open window into the flower bed beneath. But he did not. Perhaps his normal self-discipline asserted itself, perhaps he recollected the look in Woods's eyes. He merely said, 'I'd like you to carry on with the robbery case while I interview your murder suspect. You ought to have conferred with me before you made an arrest.'

'You weren't around. I had no way of knowing how long they'd keep you in hospital. Do you object to my sitting in on the interview before I start the other job?'

No, Carrick did not. Not if the alternative was an accusation of not having been even-handed. 'Perhaps you'd go

44

and fetch him,' he said. 'We can use the interview room next door.'

Despite his night in the cells, and presumably not having had a lot of sleep, Patrick Gillard walked into the interview room with cat-like grace, his expensive suit not at all creased, and smiled easily at Carrick as he sat down. During the formalities of relaying the information that the interview was being taped he remained passive, gazing into space. But when the tape was running he started talking without waiting for any questions. He spoke quietly, fluidly and with diamond clarity. He gave the impression that anger was being held well in check. For the moment.

'Chief Inspector,' he began, speaking directly to Carrick, 'I'm aware that because you know me rather well you're under even more constraint than would be usual in the circumstances to act correctly and professionally. This situation must be difficult for you, especially as I was arrested by one of your subordinates without your knowledge and orders while you were lying in hospital.'

'You cannot be aware that I acted alone in this,' Hobbs said.

There was something of the vivisectionist in the way Gillard regarded the speaker. 'I'm aware that Chief Inspector Carrick isn't a complete prat.' The final noun used was actually a different, more vivid one, and Hobbs blenched.

Gillard continued, still addressing Carrick alone, 'The tape which was found in my brother's flat and which seems to be the only evidence you're using against me *is* a recording of my voice. There's no need to play it again for my benefit but I think you ought to hear it for your own interest if you haven't already done so.'

Hobbs had provided the means and it was switched on after Carrick had nodded to him. The same voice that they had just been listening to issued from the machine. The same and yet different. The threats and insults offered were obscene and terrifying, the voice used as a weapon to intimidate. Despite everything, Carrick shivered. It was the same kind of feeling one sometimes experiences during a good stage play performed by internationally famous actors.

After listening for a few more seconds Carrick leaned over and switched it off.

'The real threat follows, sir,' Hobbs protested. 'That he's going to—'

' "Take a trusty shooting-iron and blast, blast your miserable, filthy brains all over the shithouse wall for your cow of a wife to scrub off with the hair of her scabby, scabby head!" ' Gillard obliged for him. 'Wonderful stuff, isn't it?'

'Karel Grootnic,' Carrick said to the nicotine-stained ceiling, a wonderful sense of peace having come over him. 'The dwarf Harel addressing his brother Lars in the play *Swineherd*. When was it written? About 1880?'

'1884,' Gillard said. 'Just before the illustrious author committed suicide during a drink and drugs-soaked orgy. Larry helped run theatre workshops with Bristol Old Vic. He asked me to tape that because he thought it would give the students an idea of menace. I think he'd heard me reading Shakespeare aloud at some time or other.'

'The Smith and Wesson in your briefcase was hardly of a theatrical nature,' Hobbs said.

'I'm permitted to carry a gun,' Gillard replied. 'But haven't done so for some time as my job is now mostly administrative. Word has recently reached us that someone wants to settle an old score with me and I've been reissued with a hand gun. This is not a fact that I was about to broadcast in front of my parents. Periodically I'm required to present myself for retraining and assessment in self-defence skills and that is what I've been doing for the past week. I used the weapon you found in my possession. If you wish to contact the military establishment in question to confirm this they're permitted to release that kind of information so long as the course has ended and those who took part are no longer on the premises. As for the weapon itself, it is rarely carried in a document case. For some reason I'd left the shoulder harness at Hinton Littlemoor. Now, Inspector Hobbs – is this the end of your stupidity?'

'I insist on seeing some kind of written proof that you're allowed to carry arms,' he said stubbornly.

'I can obtain it for you,' Gillard answered. 'Better still, it can be posted directly to you.'

'I also insist that you leave the gun here until it arrives.'

'No,' Carrick said, before Gillard could reply. 'I have no wish for the Somerset and Avon Force to be held responsible for the death of a security services operative.' He sat back, folded his arms and regarded the man seated opposite to him. 'Tell me about last week when you were on your way to wherever your training session was held.'

Gillard nodded briskly. 'The car's under extended warranty – I always go for that as I have to have my cars adapted slightly so there's a hand throttle. I was on the outskirts of Shepton Mallet – I don't mind you knowing that I was heading for Cirencester – when I noticed that I had a temperature warning light flashing. I stopped at a service station and checked cooling fluids and realised that the radiator or a hose was leaking. It seemed sensible, having topped everything up again, to make for Bristol where I knew there was a big BMW service place. Then I remembered that Larry was off work getting over a dose of shingles. I called in, and as I expected he was bored out of his skull with nothing to do. He offered to see to getting the car repaired and lent me his old banger.'

'You were happy about him leaving a car like that in the road in a rather run-down area of Bristol?' Carrick asked, wanting to have everything absolutely clear in his mind.

'Larry wasn't and I tended to agree with him. He told me that as soon as it was fixed he'd take it over to Hinton Littlemoor and get Dad to run him home. I said, no panic. Leave it in the garage until the weekend if he wanted to.'

'Do you think he was on the way there when he stopped by the lake?'

'Well, it's not exactly on the way, is it? But I know he liked the spot and I'd be the last person to object if he wanted to go for a longer drive.'

'I shall have to ask you about this threat you've got wind of.'

'I know no more than you do now. It's just mentioned on a grapevine we use a lot of the time – an international one. Sorry, but that's gospel, I really know no other details.'

Carrick believed him. But it was what was being left *unsaid* . . .

47

'Larry had mentioned no threats to him personally?'

'No.'

'Is there any likelihood that the threat to you could include him?'

'I wouldn't have thought so.'

'So we're talking about mistaken identity. The killer thought it was you?'

For the first time since they had started talking the urbane manner showed signs of wearing thin. 'I can't be expected to know what the killer thought.'

'You must have theories and opinions on the matter.'

'I do. But they're no more than theories and of little use to you. I have no *evidence* to give you.'

'Okay,' Carrick conceded lightly. 'So the bloke in Larry's flat who almost brained yours truly was just someone he owed for a week's newspapers?'

'I have no objection to discussing my theories with you,' was the retort. 'But not now.'

Carrick became aware that Gillard was tired, exhausted even, the very fact that this was self-evident a sign that the other's reserves were almost finished. It would be comparatively easy to carry on battering down his defences and force him to talk about subjects he clearly did not want to. To defer doing so might mean that he, Carrick, would never get to the truth. Instinct told him, however, that he would learn more by working with the man, and by respecting his wishes.

'Incidentally,' Gillard said, breaking the silence, 'it was me to whom you spoke on the phone.'

'I'm sorry you had to hear the news like that. I had no idea it was you.'

Gillard stretched his tall frame. 'Is there anything else you want to know right now? Only I'm needed at home. We have my brother's funeral to arrange.'

'No, not just now. I'll be in touch.'

Carrick brought the interview formally to a close.

Gillard got to his feet and there was no mistaking it, he now looked utterly all-in. To Hobbs he said, 'It's worse than you think, boyo. My bunch don't like it when operatives' family members are shot dead. They do a bit of investigating

48

of their own. We tend to be given *carte-blanche* – and that means *carte-blanche*. But I told my boss – and he does tend to be a little old-fashioned in these matters – that these days it's preferable for us to work closely with the police investigating the case. He's given me the job. So I'm going to be right under your feet, laddy. Right in your lap, for that matter.' And with that, he walked out.

Carrick caught up with him in the entrance lobby. 'You'll want the gun.'

Gillard turned. 'So I will. I'd actually forgotten about it for a moment.'

When he had made arrangements for the weapon to be brought from the safe, Carrick said, 'Perhaps you'd let me have this phone number in Cirencester?'

Despite his tiredness Gillard grinned. 'You run a bloody tidy nick, don't you?'

Carrick smiled back. 'Of course. I'll fix you up with a lift home too.'

'Do you fancy a pint later on?'

'You'll be asleep until this time tomorrow.'

Gillard squinted at his watch. 'Eight? At the Ring o'Bells?'

'I don't drink and drive.'

'I was going to suggest you stay the night.'

'You're on.'

Hobbs was still sitting where Carrick had left him. 'We can't touch him!' he almost spat.

'He's not guilty,' Carrick pointed out.

'You realise that MI5 has always enjoyed what amounts to diplomatic immunity? No accountability at all.'

'Not these days.'

Hobbs disregarded the remark. 'Any number of military establishments would provide him with an alibi – just for the asking. The army works like that. It's a waste of time even to chase it up.'

Carrick tossed him the scrap of paper upon which he had written the telephone number Gillard had given him. 'Phone. I want to know the exact details of the time he spent there and the name of the person who gives them to you.'

'You mean you don't believe—'

Carrick interrupted with, 'And put the interview tape with the file. I should hate it to get lost, wouldn't you?' He went back into his office, closing the door behind him, wrote a short report on the incident at the murder victim's flat and then, discovering he had been allocated an amazing number of personnel for his murder inquiry, held a briefing.

The murder victim's ex-wife, Shirley, had been given the news by her deceased husband's father. It did not occur to her – and she would not have cared – that the Reverend John Gillard had had to spend practically two hours on the phone to trace her whereabouts. He had finally run her to earth through her solicitor, whose address had been among the dead man's personal papers.

She had received the information without emotion, brushing aside his words of sympathy. And no, she had said, she would not be attending the funeral. Then put down the phone before he could say anything else.

Shirley hated them all; Larry's parents, their other son and his wife, and all the relatives of theirs she had met during twenty years of marriage. She had grown to hate Larry too, even though he had been different, more human. 'A chip off no one's block,' as his own mother had once described him. To Shirley such a remark revealed more about the person uttering it than the son to whom she was referring.

Shirley leaned both elbows on her bedroom window ledge and stared out at the view of derelict factories and, in the distance, the Yorkshire Moors. The whole bunch of Gillards were just too bloody perfect to be borne. It was the reason why Ingrid had divorced Patrick after endless rows. Yes, they had met up again and remarried several years later but that was only after the lordly Patrick had had his pride taken down more than a peg or two by getting himself blown up in the Falklands War. He had ended up having to have the lower part of his right leg amputated. And Ingrid, the silly cow, had felt sorry for him!

Larry *had* been different. More ordinary. He hadn't worried about everything at home being super-clean and tidy or that her home baking – when she did get round to it – had not been up to his mother's standards. Weekends for them had been a matter of going to the supermarket and taking things easy. They had always lived in flats so there had been no gardens to worry about. On Sundays Larry had probably taken the children to the park while she herself had a lie-in. For the rest of the time they had watched television. Shirley had always felt that she deserved a rest at weekends, reckoning she worked quite hard enough in between.

From an early age the children had gone to childminders so she could work. Friends usually. You all had to muck in together, didn't you? That's how you got by. And it was over the business of childminding that her mother-in-law had interfered. On one occasion she had told Larry that it was not good for the children to be sent hither and thither, and on another complained that the woman who had been looking after them at the time was unsuitable. There had been nothing wrong with the woman, Annie, as far as the kids were concerned. The trouble had been caused by Matthew telling tales to his grandmother about how Annie had said to them that her husband drank too much and hit her. Worse, he had also reported that Annie sometimes smelt of drink too. But people have to make a living, don't they? Elspeth, who had probably never worked in her life, should have remembered that and kept her mouth shut. Those who went to church on Sundays wearing their best hat – and more than anything Shirley hated religious posturing – had no right to preach to those less fortunate than themselves.

The flat where Shirley was now living had belonged to her mother. When Shirley had left Larry and the children she had moved in with her and nursed her through her final illness, looking after her until the last two weeks when she had gone into a hospice. Her mother had been grateful for that, she supposed, and drawn up a will leaving Shirley her home, a modernised first-floor flat in a terraced house, which she had moved into five years previously, returning to her birthplace York. Shirley had been the only child. She had never really got on with her mother; a hard, grim sort of woman who'd always insisted that life treated her very badly. Death had treated her badly too; she had suffered terribly before she had died from bowel cancer.

Shirley had never known her father. He had walked out of the house one night when she had been a few months old and her mother had never seen him again. Spiteful neighbours had whispered in the young Shirley's presence that he had been driven away by his wife's ceaseless nagging. Shirley didn't know about that and didn't much care. Her mother had always said that he was a useless wastrel and they were both better off without him. It had been very hard for her, of course, she had had to work long hours to keep them.

Marriage to Larry had initially been a wonderful escape from the grinding boredom of life in a Birmingham suburb. They had met at a teachers' conference when both in their early-twenties. Larry had been fun in those days, a rising star in the trades union movement. He had taken her to what had seemed to be endless parties in crowded bedsits where young people drank cider, argued about Marxist principles and planned to change the world.

'Such fools we were,' she muttered.

They had been married in a Register Office, having rebelled against his family's hopes for a church wedding. Larry's father, she knew, had been particularly hurt by this decision; he had hoped to marry them. But to Shirley it had been a way of getting back at the old way of things that she despised. The world of The Toffs versus The Rest.

Larry had not hated his parents, just did not share their views. So when he had landed a teaching post in Bristol nearly everyone had been delighted. Not Shirley though. She blamed the Gillards' close proximity and the way her mother-in-law interfered for the way she started drinking. She had managed to get a job in a nursery school soon after they had moved into the area but did not enjoy it. When the expensive childminder she had found decided to give up because she was expecting a child of her own, Shirley had been forced to stop working and stay at home to look after the children. She soon became bored and miserable.

Things had become more and more difficult between her and Larry too. As he grew older he changed. In short, become more like his brother. He had volunteered to take the children at the school on adventure weekends in Wales. Shirley had simply not been able to believe this news when he had first told her but he had been serious and gone on a course to receive the necessary training. The upshot of it as far as Shirley was concerned was that in the summer she had hardly ever seen him at all. He taught all week in termtime and spent most weekends and part of the holidays in the Brecon Beacons. Her life became a series of lonely binges, the gin bottle always at her elbow, the children spending more and more of their time with their grandparents at Hinton Littlemoor. Elspeth would ring her sometimes and invite her to the rectory for coffee or lunch, wanting to know if she could help in any way. Shirley had not gone, had an idea it was just a ploy to give her a lecture.

She had left home. At first she had tried to make the children go with her but Matthew, who was turning into a very difficult child, refused. He had threatened that he would run away and take Katie with him, wherever their mother took them.

'And where the hell would you go, you stupid boy?' she had bawled at him on one occasion. 'You haven't any money for train fares.'

She had never forgotten the way Matthew had stood up very straight and said, 'I'd phone Uncle Patrick and he'd send a chopper for us.'

And now Larry was dead. It was a pity really; she had not had the chance to tell him that she was making a new life for herself. Moreover, she was off the drink and had a new friend.

Chapter 5

Carrick learned nothing else of interest that day from the official inquiry even though house-to-house questioning of those who lived in the area where the deceased's flat was situated went on until late-afternoon. No one seemed to have noticed a stranger acting suspiciously anywhere nearby, or if they had, had taken no notice. This was easy to understand as there were any number of apartments and bedsits in the locality with constantly changing tenants. People tended to live their own lives and ignore everyone else.

Other than the possessions and fingerprints of the murder victim nothing else was discovered in the BMW so it was cleared for return to its owner, the relevant paperwork landing on Carrick's desk just before he left work. Although now officially off-duty he was bracing himself for what might be a very difficult encounter indeed.

There was a display of clog-dancing outside the ancient coaching inn at Hinton Littlemoor, a small crowd gathered round to watch. Both dancers and fiddlers perspired in the heat; the previous night's storm might never have occurred. Carrick watched for a few minutes, lulled by the timeless scene; the music, rooks cawing in the tall trees that surrounded the village green which lay opposite, the church clock striking the hour.

Patrick Gillard was sprawled on a bench outside the pub, a half-full glass of bitter on the table before him. 'I'm sure you prefer the pipes,' he said as Carrick approached.

'Yes, but not here,' Carrick replied. 'Not on English village greens.'

'Where have you left your car?'

'In the car park round the back.'

'I suggest you shift it to the rectory drive. It would be a bit awkward if you were leaped on by your own bunch and breathalised when you were driving all of twenty yards. There have been a few break-ins on vehicles left here all night too. What will you have to drink?'

'What's yours?'

'Wadsworth's 6X.'

'I'll have the same. Are you sure I won't be intruding? Staying the night, I mean?'

'Not at all. On the contrary, my mother will feel much more positive if you're around. Besides, she knows I'm going to be grilled by the investigating officer.'

Carrick went to move his car. It was difficult to stay one step ahead of these people, but he would have to if he was going to achieve anything.

'You could have got out the hot pincers and thumbscrews this morning,' Gillard said when he returned. 'Why didn't you?'

'While you were really under par, having had a hellish few days in Cirencester? I had no grounds to.'

'I would have done under the circumstances. Softened-up witnesses aren't often handed over on a plate.'

Carrick half-emptied his glass and came up for air. 'Are you saying in an oblique way that now you've had a rest and time to unwind you have no intention of answering any sensitive questions I might throw at you?'

'If I were the killer's intended target, any answers I gave would not be much help to you.'

'I'm trying to find your brother's murderer.'

'And in the friendliest possible fashion I'm telling you that if that *is* the case, you're unlikely to succeed.'

'Good,' Carrick said, after downing the rest of his pint. 'We're right down to basics already.' He picked up his empty tankard. 'Another?'

Gillard drank up. 'Yes. Thank you.'

When Carrick brought the drinks Gillard said, 'When does your Super return from his hols?'

'He already has.'

'I shall have to go and see him – about getting under your feet, I mean. I can't think that it'll be for more than a few days. It's really a question of eliminating unwanted information and collating everything that your team turns up. Also making sure, of course, that Larry wasn't mixed up in anything dodgy that no one knows about. If I am the real target the answer's not going to be found on your patch – people after my skin tend to be international.'

'No,' Carrick said.

'No?'

'You've just put your finger on it. It's my patch.'

Gillard's eyes narrowed slightly.

'You're not going to use me and my team and then go away and sort this out yourself. First and foremost, whatever *anyone* in Whitehall says, your brother's death is a police matter. I'm delighted to have you aboard, but you're not going to call the tune. You're not going to withhold information from me on the grounds that it's classified material. If you do, or I suspect that you are, I shall call in Special Branch. And you don't want that, do you?'

After a thoughtful silence Gillard said, 'You didn't grill me this morning in recognition of the fact that I hadn't raised hell after being arrested.'

'Correct,' Carrick responded succinctly.

'But you let me get my own back on that idiot Hobbs – you lined him up so I could walk all over him with my big hob-nailed boots. Mostly, perhaps, because you detest the guy.'

'Absolutely.'

Almost absently Gillard scanned those seated and standing nearest to them. 'I was thinking of having some supper. Have you eaten?'

'No. Do you feel safe out here in the open?'

'It won't happen in a busy public place like this. Too much risk of being caught.'

'There are such things as rifles with telescopic sights,' Carrick reminded him.

He was given a gentle, tolerant smile. 'Permit a soldier to work out his own defences. I'm in visible range only from the top of the church tower, and believe me I've put a *very*

56

good padlock on the door at the bottom of the stairs that lead up to it.'

'Why don't you just disappear for a while?'

'That solves nothing. And I've Ingrid and the children to think of.'

Carrick leaned forward and spoke quietly. 'Aren't they in danger too?'

'Ingrid might be – that's why she's staying with a friend in the States for a while after seeing her publisher. I've asked her not to come home for the funeral. Naturally, she's not too happy about being away from the children for longer than planned but I've arranged for them to be taken to an hotel in the Lakes by their nanny tomorrow. She'll have armed protection that she doesn't know about yet. I'm staying right away from them.'

'So who are we talking about?' Carrick wanted to know. 'Organised criminals? Terrorists? Someone you put behind bars years ago?'

'I was on the line when I said I didn't know. As I said this morning – it's just a rumour on the grapevine. But nevertheless a rumour that I'm taking very seriously.'

'*More* than a rumour now Larry's dead though.'

Gillard got to his feet. 'Shall we go in and find a menu?'

They found an unoccupied corner table and ordered their meal.

Mildly, but determined not to be sidetracked, Carrick said, 'Might this be anything to do with Operation Rookshoot?'

'No,' Gillard said shortly.

Carrick had observed the blaze of anger in the other's eyes. 'Sure?'

'Sure. Who mentioned such a name to you?'

'Someone who's been in your house and unavoidably heard you talking to a colleague – Terry.'

'Shit,' Gillard whispered.

'So *is* there a connection?'

'No. The maggot in that particular apple's dead.'

'Did he have any friends?'

The army officer uttered a strange snort, almost a laugh. 'Probably not.'

'I was told that your brother was shot and wounded in an

57

incident connected with the episode. I'd like you to tell me about it.'

For a full minute there was silence between them, Gillard tapping his fingers on the table-top, gazing into space. Carrick was aware though that they were not engaged merely in a battle of wills. This was a subject about which Gillard was very reluctant to talk.

'If you're right and there is a connection,' he said eventually, speaking slowly and deliberately, 'then it boils down to whether I get shot or go to prison for quite a long time. Or even both.'

'Therefore my being a copper doesn't help you a lot.'

'No,' Gillard said under his breath.

'I suggest to you that it's now you who are being old-fashioned. My being a copper with resources at my disposal gives us every chance of solving the problem.'

'Try this then,' Gillard replied. 'The guy who died was a top-ranking policeman, a Commander in the Anti-terrorist Branch. He'd thought up a wonderful scheme to trap all the world's most wanted terrorists and the top brass let him get on with it. It was the most wicked thing you've ever heard of. I had him topped.'

'There now, officer,' Gillard said, watching Carrick's face. 'Perhaps you spoke a little glibly and hastily.'

'Does Daws know about this?'

'You *have* been busy. No. At least, he's aware of the man's real identity – which is more than I am – and that he was drowned on a fishing trip while on holiday in Scotland.'

'Daws told me that you look after your own.'

'I assure you he'll not kiss my arse if he hears the truth.'

Carrick waited until they had eaten before asking any more questions – mainly to give himself time to think – but was forestalled by Gillard saying, 'I shouldn't have told you. It achieves nothing and puts you in a very awkward position.'

'But you have,' Carrick said. 'Give me some of the background information. Why were you so opposed to the man's plan?'

'Heard of Anton Lyndberne?'

'Yes. He was wanted for all kinds of crimes on the continent, mostly of the bombing and murder variety. He was captured in this country and extradited to what was then West Germany, who had first bite of the apple so to speak, then sent to prison.'

'That was him. The identity was created for him. He was blamed for a few real crimes and they set up a few phonies. Afterwards he set up a so-called survival school in Wales, in the Brecon Beacons. In actual fact it was a school for terrorists. There are quite a few around the world, as you probably know – mostly in places like Libya. The front, the survival school, was a very good one and for part of the year that's what it was, a bona fide business. But for a week in the summer, a couple of years ago, Immigration let in people travelling under false passports – folk who were booked in to sharpen up their terrorist skills.'

'Knowingly?'

'Oh, yes. They were ordered to by the Home Office. The plan was that the students would all be grabbed when they tried to leave the country again. Only it didn't work out like that. Mostly because my department became involved. You must understand that Daws didn't discover that the whole stupid idea had official backing until *afterwards*.'

'Go on.'

Gillard poured cream into his coffee. 'My brother was engaged in Outward Bound-type trips with the children at his school. They started to have trouble. Kit was damaged, tyres slashed on the van, climbing ropes almost severed. Other groups suffered too. He asked me for help after someone took a pot-shot at him during a mountain walk. I organised an adults-only trip with someone carrying a gun. It got worse and we ended up on the scene after two children staying at a local youth hostel were deliberately mown down by a maniac driving a Volvo. They both died. Then a bloke was found dead in the same car and it had been made to look like suicide. But it was a German hoodlum by the name of Friedrich. He'd not been famous for his soundness of mind. Lyndberne had shot him when he got out of hand.'

'Had he been responsible for the other incidents too?'

'Probably not. Lyndberne had merely ordered that efforts

59

be made to rid the immediate area of outsiders. Obviously, he hadn't reckoned on tourists in a National Park.'

'So the police went in?'

'Nothing so sensible. No, the police had no evidence to enable them to do anything. Ingrid and I went in. We closed it down.'

'At great personal cost?' Carrick asked sympathetically, noting the way Gillard had spoken; in staccato sentences, his voice a little hoarse.

There was a wry smile. 'Yes, we were captured and he took pleasure in torturing us. I managed to turn events round by subverting the so-called students. Terry and a friend of his helped us to get out and there was a fairly satisfying war during which . . . No, I won't go into details. Suffice to say that most of them were killed. Lyndberne gave himself up to the police after I'd played fair by not shooting him. If I'd known then he was actually a copper I'd have shot him on the spot.'

'He had permission for *everything* he did?'

'It can't have been known the lengths to which he'd gone or the way he relished his rôle. Believe me, this man was barking mad. He'd turned himself so thoroughly into a criminal he no longer knew the difference between right and wrong. But official reaction afterwards was that the operation had served its purpose and had been worthwhile. He was going to be given another go at it somewhere else after presumably escaping from prison. After *that* they were going to give him a new identity – in case anyone traced what had happened back to him.'

'You mean a whole new *real* identity.'

'Yes, sorry. The works – cosmetic surgery, new name, a posting to a police force well away from places he'd been seen previously. He would probably have ended up a Chief Constable somewhere. Only I had his rowing boat capsized and he couldn't swim.'

'Bloody hell!' Carrick murmured. 'And I suppose the name of the man who obeyed your orders will go with you to the grave?'

'I issued no orders. When you've served with people you

60

do one another favours. But yes, basically, you're quite correct.'

After a pause Gillard asked, 'What are you going to do?'

'I don't know,' Carrick answered, honestly. 'Was your name mentioned?'

'Too right. It's plastered all over his, Commander X's, reports. It wasn't worth trying to conceal who I was – he already knew.'

'And would you have expected that?'

'No, but don't forget he was pretty senior in the Anti-terrorist Branch and had the backing of his bosses. They would have been able to identify members of MI5 with whom they'd previously liaised.'

'Were the circumstances of his death regarded as suspicious at the time?'

'The verdict was Death by Misadventure. God knows what was thought privately. Would you care for a dram?'

'I'm on home ground there too.'

Gillard chuckled, a degree of malevolence contained therein. It was small but nevertheless detectable.

The rector was out, visiting a dying parishioner, but Elspeth was still up, reading in the living room. Carrick's first thought upon seeing her again was that it would have done her good to have joined them in the pub for a square meal and try to forget her sadness for a short while. But she would no doubt feel that such an outing was impossible at the moment. He wondered if she was angry with Patrick for socialising so soon after his brother's death. It soon became obvious that this was not the case.

'James!' she exclaimed upon first seeing Carrick. 'Your head! Patrick said that someone had attacked you but I had no idea it was so bad. And here's me telling him to take you out for a spot of supper as I knew you would want to talk to him. Beer might cure a few ills but not a headache, surely!'

'It's a good local anaesthetic sometimes,' he assured her gravely. 'And then you go on to the real stuff and don't feel a thing – until the following morning, that is.'

She eyed them both with clinical gaze. 'So is it whisky you're still drinking or have you reached the coffee stage?'

'I promised him a taste of the Glen Esk,' Gillard reported smoothly.

'I rather thought that was your father's Christmas present.'

Her son beamed in placatory fashion. 'Dad's not too fond of single malts. I'll buy him a blend.'

'Well, I don't mind, dear. And I think I deserve a dry sherry, if you'd organise it for me.'

No, Carrick could not possibly have imagined it: she had given him a heavy wink. This family seemed to operate on a completely different plane from all the other people he knew. Not that he had not realised what she meant to convey to him.

Patrick having been despatched to organise the drinks, Elspeth said, 'Please, do sit down. I know that the last thing you must want to do is talk shop but are you any nearer to discovering who shot Larry?'

Carrick had no intention of revealing that he had been struck down in Larry's flat. He thought of giving her a breakdown of all the mostly negative information but in the end merely said, 'No.'

'That man Hobbs... Surely he had no real grounds to suspect that Patrick had anything to do with it?'

'He thought he had but again, no. He was barking up the wrong tree altogether. Tell me, did Patrick and Larry always get on well?'

Elspeth had known she would be asked this kind of question. 'No, by no means. When they were young they fought like cat and dog. It was really only recently that they buried the hatchet. Lorna Templeton had a lot to do with that – she worked wonders with Larry during the time they were together. I was very sad when they broke up. Shirley stirred up a lot of trouble between my sons. She had a way of opening old wounds. Don't ask me why – but then again I never understood most of the things she did.'

'What was the reason for the brothers not getting on?'

'Mainly, I'm afraid, because Larry was such a little creep when he was a child. He was lazy, solitary, and a teller of tales. I relied on Patrick more and more as he grew up. I had an impractical husband whose head was full of theology and the dates of Synod meetings but didn't even have time to chop sticks for kindling for the open fires. Rectories always used to be freezing barn-like houses with terribly old-fashioned facilities. Patrick learned to mend fuses and could deal with the dead mice in the traps that we had to have everywhere in one house. Larry labelled him "Mummy's boy" and Patrick would lose his temper and next minute they'd be going at it hammer and tongs.'

She did not want to elaborate further on Patrick's temper; those terrifying moments when he lost control and wasn't quite sane. She herself seemed to be the only one able to make him return to reason; even Ingrid had sometimes to leave the room and stay away for a while. Over the years a reiterated request had been, 'Please come and throw a bucket of water over Patrick. He's gone right over the top again.' And so naturally circumstances made her wonder. What if . . .? No, it was too dreadful to contemplate.

Carrick said, 'Presumably Larry would have shared any worries he had with Patrick. For example, if someone was threatening him or he was in any kind of trouble.'

'I would have thought so. Especially after Patrick helped him sort out the problems he had with the Brecon Beacons trips.'

'We spoke about that.'

'Well, you must know more than I do now. Ah, here he is. I hope you put some ice in my sherry?'

Patrick hadn't and went away again.

Much later, after John had come in and both he and Elspeth had just gone to bed, Gillard said, 'So who *was* this guy who laid you low?'

'I'd left the front door open while I went outside for some fresh air and to phone your mother. It could have been someone who'd sneaked in hoping to steal something – to be expected in that part of the city.'

'You didn't see who it was?'

'No, just a dark shape in the hall. I'm not actually attaching a lot of importance to it – not as far as Larry's death's concerned, that is.'

63

'I agree with you up to a point. But I'm not too keen on the possible existence of a Mystery Someone.'

'Who might be the killer. Yes, we must bear it in mind.'

Later again, when the whisky bottle, which had not been quite full to start with, was almost empty, Carrick regarded his host with a smile. 'You live on the edge of Dartmoor,' he said.

Gillard's eyes were slightly unfocussed. 'So I do,' he muttered. 'I always knew you were a good detective.'

'What I mean is, there's a chance that another terrorist school might be going to be set up in another national park. Are they trying to get rid of the known opposition?'

'You tell me.'

'To whom is Daws answerable?'

'The Prime Minister.'

'Alone?'

'Yes.'

At a little after two a.m. Elspeth heard a light step on the landing and the hinges on the spare room door squeak as it was closed. There were no other sounds and she drifted off to sleep secure in the knowledge that Patrick had remained downstairs.

Men were so predictable. But what on earth had he been thinking of, imagining he could drink James, a Scot at that, under the table? The wider implication of what had transpired that evening escaped her just then. It was only later that she became aware that her son had finally met his match.

Chapter 6

Higher authority having returned from golfing in California with a fetching tan and apparently boundless energy, the area in and around Bath's Manvers Street police station was throbbing with activity when Carrick arrived the next morning. Immediately summoned to a meeting, Hobbs included, Carrick was waylaid by a jubilant Ingrams.

'Really?' he exclaimed when the Sergeant had relayed some information.

'All sorts of stuff, sir. And we've photos of some of the silver items that the owners sent in after the burglary that we can match up with what's been found.'

'Cranthorne Manor, wasn't it?'

'That's right, sir. And there are wallets containing credit cards and even cameras with the owners' names on them.'

'Good work, Bob,' Carrick said, clapping him on the shoulder. 'But, look, I must dash. I'll get the details from you later. One thing though – check if a Mr and Mrs Hausner are still staying at the Royalty. If they are get them along to see if they can identify any of the stolen stuff as theirs.'

It was gratifying, during the meeting, to be able to report that, following several complaints from members of the public about a noisy party in a house in Twerton where drunk guests were damaging parked cars, the police had discovered a large number of stolen goods in an upstairs room. Suspecting that drugs were also in the house, they had made a wider search and more stolen property was found in a garage. Three people in the house had had banned substances in their possession and were arrested, together with the owners. Initial investigations suggested that the property represented the proceeds of several burglaries and muggings in the Bristol and Bath areas.

'Do we know any of these people?' Superintendent Buller snapped. 'Have they form?'

'Two have,' Carrick answered, relying on his good memory. 'Drug pushers. The others are probably new to the district. I'll get full details from Ingrams later.'

'I want a detailed report. I will not have louts coming here thinking that Bath is an easy option. And I've had a fax from Whitehall. Do you know anything about this MI5 man who's been sent to plague us after his brother was shot?'

'Yes, sir.'

'Well, I'm glad somebody does. He is *not* to assume any kind of authority. I simply won't have it. I don't care who he is. If he gets stroppy, send him to me and I'll put him in the picture.'

Hobbs said, 'I'm awaiting confirmation from London, sir, that this man's permitted to be armed.'

'Armed?'

'I found a Smith and Wesson revolver in his possession. He was interviewed because tapes were found at the deceased's flat. Recordings of his voice. Threats. There has been a satisfactory explanation for that, though.' Hobbs did not make it sound as though he had found the explanation very satisfactory.

'A tape,' Carrick corrected.

'Are you completely happy about the explanation?' he was asked.

'Yes. It was a quotation from a nineteenth-century play used for a theatre workshop.'

'You know him better than I do, of course,' Hobbs remarked slyly.

'Oh?' said Buller.

'Patrick Gillard is a friend of mine,' Carrick was forced to admit.

'And have you satisfied yourself completely that, quotations from plays apart, this man did not threaten his brother?'

66

'He did not.'

'I rather thought he was supposed to be here first thing this morning. Perhaps you'd be so good as to find out what the hell's happened to him?'

Carrick knew that that meant now, at this very moment, so left the room. He could hardly say that, to his certain knowledge, the highly trained and totally worn-out operative of MI5 was still sound asleep on his mother's sofa.

Not so, however.

In the lobby, Woods was being bombarded with a stirring excerpt from *Henry V* by a drunk. This individual, dirty, unshaven, with slightly bloodshot eyes, was swaying just a little, as he did so sprinkling the contents of a lager can over the polished floor. He was dressed in filthy jeans, trainers and a fraying green sweater. His hair had grass and leaves in it, a state of affairs that spoke of days and nights spent living rough in Victoria Park.

'Oi!' Carrick called.

The drunk reeled in his direction having first, lovingly, presented Woods with the now empty can. The desk sergeant, who no doubt thought Carrick was going to show their visitor out the back to sleep off his excesses in the car park, thanked him warmly and went on to make a phone call.

The meeting was breaking up, no one paying much heed to what was going on in the corridor. Hobbs did not even spare a glance at the man whom Carrick was escorting towards the rear of the building. The pair took a left turn and entered the comfortable, carpeted office at the end of the corridor. Once inside Patrick Gillard flopped into an easy chair with a relieved sigh, wiped most of the earth off his face with his handkerchief and ran his fingers through his hair, showering grass and leaves all over the pale grey Wilton carpet. This small flurry of vegetation was still in progress when the regular incumbent of the room appeared in the doorway.

'Lieutenant-colonel Gillard, sir,' Carrick said, and was not surprised when his superior gave every sign of being lost for words.

'Sorry about the need to be slightly undercover,' Gillard

said, getting up and shaking the bemused man by the hand. 'I'm sure the Chief Inspector will make you aware of the difficult situation I've found myself in. I've had a bit of a rethink concerning the most appropriate way for me to conduct my own investigations and have come to the conclusion that it would be better to keep a lower profile than I have done of late. I do not intend to liaise openly with your personnel and this will be the last time you will see me on these premises until the case has been brought to some kind of conclusion. Are you happy with that?'

The Superintendent had recovered most of his composure but was having difficulty in dragging his gaze from the visitor's disintegrating sweater. 'Er – yes, I think so. I suppose you'll be using your own personnel?'

'That's correct.'

'I think on reflection that I'd prefer it if you liaised with *someone*. I ought to be kept closely informed of anything relevant to the case that you learn. I'm afraid I shall have to insist that you keep in close contact with Chief Inspector Carrick who will report to me anything of value.'

'As you wish,' said Gillard. He gave them both a curt nod of farewell and turned to leave. 'Oh, when can I have my car back?'

'Tomorrow,' Carrick told him. 'I'll see you out.'

They went out of the rear door, meeting no one.

'That was neat,' Carrick said.

Gillard smiled reflectively. 'I'm sure you wanted things kept simple too. Although what will happen if it comes to conflicting interests I don't know—'

'Look, the Home Secretary might be my ultimate boss but that doesn't mean I'm going to go along with a police scheme that risks the lives of innocent people!'

'If one even exists,' Gillard said with a shrug. Somewhat warily, he added, 'I made you what amounts to a confession last night. I think it's only fair that you intimate what you intend to do about it.'

'What confession?' Carrick said.

Elspeth, who had finished her shopping in Sainsbury's in good time and was waiting in her car for a passenger, observed the ruinous down-and-out coming in her direction. Other shoppers removed themselves from the path of her son. They could not conceal their surprise when he got into the car belonging to the respectable-looking woman and kissed her cheek.

'I can have the car back tomorrow,' he said, settling down for a doze. 'Do you have any headache pills at home?'

'Yes, and thank goodness he had the sense not to let you have it back today!'

Carrick had made his decision quite cold-bloodedly. No, he knew nothing of confessions. Not until a confession became relevant. There had been an inquest on the Anti-terrorist officer in question which had recorded a verdict of Death by Misadventure. There was no evidence to support any claim that the man had been unlawfully killed. For he himself to suggest otherwise at this stage and use it to support a theory that Lawrence Gillard had been shot by mistake in some kind of revenge killing would be not only wrong but foolhardy. He could imagine the furore if anyone even hinted that a police department went gunning for MI5, especially if there was no real evidence to back such an allegation. One would have to tread very carefully.

All this was going through Carrick's mind as he drove north on his way to interview Larry's ex-wife. He had obtained the address and phone number from John Gillard.

He had not asked Gillard what he intended to do next and had no choice but to trust him to make any findings known. He was a man whom you could trust with your life but when it came to plumbing the murky depths of national security Carrick was not so easy in his mind. Having seen Gillard's endeavours the previous morning he was not so concerned for his safety. He had not so much disguised himself as a drop-out as *become* one. False hair or whiskers played no part in this type of undercover work – Carrick had an idea that such ploys would be regarded as time-wasting and cumbersome. No, this was all about acting; stance, body language and mimicry. The Shakespeare had been quoted in as rich a Dorset dialect as Carrick had ever heard. And Woods was a Dorset man, born and bred. Presumably a keen ear had detected this and the knowledge been used as a little insurance against being arrested for being drunk and disorderly. Or, on the other hand, Gillard might merely have been enjoying himself. Carrick thought that even more likely.

When he had rung the telephone number he had been given a man had answered. He had offered no name but had gone to fetch the person to whom Carrick wanted to speak.

A full half minute later Shirley had come on the line. She was using her maiden name now, she told him: Huggins. She had gone on to say that she saw no reason for him to travel all that way. Could he not just ask her a few questions over the phone?

'Sorry, no,' Carrick had informed her. 'That would not be at all satisfactory. Would tomorrow afternoon at two-thirty be convenient?'

She had had no choice but to agree.

It was an overcast, muggy sort of morning, mist hanging over the city. Notwithstanding the warmth, the grey light made it look like a November day. Carrick found the road he was seeking quite easily; for some reason John had known it was near the Railway Museum. Number twelve looked like all the rest – rather drab. The first-floor flat had its own entrance, round the side of the end-of-terrace house, an open doorway leading directly to stone stairs. He rang the bell of the door at the top.

Distinctly, he heard hushed voices within and the sound of an interior door closing. He glanced at his watch; he was a minute early. Then the front door was opened.

The murder victim's ex-wife was a surprise. He had been prepared, after what people had said, to be confronted by someone coarsened by drink. Lorna Templeton had described Shirley as a big woman with a red face and a loud voice. She did have rather a high colour but must have dieted to lose weight and when she spoke her voice was not so deep as it had sounded over the phone and could not be described as unpleasant.

Carrick felt that she might have dressed for the occasion, the formal unfashionable dress in a shade of green not at all suiting her dark colouring. Strangely, her hair, dark brown and glossy, was cut in a style that Joanna had recently told him was up-to-the-minute and all the rage, a short layered bob with a whispy fringe. Shirley's eyes were also dark brown, almost black, and were regarding him with suspicion.

'I think you're wasting your time, Chief Inspector,' she said, leading the way into a small living room. No, perhaps not so small, Carrick decided when he had accepted the invitation to seat himself, the room was merely stuffed full of furniture of various kinds. There was a leather sofa in a somewhat grim red, like raw liver, two armchairs with fabric covers in a different shade of red, a drop-leaf table against one wall, two bookcases filled mostly with Readers' Digest condensed books and piles of women's magazines. Several more sets of shelves and a whatnot were fixed to the walls, all crowded with small ornaments; holiday souvenirs, tropical shells and china figurines. The two pictures in the room set Carrick's teeth on edge: lurid Tyrolean mountain streams with sunsets looking like an oil refinery blowing up.

'This was my mother's flat,' Shirley said, noticing his interest. 'I've kept it just the way she left it.'

'How long have you lived here?' Carrick asked. He thought he was probably wasting his time too but the business of the voices in the hall was intriguing.

'Since she died and left it to me in her Will.' Her full lips had a way of falling into a petulant pout that he knew he would soon find irritating. 'About two years ago, that was. I was the only child, you see.'

'I'm very sorry about Larry.'

She shrugged. 'It was a shock. But, honestly, I'd almost forgotten about him. Him and me, I mean. *Us*.'

'You've made a fresh start then.'

'You have to, don't you? I'm sure his parents told you all about my drink problem. They're the sort of people who would. But it's all behind me now. I don't have to think about Larry and his wretched family anymore. They all used to worry me to death. That's why I started drinking.'

'In what way did they worry you?'

Again the pout. 'I was never good enough, was I? I know

71

I didn't come from the same background – my dad was on the railway – but Larry never put on airs. We met at a teachers' conference – I was a nursery teacher in those days – and we just clicked. Then he took me home to meet his family. The Gillards lived in Bristol at that time where John was curate at a church in the suburbs. It was awkward from the start. I was made to feel very aware that the male line had always gone into the services or the church. Larry was the black sheep, you could tell that. Elspeth simply couldn't stick his long hair and casual way of dressing. John couldn't either – he kept going on about it. Patrick, the elder brother, didn't speak to him much at all and didn't really waste his breath making conversation with me either. The whole boiling lot used to stick in my gullet.'

Carrick decided that it might be more profitable to change his line of questioning. 'Did John tell you the whole story? That Larry had been shot?'

'Yes, when he was driving Patrick's car. It's obvious it was a case of mistaken identity. Stands to reason with the things he gets up to in the name of Queen and country.'

'Surely soldiers have to obey orders?'

'I don't mean it like that. The bloody man has a screw loose! He once pointed a loaded gun at me, you know. It was on the day of Justin's christening. There was a chum of Patrick's there too. Terry, I think his name was. He married Dawn, the nanny they had then.'

'Why on earth did he point a gun at you?'

'Terry had had a run-in with someone outside. They'd all been drinking. I was all for rounding up the children and going home but Patrick said no, stay. And pointed this gun at me. Well, I couldn't argue *then* but we did go home, I assure you. Just as soon as we could.'

Carrick made a mental note to dig a little deeper into this fascinating episode.

'The point I'm making,' Shirley continued, 'is that he's upset a lot of people. You don't cross Patrick and get away with it. When he loses his temper he's not safe to be near. I bet Elspeth didn't tell you about that, did she? And *language*! No, if you ask me, someone had it in for Patrick

72

and got Larry by mistake. Larry wasn't the sort to make enemies.'

'But you left him?'

'That wasn't the same. He was a very irritating man for most of the time and I got so I couldn't stay in the same house with him. I just reached the stage where I couldn't take any more.'

'The brothers never got on when they were young, I understand?'

'No, they didn't. Larry didn't say much but I reckon that Patrick used to be as big a bully then as he is now. He probably used to beat Larry up. I'll admit that they made it up quite recently but it wasn't all sunshine and roses.'

'How do you know this?'

'Larry told me. He rang me up sometimes to let me know how the kids were getting on.'

'Do you have regular access to the children?'

Her gaze, which had been fixed upon Carrick unwaveringly and in a fashion that he found slightly unnerving, dropped. 'That was one of the conditions of Larry being given custody. But it didn't work out in practice – the kids didn't want to come. He brought them once or twice in the beginning but it was dreadful. It's Matthew . . . he's turning into a right little rebel. We'll have trouble with him in the future, I'm sure.'

'We?' Carrick asked.

'Those who look after him, I mean,' Shirley said, flustered.

'Have you given any thought to their future?'

'Yes, if it's any business of the police's. Children of that age belong with their mother.'

'Do you live here alone?'

'Yes.'

'Only I thought I heard voices just before I rang the bell.'

'I had the radio on in the bedroom,' she replied angrily. 'It seems you've come here to snoop as well as ask about Larry. Well, Mr Policeman, you can damn well go back to Bath and leave me in peace. Larry's death was nothing to do with me and I don't care a toss now he's gone.'

'I'm conducting a murder inquiry,' Carrick told her serenely. 'If I think you're hiding anything I'm quite within

73

my rights to take you back to Bath for a formal interview. Where were you last weekend?'

She looked at him with pure hatred. 'Here.'

'Alone?'

'Yes.'

'You stayed in all weekend and saw no one?'

'I went shopping on Saturday morning and for a walk on Sunday. I like being quiet and away from people in my free time.'

'So you work?'

'Part-time in Boots – mornings. I have to, to make ends meet.'

'You didn't get an allowance from Larry?'

'No. Because of being left the flat and a small sum of money by my mother. He said he couldn't afford to let me have anything on his pay, with having to feed and clothe the children.'

Carrick got to his feet. 'Please don't leave the area. I may want to talk to you again.'

He left and drove away. But not very far, turning round and returning to a parking space farther along the street where other vehicles concealed his own. But by sitting in the front passenger seat he could observe the house.

As soon as her visitor had gone Shirley burst into the bedroom of her flat, shouting: 'He suspects me, you bloody moron! You swore to me you hadn't done anything and now a senior cop comes all these hundreds of miles to talk to me.'

The man who had been hiding in a built-in wardrobe emerged sheepishly. 'Quit yellin' at me. I didn't do nothin'.'

'Where were you last weekend then?'

'Fishin'. I told you I was goin' fishin'.'

Shirley went right up to him, several inches taller than the overweight, slouching figure she was addressing. 'Tom, I don't think I believe you,' she said, speaking quietly but venomously. 'We'd been talking, hadn't we? About how Larry was stopping me having the kids and I said that my mother had given him a lot of her jewellery for Katie when she grows up that ought to have come to me. And a watch that was once my dad's.'

Tom shook his head. 'Nothin' to do with me.'

'I'm beginning to wish I hadn't clapped eyes on you in that clinic and fallen for your hard luck stories.'

'Since when?' he exploded. 'You were all sweetness when I took you out for a meal last night.'

'Since now. Things have become sort of clearer to me. You've done time. Now you might even have killed Larry.'

Tom had been good-looking once and his blue eyes were still bright and clear in the wreckage of his features. 'You want to make up your mind, woman. One moment getting rid of your ex is a good idea because the jewellery's valuable and the watch was an antique, and the next . . .' he broke off with a gesture of disgust.

'You know perfectly well I was just talking,' Shirley yelled. 'Tell me!'

He rounded on her. 'Tell you bloody *what*? Okay, you want to know if I killed him. No, I didn't.'

'You went to the flat though, didn't you? Look me in the eyes when you're talking to me, you bastard!'

He gave her a humourless grin, displaying broken teeth. 'There wasn't no jewellery. He must have sold it.'

'I don't believe you,' she said.

Tom brushed past her and walked out, slamming the front door.

75

Chapter 7

Carrick had wondered fleetingly if Patrick would risk attending his brother's funeral and concluded that it would take more than death threats to prevent him from doing so. This proved to be correct but there were precautions taken; he, Carrick, receiving a formal request for members of the Territorial Support Group to be present in inconspicuous fashion. Thus there were no armed men on the church tower or anything, for that matter, that detracted from the solemnity of the occasion. Patrick Gillard was present and no more prominent than any other man who attended wearing a dark suit, slipping quietly into his place next to his parents after acting as one of the pall bearers. The Bishop of Bath and Wells took the service.

Afterwards there was a small family gathering at the rectory. Although invited, Carrick excused himself gracefully and returned to work. In his capacity as a policeman he would merely be an intruder. The previous evening though he had called in and spoken to the dead man's children: Matthew bravely taking on a man-of-the-family rôle for the benefit of his younger sister; Katie, also very mature for her years, helping her grandmother in the kitchen. Neither, on being questioned with the featherweight touch that Carrick was not aware he possessed when dealing with children, had confirmed seeing any strangers hanging about the area where they lived nor did they know of any particular concerns that their father might have had. Other than the surprise holiday in Wales there had been no change in their routine. It emerged that both desperately missed Lorna and her small but homely cottage.

'I thought they were going to get married,' Matthew had confided sadly. 'That would have been super. Do you think they'll let us stay here?'

'I expect your grandparents would love to have you,' Carrick had said.

'No, I mean *they*, the social workers. Mum tried to make us go with her when she left but we wouldn't. I told them that we'd run away wherever she took us so we were allowed to stay with Dad. She'd said he wasn't able to look after us but it wasn't true. You don't think we'll be *made* to go and live with her, do you?'

'I can't tell you what will happen,' Carrick had admitted, seeing with regret the misery his answer generated. To this boy he was part of the officialdom that might now control their lives, perhaps one of the enemy.

Shirley had not attended the funeral.

The murder inquiry had gone stone cold and Carrick could not remember a case where he had less to go on. He was satisfied that the killer had not thrown the gun into the lake from the shore as an extensive underwater search had drawn a blank. Forensic evidence did not point to the body's having been carried in the BMW so it could only be assumed that Larry had met his death in the area where his body had been found. The shore had been dug over in an effort to discover the bullet and metal detectors had also been used. Nothing had come to light.

'It's a professional job,' Carrick commented, glancing up from the case notes as Hobbs entered his office. Their paths had not crossed for two days.

'The Gillard murder?' said Hobbs with a smile. 'Yes, naturally.'

'Naturally?'

'Anyone going after Patrick Gillard *has* to be a professional – otherwise he doesn't stand a cat's chance in Hell.'

Carrick's keen hearing had caught the insincere nuance of his tone. 'If you know anything that I don't, I should be grateful to be allowed to know the secret,' he said heavily.

Hobbs appeared to think about it. Then he sat down and

said, 'As you instructed I telephoned the number Gillard gave you. Someone, a Captain Dean, was far more helpful that we'd been led to expect he would be. Gillard was on site from four-thirty pm on the Wednesday before his brother was killed until nine-thirty am on the Wednesday following.'

'And?'

'Everyone on the course, all eight of 'em, were let out on the Saturday evening for what the navy calls a run ashore. They left at seven-thirty and were required to be back in barracks at midnight. They all were. But Gillard didn't go with the rest – apparently the others departed in someone's Range Rover – but went on his own. He got back alone too.'

'Well, he'd have had to have done, wouldn't he? He could hardly have left his brother's car outside a pub somewhere.'

'A bit unfriendly, wasn't it? Unless he didn't go for a drink at all. Perhaps he drove over to Chew Valley Lake. It's no distance at all—'

Carrick knew that it was important to hang on to his temper. 'Okay. So why did he kill his brother? What possible motive did he have?'

'Perhaps the guy made a pass at his wife,' Hobbs said with a crafty smile.

'Sorry, you'll have to do better than that. How about some evidence?'

'I read through the case notes. The Templeton woman said that Lawrence was an ordinary bloke who didn't drink or smoke but sometimes had a few beers at weekends. By that I presumed she meant he might go to the local when the kids were over at their grandparents' place. So I asked a few questions in the pub nearest to where he lived. They knew him all right, he was going out with the barmaid. Her name's Sapphire apparently and as the landlord put it, she's very nicely set up. According to him they had a relationship. It occurred to me that someone like Patrick Gillard isn't likely to be too happy about his niece and nephew being around while their father has it away with a barmaid.'

'Did you speak to the woman?' Carrick asked.

'She's on the Costa del Sol with her mum until late tonight.'

'I see. Well, *Crispin*, perhaps you'd care to allow me to carry on with this and concentrate on the job I gave you to do.'

'It's a London mob,' Hobbs said, unperturbed. 'I'm sure of it. They've worked their way down through Surrey and Wilts. The MO is almost identical every time.'

'Then we need to catch them red-handed next time,' Carrick told him. 'Try to guess where they'll strike next.'

'The new computer shop in Heron Mall in Bear Flat might be up for grabs.'

'Is that a guess or actual knowledge?'

'It's a guess. But a fairly intelligent one.'

'Then make sure a few people keep an eye on the place.'

Hobbs left the room, a small smile on his face.

Carrick put his head in his hands. No, Larry's death was not going to be solved using conventional methods, not while he had to contend with idiots like Hobbs muddying the waters. Admittedly, the news of the barmaid was interesting, especially if such a lady had a disgruntled boyfriend in the background. There was nothing for it but to find out.

'What's the name of that pub?' he called into the main office a couple of minutes later.

'The Frog and Thicket,' Hobbs answered.

'The *what*?'

'I think it used to be called The Bell. It's been revamped. Quite nice too.'

Buller was in his office and hurriedly put in a drawer the small mirror he had been using to examine a spot on his nose. 'Progress, James?' he asked. This was his usual greeting.

'No,' Carrick said tersely. 'And there won't be any if I stick to the rules. I need to work *with* Patrick Gillard to get to the bottom of this.'

'Do you know where he is?'

'Just for today.' He leaned both hands on the desk, eye to eye with his superior. 'I hope, sir, that you've been straight with me and would tell me anything I need to know about this case.'

The man was not one to bluster or pull rank in moments of what he felt to be other people's crises.

'You have my word on that – naturally. But what—?'

'I want permission to act either alone or with Gillard for a while.'

The Superintendant's chunky fingers tapped the desk. 'I can give you a week. But no more than that. And if you haven't got results by then I'll have your hide.'

The gathering at the rectory at Hinton Littlemoor had dispersed when Carrick arrived, relatives and friends having departed on foot or in their cars leaving the house sad and silent. Elspeth was gathering used crockery in the living room, John replacing clean glasses and bottles in the drinks cabinet, Patrick in the kitchen feeding a dishwasher while almost absent-mindedly finishing off a plate of small, dainty sandwiches.

'It's that nice policeman,' Matthew announced. At his grandmother's request he had answered Carrick's ring at the door.

'So it is,' Elspeth cried, cheering up. 'James, I'm sure you'd like some supper. I know I do. I feel quite strange if I go to bed on tea and sandwiches.'

Carrick produced his gift, the latest Disney video, and the two children became all smiles and carried it gleefully away to watch it upstairs.

'That was really kind,' Elspeth said. 'If you want to talk to Patrick he's in the kitchen.'

Carrick picked up the tray of crockery and carried it through.

'I was hoping you'd look in,' Patrick said. 'Fancy a pint?'

'Your mother's invited me to supper.'

'Even better.' He looked at his watch. 'We've time for a quick one.' He swiftly loaded the crockery that Carrick had brought into the dishwasher, closed it and set the programme. 'Did you personally go through the stuff at Larry's flat?'

'Only some of it,' Carrick said. 'But SOCO listed everything and I read it through afterwards. Why do you ask?'

'Well, as you know, we've been given the really personal

things: his papers, watch, a couple of pairs of cufflinks, photographs. But Mother's worried about some jewellery that Shirley's mother gave to Larry for Katie when she's older. There was a watch too, for Matthew.'

'There was no jewellery on the list – nothing like that.'

'He probably put it in the bank. Don't worry about it.'

'But you'd have the receipt with a deposit box number on it.'

'Forget it. I'll have another look tomorrow.'

Carrick perched on a chair. 'No, this is important. Do you know exactly what the jewellery consists of?'

'Mother does.'

'It wouldn't have been on the premises when I was knocked down. Everything valuable or private had been taken back to the nick by then.'

'So your man in black wouldn't have got it. That's something.' He went away for a few moments to fetch a jacket. 'Have you spoken to Shirley?'

Carrick nodded. Speaking quietly he said, 'She had a man in the flat with her but I've no idea if he lives there. I wasn't allowed to meet him, he was skulking somewhere – probably in the bedroom. I parked farther down the road when I left and watched the place for a bit. He came out – a bit rough to say the least.'

'Pity we don't know who he is.'

'We do. He got in a car and I had the number checked. His name's Thomas Lee. His last known address is in a village nearby and he's got form for burglary, demanding money with menaces, motoring offences and assault.'

'Nothing drink-related?'

'Yes, the motoring offences. Drunk in charge of a car, driving while over the limit, driving while banned. Quite a clutch of them.'

'So she probably did meet him at the drying-out clinic. That's why I asked.'

Elspeth arrived, framed in the doorway. 'I suppose you're going for a beer first?'

'We were mulling it over,' said Patrick.

'Don't mull too long. I'm making pasta with chicken and prawns so if you're one second longer than half an hour it'll

81

be either ruined or all gone.' A little hesitantly she added, 'Am I right in thinking that you're working together on this?'

'We are,' Carrick replied. 'But I'm not going to get under his feet and it won't be for more than a few days. It's really a question of eliminating unwanted information and collating everything that his team turns up.'

'Splendid!' Elspeth exclaimed. 'What a good idea.'

'Your round,' Patrick said grimly when they had arrived at the Ring o'Bells. 'And I'll bloody well have a double of The Macallan.'

'Is someone still watching your back?'

'Several someones. But only until midnight. After that I'm on my own.'

High on Dartmoor, on the road from Yelverton to Princetown, a car was parked without lights in a lay-by. It was a warm night and both front windows of the vehicle had been opened. There were no lights within either.

'There has to be some kind of working code of practice,' Patrick Gillard said. 'Otherwise there might be confusion, and confusion in any kind of difficult situation can lead to failure and even death.'

'What do you suggest?' Carrick asked. They were seated in his car and, as directed, he had done all the driving. The BMW had been spirited away by a man who had walked from the shadows of the rectory garden at one minute past midnight precisely.

'I suggest we play it like I have before when working with non-military personnel. We stick to our own particular fields of reference whenever possible and confer on and discuss every move. I'm quite prepared to take your advice on matters about which you know more than I do. But when I shout – when I'm in the position to be aware of impending danger and where my training counts – you jump. When I shout, you do as I say.'

'Agreed,' Carrick said. 'Now tell me what we're doing here.'

'I have a bolt-hole not far away. Not even Ingrid knows

about it. I asked you to pull in here to make sure we weren't being followed but as no one has passed us I think it's safe to continue. Please turn round and go back the way we came for about half a mile.'

'Big words – failure and death,' Carrick murmured, turning the key in the ignition.

'I now know with whom I'm dealing,' Gillard responded evenly. 'He's a big guy.'

Carrick turned the car and, obeying instructions, slowed right down on a bend, taking a rough track that took them steadily uphill. They bounced slowly over the ruts, Carrick not daring to drive too fast in case the vehicle grounded. Trees and bushes on either side brushed against the bodywork.

'Remind me to swap this for a four-wheel drive vehicle if we pop into Tavistock,' he said under his breath.

Gillard chuckled. 'It's not far. Yes, we're here. Take the right fork and then swing in and park in front of the barn.'

The barn was two-storied, the lower part a cart shed with wooden doors. Gillard got out of the car and opened them to enable Carrick to drive in. The doors were closed immediately the car was safely within. Lights were switched on.

Revealed was a tidy, beamed garage, the walls whitewashed, quarry tiles on the floor. At one end was an open-plan staircase.

'If you don't have the key the doors can't be opened from the outside,' Gillard commented, leading the way up the stairs. 'Unless you take a chainsaw to them. Come up. I'm sure you could do with some coffee.'

'I haven't brought an overnight bag or anything like that,' Carrick said. 'I wasn't expecting to be heading off tonight.'

'You should do as I do and keep one packed ready in your car. But it doesn't matter – everything you'll need is here.'

The steel door at the top of the stairs had impressive locks. There was also an electronic locking device that Gillard deactivated by keying in a series of numbers. The door opened into a surprisingly large room with a kitchen in one corner. He switched on more lights.

'All self-contained,' Gillard said. 'The loo and shower are

83

through there. I bought the place from a farmer who put in electric and water so his son could use it to build a boat. As far as he's concerned I escape from the wife when I can to write a book.'

He went on talking, making the coffee as he spoke, explaining where everything was and how the bench seating doubled as beds. Pillows, blankets and linen were to be found in the lockers beneath.

'You fitted this all out yourself?' Carrick wondered aloud.

'Some of it was here already; the kitchen units and the shower room. Terry helped me with some of it – carpentry was never a strong point of mine. Sorry about the bars over the windows. They were put in by the farmer's son after someone broke in and nicked his tools.'

'So how do you get out in a hurry? If the enemy get in downstairs and light a fire under you, for example?' Carrick was only half serious.

'The escape hatch is through the cupboard next to the sink. It was the old chute for fodder which we redirected. You end up by crashing through what look like metal bars in the outside wall. Only they're made of plywood, painted black.'

Carrick smiled. 'To land right in the lap of the enemy?'

Gillard actually looked annoyed. 'Look, if it gets as *meaningful* as that you go down with a knife between your teeth and cut the throat of anyone loafing around at the bottom.'

From the point of view of his chosen career Carrick fervently hoped that no situation would get 'meaningful' while he was around. But all the same, a tingle of excitement travelled slowly down his spine.

'Not that I intend to declare war on a secret unit of the Anti-terrorist Branch, the continued existence of which my department has only just discovered,' Gillard added, pouring coffee. 'The trouble is, they appear to have declared war on me.'

'You know that for sure now? How?'

'Because of something that was left in my car.' He dug in a pocket and produced a small, round metal object that he slapped down on the kitchen worktop.

'A St Christopher medal?' Carrick said, looking at it. 'I

noticed it. It was stuck to the bottom of the inside of the windscreen on the driver's side.'

'Not mine.'

'Whose then?'

'That's not important. He used to call himself Christopher Ladd. He was big, blond, good-looking and couldn't put a foot wrong so was nicknamed St Christopher. It stuck, even when he was made major. He used to give his friends medals like this, for presents, – birthdays and so forth. Silver or even gold. Then he left the army and joined the police and I lost track of him.'

'I could check.'

'A pound to a penny he isn't calling himself that now. Especially if he's in some kind of *carte-blanche* unit that set up the survival school in Wales. It's not impossible that Commander X – Lyndberne – was a friend of his.'

'Do you know this man well?'

'As well as anyone who served with him. The down side is that when I was an instructor in Special Operations I taught him all he knows.'

'You mean, the outfit at Cirencester that you have to attend for annual assessments?'

'It's part of it.'

'And he's clever.'

'Clever in the sense that he's strong, single-minded, ambitious and with a cruel streak that caused me to dislike him. He would be dangerous to cross.'

'You told me you weren't going to lie low.'

'I'm not. I've come here to have a good think – weigh everything up. But, to be honest, I already knew what I was going to do. Really, I have no choice.'

'Care to tell me what that is?'

'I feel I must run him to earth and find out if he did kill Larry, mistakenly or no. Then stand back and let you arrest him.'

'Chief Inspectors don't normally get to have the top brass for breakfast,' Carrick pointed out. 'If he is top brass, that is.'

'But his rank wouldn't prevent you from arresting him?'

'Not at all. Chief Constables have been hauled in for driving over the limit before now.'

'The problem with this one – assuming that all my guesses are correct – is that he'd arrange to have you chucked off the nearest suspension bridge as soon as you had him in your sights. He won't play legal any more than Lyndberne did.'

'I'd have to make it official. Remember, I don't work undercover and largely unsupervised like you do.'

'But *he* will be. With official backing. You might even be warned off by your own superiors. That's why I didn't really want you to be involved. Hell, I don't want you to put your job on the line on account of my brother.'

'Larry was a murder victim. If someone warns me off finding out who killed him I shall resign and go after him privately. I didn't join that kind of police force.'

Gillard's response to this was a grave nod.

'Which makes it even more important that I have all the facts,' Carrick said. 'And I need *more* facts – from you.'

'Can't it wait until we've had a couple of hours' kip?'

'No.' When silence greeted this reply, Carrick continued, 'I want to know why it was once necessary for you to point a gun at your one-time sister-in-law.'

Gillard could not prevent an angry shrug. 'She's never forgiven me. It happened the day of Justin's christening. A local man – he was a government scientist – attended the service but did not come to the house afterwards even though most of the village did. Everyone was leaving and my family were in the kitchen clearing away when he burst in, saying that some men on a motor bike were after him. Terry was outside doing something or other and the next moment we heard a bike in the drive and he almost fell through the door and then collapsed. He'd been hit on the head – with a spanner, we discovered afterwards – actually causing a hair-line fracture of the skull. I pulled Terry's gun from his bag that he'd dumped in the kitchen – we were all armed in those days – and prepared to repel boarders.

'Shirley had hysterics and was all for grabbing the children and Larry and heading for home. I told her to stay where she was until it was safe to leave. She was all for bolting through the door and it was a case of either slap her face or point the gun at her. I only had time to do the latter and it's just as well I did as the madmen outside were part of a group of Hell's Angels working for an international gang bent on murdering the scientist. They'd mistaken Terry for him in the dark. You can check it out – just ask Daws.'

'Talking of Daws . . . Are you going to keep him in the dark over this affair?'

'I haven't decided yet. What else do you want to know?'

It was as if a NO TRESPASSING notice had been erected, sparks of anger visible deep in those grey eyes.

Carrick made himself more comfortable on the bench seat. 'On the Saturday when you were at Cirencester you were all allowed out during the evening. You went alone. Why?'

'The others were all bloody bores, that's why.'

'Where did you go?'

'To a little pub for supper.'

'Sorry, you'll have to do better than that.'

Anger was overlaid by resentment. 'Look, you'll be saying next that—'

'Did you know that Larry was going out with a woman called Sapphire? The barmaid at his local?'

'He said something about a new girlfriend. James, I did *not*—'

'And there's that awe-inspiring temper that your mother didn't mention. How long do I have to wind you up before you lose control and are too dangerous to be in the same room with? Was it the last straw when the children were removed from an idyllic country cottage belonging to a really pleasant girl and taken to a grim flat in the city? And about their father having an affair with a bit of a trollop? Did you go back to Bristol to have it out with him and just happen to pull the trigger?'

Gillard blinked rapidly several times and then said, 'There was no question of my taking a firearm out of the establishment that night.'

'But I thought you had been given permission to carry a gun for personal protection purposes?'

'That's right. But nevertheless, that night—'

'I can just picture it. You might have given him a ring and offered to meet him at the lake. Perhaps the idea was that

87

you'd have a pint together and exchange cars. But instead you had a heated argument on the lake shore. It was just like the old days and he became very offensive. All the old dislike was rekindled. You were damned if this man was going to carry on being responsible for your niece and nephew. Before you realised it he was dead at your—'

'No!' Gillard shouted. He shot to his feet and every muscle in Carrick's body tensed. But the other man had flung himself away to the far end of the room and now stood with his back to him, gripping the top of a wooden chair. Carrick could almost hear the tendons of his fingers creaking.

'It would be a clever ploy to create a Mr Big who's vowed to get even with you,' Carrick went on. 'And because of your job you're in such a unique position that it would be virtually impossible to disprove anything you've said. I'm sure that no end of disgruntled terrorists whom you've shoved in the slammer are out and thirsting for your blood. Then why, I hear you say, didn't I simply blame it on someone like that and not a real-life copper? I'll tell you why – because you're bloody arrogant. Creating webs of intrigue around yourself is your stock in trade. Sometimes you do it to amuse yourself or entertain others, like when you pretended to be a drunk at the nick. You weave around yourself a whole fabric of make-believe and lies. It's second nature to you now. Ingrid once said to me that she sometimes has the disturbing thought that even *she* doesn't know what is the real you.'

Slowly, Gillard turned.

'And then there's fear,' Carrick continued, experiencing the sensation of a man facing his firing squad. 'As I said just now, that temper. People dare not push you too far, not even your own family. You punish with scathing wit or foul language, depending on whom you're up against. Or even, perhaps, physical violence. Then what do you do? Shoot all the rooks out of a tree in the garden if they keep you awake? Kick the cat? Wallop Justin?'

Astoundingly, tears sprang to Gillard's eyes. 'That's outrageous,' he whispered. 'I've never laid a finger on Justin. Or on Pirate for that matter.'

88

Carrick went up to him. They stood face to face. 'Then perhaps it's sheer presence,' he said, just as quietly. 'I'm king. Worship me. Your men worshipped you when you were on active service, didn't they?'

'It's called leadership.'

'You can't hide behind that now. *I meant what I said.* You're not calling the tune. You're not leaving out things you don't want to tell me. Give me the whole story of what you did that Saturday night or I'll walk right out of here and put out a warrant for your arrest.' After fully ten seconds' dead silence during which, somehow, his nerve still did not break, he added, 'And if you push my teeth down my throat, I'll have you for grievous bodily harm too.'

'What kind of a man do you think I am?' Gillard said hoarsely after another agonising silence.

'That's just the point I'm making,' Carrick said. 'I'm not at all sure.'

Jerkily, like a puppet on strings, Gillard went to a wall cupboard and opened it. He took from it a whisky bottle and two glasses and splashed some of the golden liquid in each. His hand shook just a little. He passed one over to Carrick and downed his in one, pouring himself a refill.

'I'll tell you,' he said. 'Yes, I went to the lake. I'd rung Larry to find out if the car had been fixed or whether there had been any problems. He suggested meeting up for a beer – he knew I wasn't all that far away. There was something in his car that he wanted – he'd left it in the boot. It was a project file for his class or something like that. We met and for some reason he started talking about the woman, Sapphire. He got a bit crude, telling me that she was a real goer in bed. I said that mother would be upset from the children's point of view. He said that she knew, and was, but it didn't make any difference, he could do as he liked. It was just like you said. It seemed to trigger all his old resentment and he went on and on. Getting offensive, deliberately winding me up. He'd been in a bad mood from the beginning as he'd left his wallet behind and had no money on him.'

Carrick had not touched his whisky. 'And?'

'I just got out. I knew I was coming to the boil. I was so

upset I got back in the car – *his* car – and drove back to Cirencester.'

'And the gun?'

'I told you the truth. It was secured in a locker at the barracks.'

'Do you have any proof of that?'

'No. It's for my own personal use. I don't have to sign it in or out or anything like that.' He sat down suddenly. 'I keep having nightmares that I did kill him,' he muttered. 'I shot him but he didn't die. He just waggled a finger at me and jeered, "You missed! You missed!" Then he walked away, blood spouting from his head like a fountain... It's ghastly, disgusting.' Gillard retched, shuddering violently. 'You're a bastard,' he succeeded in saying.

Nothing else was said as they settled down for a couple of hours' sleep. When Carrick awoke he was alone.

Chapter 8

The hot summer sunshine beat off the pavements, turning the streets of London into furnaces, the taste of car exhaust constantly at the back of Carrick's throat. There had been no rain here and a light breeze that did not cool or freshen blew dust into little edies that rose and got into the eyes and between the teeth. Litter lay underfoot, kicked aside by the throngs of tourists.

Carrick entered the new MI5 building and went up to the reception desk, the sudden change to an air-conditioned environment causing him to shiver.

'I would very much like to see Richard Daws,' he said to the security guard who gazed at his warrant card dubiously. 'My apologies for not being aware of any title due to him but I've only spoken to him once and that was over the phone.'

'I'm afraid, sir, if you haven't an appointment . . .'

'Be so kind as to give him a ring. Tell him I'm here and ask if we may have a chat about survival schools.'

'Survival schools?' said the man blankly.

'That's right. He'll know what I mean.'

Carrick carried on staring unblinkingly at the man and won. Five minutes later he was being ushered into an outer office on the fifth floor where a secretary gestured to an armchair and asked him to wait.

'It's colonel,' the security guard had called after him.

After only a few minutes had elapsed the phone buzzed on the secretary's desk.

'Please go in, Chief Inspector,' the woman said, indicating one of the three panelled doors in the room.

The office that Carrick found himself in was far more plush than that belonging to the Chief Constable at HQ in Portishead and twice as large. Carrick had time to assimilate a long case clock of magnificent aspect and a display case containing a collection of small jade ornaments and then went forward to shake hands with the tall man who rose from his chair behind an antique pedestal desk.

'You're lucky,' Daws commented when they were both seated. 'I only work part-time now and this is the first day of my transfer here. The department used to be housed in a building overlooking Horse Guards Parade – and a damned sight more pleasant it was too. Am I to understand that you want to talk about the late Anton Lyndberne?'

'Actually, I think I'm more interested in friends of his.'

Daws was probably in his early-sixties. He had piercing blue eyes and fair greying hair that tended to flop over his forehead. He scooped it back impatiently. 'Ah,' he said, frowning. After a few seconds during which he studied Carrick gravely, he said, 'The man who actually tipped the Commander out of his boat and then held him under until he drowned died in Bosnia. He'd become a mercenary and was fighting for the Croats.'

'Is Lieutenant-colonel Gillard aware of that?'

'Probably not. Whether you tell him or not is up to you. But from the point of view of any investigation you're carrying out that line of enquiry has to be regarded as closed.'

'He was requested to put an end to the Commander's fishing trip,' Carrick pointed out.

'I'm aware of that. But there's no evidence to support it and the inquest recorded a verdict of Death by Misadventure.'

'Gillard does not appear to be aware that you're in possession of the facts.'

The Colonel smiled grimly. 'It's irrelevant to your inquiry what facts I'm in possession of but since you ask I'll explain the situation a little. For practically all the time I've known him Patrick Gillard has believed he could stay one step ahead of me. Occasionally he succeeds. But he forgets that my army career spans many years more than his. I have built up extremely close links with all aspects of things military. If you like, I'm one of the people who tend the grapevine. If someone in the security services asks someone else to remove a senior police officer from the land of the living it does *not* remain a secret from me.'

'And if the friends of the policeman go gunning for the perpetrator?'

'It's worrying, I agree, if others are aware of the truth,' Daws replied blandly.

'I'm sorry but that sort of answer simply won't do. I'm looking for Lawrence Gillard's killer. Someone shot him and threw his body into a lake.'

Daws shook his head sadly. 'I don't see how I can help you.'

'I need to look nearer to home then?' Carrick asked baldly.

'Alas, I'm not an oracle.'

'You did not approve, I presume, of the survival school idea?'

'At the time I thought it innovative and quite clever. But not after I had read all the reports and had time to reflect. We would all like to be given free rein to put our most cherished ideas and plans into practice but such plans should not involve serious risk to the public. Criminal irresponsibility is the way I would describe it now.'

'And what if they're going to do it again?'

The urbane manner was slightly shaken. '*Are* they? Do you have evidence to support it?'

'Gillard has not discussed this with you?'

'I cannot reveal what I discuss with my subordinates.'

Carrick hung on to his temper. 'Colonel, I can't work in a mass of red tape. Patrick Gillard has come very close to being charged with his brother's murder and I'm moving heaven and earth to get to the truth. If someone has shot Gillard's brother either by mistake or as a warning to him to keep out of the way while some ruse to catch terrorists is set up then it's your duty to tell me anything you know.'

Daws smiled, real humour breaking through for a

93

moment. 'I wish I worked to such clear-cut precepts,' he said. 'I would help you if I could but must point out that the red tape, in this case, is on your side of the fence.' When he received no response he added, 'I have not discussed this with Gillard and am not aware of any reason to think what you say might be true. Perhaps you would be kind enough to tell me what you know?'

Carrick was unaware of doing so but thawed slightly. 'A St Christopher medal was left in Gillard's car, presumably on the night Larry was killed. Patrick once knew a Christopher Ladd who gave out such keepsakes and now works for a police department. Patrick trained him – in other words he's dangerous. If he now works for the undercover unit of Special Branch that set up the Brecon Beacons scheme...' Carrick left the rest unsaid.

'Can *you* find out about him?'

'Not without making undesirable waves – assuming, that is, that the suspicions are borne out.'

'They wouldn't bloody dare,' Daws said under his breath. 'It was fully sanctioned.'

'By the Home Office. But I don't suppose the Home Secretary was told that children had died as a direct result of his signature on that particular piece of paper.'

'And the Prime Minister was dead against it?'

Carrick received a fierce stare for this sally and knew that he was correct.

Daws said, 'The Avon and Somerset Police can't get involved in a difference of opinion between the Home Office and Downing Street.'

'I'm fairly sure we can. Especially if the Chief Constable wades into the fray.'

'You realise that if all this becomes public knowledge Patrick Gillard might go to prison for being an accessory to murder?'

'He seems willing to risk a lot more than that to find his brother's killer.'

Daws went off into a world of his own for a moment and then said, 'Are you working together?'

'Very quietly,' Carrick replied, not about to reveal that Patrick had gone off in the night taking his, Carrick's, car.

94

'All I can promise,' Daws said after a pause, 'is that I'll keep my ear to the ground. *Provided* that anything I discover is not prejudicial to the safety of personnel in this department I shall inform you accordingly. Er – this Christopher Ladd . . .'

'He might be using an alias these days.'

'That's possible. But if you think you've seen him . . .'

'I can't guarantee anything.'

'We both work on the side of law and order, you know.'

'Quite,' Carrick said enigmatically, taking his leave.

Carrick had solved his transport problem, initially, by walking back to the main road, very early, and thumbing a lift from a lorry driver to Plymouth airport and from there had flown to Heathrow. The barn hideaway had locked itself up satisfactorily behind him, not that he had been too concerned right then for the safety of Gillard's possessions. In fact he had 'borrowed' a clean shirt, an extremely smart fine cotton one he had found in a drawer, and made full use of his vanished host's toiletries in the shower room.

He was hurt and also angry. This was partly because he felt that Gillard had reacted to his close questioning with an uncharacteristic fit of pique and also with himself for failing to wake up when Gillard had departed. He had left no note or explanation and that was what hurt most of all.

Fortunately Joanna had gone to her summer school in Manchester by train so Carrick went straight home by taxi from Bath station and collected her car. Then, and by this time it was three in the afternoon, he set out for Hinton Littlemoor, having made himself a sandwich and downed a glass of orange juice. He decided to make a slight detour and call in at Manvers Street on the way.

'Why do nicks always stink of fag smoke and chips?' he asked Ingrams when they met in the lobby.

Ingrams clearly felt that he was not required to explain one of the mysteries of the universe, responding to the question with a fleeting smile. Then he said, 'We've had an anonymous tip-off about the Gillard case. Someone rang to say that Thomas Lee burgled the victim's flat on the night he died.'

95

'He's the man the ex-wife's friendly with.'

'I know, guv. You'd written it all down in the file. I rang York CID and they said he has Pre Cons as long as your arm and we could have him with their love. It just so happens they have good reasons for a search warrant anyway so they're going to turn his place over. I'm expecting a call any time now as to what they've found, if anything.'

'Was it a man or woman who rang?'

'Hastie took the call. He said it was a man.'

'Shirley has a deepish voice. And if she'd muffled it with a scarf or something ... We'll have to bear in mind that it could be a malicious call – the woman seems to be pro-grammed that way.'

Carrick thanked Ingrams and went into his office. There was no sign of Hobbs and he seated himself with a sigh of relief and reached for the phone. He would have to ask his questions right away instead of using valuable time to make a personal visit. A few minutes later he had all the infor-mation he wanted. The jewellery intended for Katie was all Victorian and consisted of two woven filigree gold rings, a brooch set with jet and very small diamonds, an amber necklace and a pair of coral and pearl earrings. The watch for Matthew was more valuable but the only details that Elspeth knew was that it was a gold fob with the maker's name ingraved inside. John had then come on the phone to say that he was fairly sure that the watch had a chronometer movement.

'If that's the case it's likely to be very valuable indeed,' Carrick had said.

'If my memory is as good as I hope it is – and you understand I've only seen it once – it's very similar to one auctioned in Bristol recently that went for twenty thousand pounds,' John had finished by saying.

'And you're quite sure these items aren't in a bank?'

'No, although if I'd known the value of it before I'd have mentioned it to Larry and advised him to keep it safe. I rang his bank to double-check and there's nothing in safe deposit boxes. I can't believe that Larry would have been stupid enough to hide these things under the floorboards.'

'I'll send someone over to make sure,' Carrick had promised. 'But SOCO are usually very thorough and check for loose boards.'

Carrick offered up a quick prayer that none of the missing items had been lavished on the athletic Sapphire. This reminded him that the woman had still not been interviewed and he sent Ingrams off to make good the omission, emphasising that he should press her about any gifts she had received from Larry.

'Surely he wouldn't have given her stuff meant for the kids?' Ingrams, a staunch family man, protested.

'Has a man ever made a fool of himself over a woman?' Carrick countered and the Detective Sergeant went away, shaking his head.

Carrick had asked Elspeth if she knew whether Sapphire had been invited to Larry's flat. There was a chance that the woman had helped herself to the jewellery.

'Oh, yes. Matthew told me. He and Katie would be in bed when she arrived but he could hear them talking and laughing together. Sapphire stayed the night. Matthew knows *precisely* what that means. It was what upset me so much and made Patrick so furious. I wish I hadn't told him now.'

Carrick had forced himself to ask one last question. 'Are you quite sure, in your own mind, that Patrick didn't lose his temper and kill Larry?'

It had obviously come as a shock and there had been such a long silence that Carrick thought they had been cut off. Then Elspeth had said, 'Yes. He's always told me the truth even when he's been in dreadfully hot water. If he'd done it he wouldn't be able to look me in the eye. That's not what I meant when I said that I wished I hadn't told him. I meant that it only made matters worse between them.'

Carrick was still no nearer to finding a murderer.

Thomas Lee sat hunched uneasily in the back of the patrol car, his thin lips pressed into a grim line. Constable Peter Hepplewhite, at his side, had removed the handcuffs while the car was in motion as it was not thought that Lee would make a wild bid for freedom and risk instant death while the vehicle was travelling at a little over eighty miles an hour in the fast lane. There had been a stop for refreshment near Birmingham when Kevin Strong, who was driving, had gone for sandwiches and tea while Hepplewhite had escorted Lee to the toilet. The food had been consumed in the car.

Strong's right foot was nearer to the floor than was perhaps necessary because not only was he missing night duty but there was the prospect of a night out, on expenses.

'This isn't the Batmobile,' Hepplewhite observed from the back.

'Just call me Robin,' Strong said, but slowed slightly, pulling over into the middle lane. Pete was always the one to urge caution. Strong gave his friend a grin in the mirror. Pete was right, of course. It was why Sergeant Crumlyn had put them together; the quiet methodical History graduate from Barrow-in-Furness and Strong the local boy, ambitious, headstrong but intelligent enough to know when to take advice.

'Where do you fancy going tonight?' Strong asked.

'So that's why you're in such a hurry. To a pub. Where else?'

'Naturally. But where? Do you know Bath? Ever been there before?'

'No. But it's a tourist trap. Must be thousands of good pubs and restaurants.'

'It's not the sort of place to have strip shows, is it?'

'No,' Hepplewhite said with just a trace of regret.

'How about Bristol?'

'That's a different kettle of fish altogether. But don't forget, we haven't anywhere to stay yet. We're relying on the people at the nick in Bath to organise something for us.'

'The Sarge said he'd fix it.'

'Good old Crumbles.'

Strong threw a glance over his shoulder at their passenger. 'Are we taking him back with us tomorrow?'

'I doubt it. Not after the rings and necklace were found at his place. They fit descriptions of stuff stolen from the flat of a guy who was shot.'

'That bloody woman . . .' Lee muttered.

'They didn't find a gun then?' Strong continued.

'No.'

'I've never had no gun,' Lee said. 'I've never had a gun in my *life*.'

'Who knows? You might be in the frame for murder,' Strong taunted.

They were on the south side of Gloucester now, heading towards Bristol. Strong relaxed, daydreaming, unconsciously putting on speed again. The traffic had thinned out considerably now they had cleared the Midlands and they almost had the road to themselves. The sun was shining and everything in the world was very good.

Lee spoke all at once, breaking into his reverie.

'Suppose a bloke *did* go into someone's place and pick up a few bits and pieces,' he ventured nervously. 'But not by breakin' in – the door had been left unlocked.'

'It's still unlawful entry and stealing,' Strong informed him in amazement.

'Suppose he did,' Hepplewhite encouraged. 'What then?'

'Well, suppose the bloke what wandered in surprised someone who wasn't the person who lived there – someone who was in a room the bloke hadn't gone in on his way up the hall and who did a bunk as soon as he saw he was no longer alone?'

'How did you know he wasn't the person who lived there?'

'I've just told you. He ran off.'

'You probably scared the living daylights out of him. He went away to phone the police.'

'But you've already said that the bloke who lived there was dead.'

Strong said, 'He was alive until you got there and you shot him when he saw you.'

Lee's battered features screwed up into a mask of hatred. 'Trust a soddin' copper to turn everything round. So I'm in the frame already, am I? I wouldn't have said anything if I'd threatened him or whatever, would I? It wouldn't have seemed so strange, him doin' a runner.'

'So this man ran off?'

'Yes, but not in a panicky kind of way. I only saw him out of the corner of my eye. He sort of went quickly and quietly. He had no business to be there – I could tell.'

'Spoken by a master of the art of furtiveness,' Hepplewhite said dismissively. 'I think you're trying to get your head out of the noose.'

'You're a real smart-arse, ain't ya?' Lee bawled in his ear.

'Cut it out!' Strong ordered sharply. He had received the full benefit of Lee's bad breath. 'What did this character look like?'

Lee simmered for a few moments and then said, 'He was just a shape in the hall and as he went through the front door. He might have been wearin' a long sort of mac. Dark, it was.'

'Was he big, small, tall, thin, fat?'

'I don't bleedin' know,' Lee whined. 'I've just told you – he was just a dark shape.'

'Good try,' Hepplewhite said.

Lee did not reply, lapsing into a sullen silence.

Bob Ingrams expected to find his quarry in the Frog and Thicket and was not disappointed. He ordered a half of lager and positioned himself at a quiet end of the bar where he could wait until she was less busy.

Yes, he rapidly concluded, Sapphire was definitely the kind of girl whom men prefer to bed rather than marry. Her figure was well-rounded, her complexion surprisingly pale in view of her having just returned from a holiday abroad. Her blonde hair was worn up in a bun which rather accentuated her short neck and rounded shoulders but she had fine hazel eyes and could fairly be described as very attractive. Her age, Ingrams supposed, was just the right side of thirty. His wife would think her clothes – a very short leather skirt and tight tee shirt – 'brazen hussyish' and he had an idea that his spouse would follow this up with a remark that the woman wasn't very bright either.

What on earth had attracted her to Larry Gillard?

'I'd like a quick word,' he said when she was free and leaning on the bar near him with a pensive pout on her full, bright pink lips.

Sapphire glowered at his warrant card. 'What about?' she snapped.

Ingrams forced himself to concentrate on the questions

he was going to ask and not on her burgeoning bosom. 'First of all tell me your full name.'

'Sadie Bartlett.'

Ingrams's eyebrows rose. It was a mannerism he had copied from Carrick, only the DCI could make just one eyebrow quirk questioningly, something Ingrams felt to be really cool, as his young son would say. He himself couldn't achieve that yet. He practised in front of the bathroom mirror.

'Me mum called me Sapphire as a sort of nickname. She used to watch a programme on the telly: *Sapphire and Steel*, with Joanna Lumley. Mum thought I looked like her.'

'I understand you used to go out with Lawrence Gillard.'

'Just for a little while,' she answered defensively.

'You know that he's dead?'

Her expression had not changed to one of regret or sadness. 'Yes, I heard. Poor Larry.'

'How did you find out about it? His name hasn't been revealed to the media.'

'The woman who lives upstairs rang me – upstairs to Larry, I mean. She heard all you lot coming and going and then someone knocked at her door and asked when she'd last seen him. She overheard a copper talking on the stairs – talking about a body.'

'You didn't try to find out more? The woman might have made a mistake.'

'No. We'd split up. Not that we ever hit it off really. He wasn't my sort.'

'When did you split up?'

'Not all that long ago.'

'Be more specific.'

'It was towards the end of last month – round about the twentieth.'

Ingrams consulted his notebook. 'That was two days before he was murdered.'

'Murdered! You didn't say anything about murder.'

'He was shot out at Chew Valley Lake. Did you have a row?'

'Not really.'

'It must have been a bit final, though. On the Saturday

101

morning he rang an old girlfriend and asked if she wanted to go for a drive.'

'You don't say?' Sapphire commented in a bored-sounding voice.

'Did you split up before or after he took his brother's car to the garage?'

'God knows. He didn't tell me anything about a car.'

'Okay, was it in the morning or the afternoon?'

'The evening. We went to the pictures.'

'And then you parted. Just like that.'

'Yes.'

Sapphire went away to see to the needs of some customers. When she came back Ingrams asked, 'Did you have a set of door keys to his flat?'

'No, we weren't *that* close.'

'But you used to visit his flat and spend the night with him?'

'Only sometimes. Look, have you almost finished? The boss is giving me funny looks.'

'We could carry on talking at the nick,' Ingrams retorted. 'Did you receive any gifts from him?'

'What sort of gifts?'

'Straight answers,' he snarled. 'Or you're coming right back to Bath with me *now*.'

Sapphire began to look alarmed. 'I don't know what you're getting at. He gave me some flowers once but I threw them away as they make me sneeze. And some chocolates for my birthday.'

'No jewellery?'

'No.'

'Think very hard. Did he ever mention jewellery to you or show you any that would be his daughter's one day?'

'No. Never.'

'So why Lawrence Gillard then? You've just said he wasn't your sort.'

Sapphire bit her lip. 'I can tell you now he's dead. . . . I went out with him to make my boyfriend jealous.'

'Name?' Ingrams went on inexorably.

'Here, you can't bring him into this. He'd kill me if—'

The Detective Sergeant shut his notebook with a loud snap, patience exhausted.

'He – he's a wrestler,' Sapphire stuttered. 'Like the side of a house. And he'd been chatting up this girl at the chemist's. And when Larry asked me to go out with him for a meal—'

Ingrams interrupted with, 'Suppose this wrestler like the side of a house didn't just get jealous but decided to put an end to the matter in a very final way?'

'No, Tip wouldn't. He's gentle really. When you get to know him. Oh, dear ...'

'Tip O'Shea, no doubt,' Ingrams said triumphantly. 'I seem to remember we once had good reason to charge him with attempted murder.'

'But he was innocent, wasn't he? He was cleared. He'd only chased ... I mean, the man was only injured because he ran out into the road in front of a lorry. Tip hadn't—'

'Hadn't tried to break his neck first? That was what a few very reluctant witnesses said afterwards. It was odd how they changed their story when it came to court though, wasn't it?'

At this point Ingrams decided to refer his findings to higher authority. He was not ashamed to admit that he preferred to have Carrick with him when he interviewed the likes of O'Shea. Carrick could look after himself.

Chapter 9

Constable Strong had taken a wrong turning in the maze of motorway interchanges in the Bristol area and found himself heading for the city centre. As it happened the mistake was not a disaster by any means but until this became apparent he spent a miserable half-hour, cursing his own stupidity, stuck in slow traffic. The situation did not really warrant the flashing blue light and siren treatment and he knew anyway that Pete would not approve. His anticipation of a good night out began to fade. By the time they had gone through the formalities of handing Lee over and found out where they were staying . . . He ground his teeth with impatience. It was well after five already.

Soon, however, they were on an open road again, fields and hedgerows bright in the late-afternoon sunshine.

'You did the right thing, Kev,' Hepplewhite said. 'I reckon that if we'd stayed on the motorway we'd have done a huge loop into the sticks that we didn't need to. The nick's right in the middle of Bath anyway.'

Then they came to houses, modern developments and the occasional small industrial estate. The closer they got to the city centre the older the property became and soon they were in sight of curving Regency terraces, the bright light causing the buildings almost to glow. And everywhere there were flowers; in window boxes, hanging baskets, horse troughs, front gardens and all kinds of containers.

'My dad would enjoy this,' Hepplewhite pronounced. 'He's a real wizard at growing carnations – wins prizes at

104

the local shows. The sideboard at home groans with the weight of cups he's won.'

'Where's the nick?' Strong asked, mind on present concerns.

'Near the railway station. Just follow the signs for that.'

It all seemed to be one-way streets but after one one small error and having to circumnavigate a roundabout twice they swept past the station and turned into Manvers Street. Seconds later they were drawing into the forecourt of the police station.

'Drop us off here,' Hepplewhite suggested. 'I can go in with chummy while you park at the rear.'

But a van had pulled in right in front of them, blocking their path, so Strong reversed into a vacant parking space, the capital letters CF painted in white on the ground.

'CF won't have to mind,' Hepplewhite said, undoing his seatbelt. 'See you in a mo.'

Strong yanked on the handbrake. He then released his own seatbelt and bent down, scrabbling under the front seat for a chocolate bar he had opened earlier that had fallen from his lap.

Above him, the windscreen crashed in in a hail of broken glass, explosions ripping into the vehicle. Then the driver's window smashed in on him, the fragments hitting his head in a stinging shower. A white hot pain hammered into his right leg and he screamed, cramming himself into the footwell as far as he could go. He knew now that what he was listening to were shots.

Silence.

Then there was the howling noise of a vehicle going very quickly in reverse. The sound headed for where he was and he caught a glimpse of the van roaring past as he craned his neck to see. It clipped the car, rocking it violently, slamming his head into the side of the glove compartment.

'Got to get out,' he heard a voice mutter. 'The petrol tank, the sodding petrol tank might . . .' It was his own voice. 'Pete!' he hissed. 'Pete. Are you all right?'

Got to get out.

He tried to sit upright but his limbs would not obey him. Reaching up with one hand he groped for something he

105

could use to haul himself up but encountered only thin air. Then he touched what appeared to be the edge of the window but it was all jagged edges of glass.

Got to get out.

He could hear something dripping and then smelt the spilt fuel.

The door behind him must have opened because something brushed against his groping hand and a breeze wafted around the back of his head. Perhaps if he tried wriggling out rear first . . .

No, he was stuck. His feet were jammed under the pedals.

Hands grasped him, touched his leg. It had been numb in an odd sort of way but now searing agony flared into his knee and calf. He could not stop the cry that burst from his throat.

'Take it easy, son,' said a fatherly kind of voice with a country accent. 'Just relax and I'll soon get you out.'

Strong tried to go as limp as possible, recognising the authority in the tone and also the the urgency. Then pain the likes of which he would not have believed possible scythed into his leg and he blacked out.

The petrol tank exploded just as Woods had run with his burden to the comparative shelter of the main entrance doors, blowing him off his feet and into the arms of those running to help.

'Never mind us, get to the others!' Carrick yelled from somewhere underneath. 'Get that bloody fire out!'

Fire drills and bomb alert exercises, no matter now well organised and imaginatively planned, cannot quite prepare those involved for the real thing. There had even, recently, been a full-scale mock-up of a train crash, the venue a private railway in East Somerset. There had been blazing overturned condemned carriages, courtesy of Great Western Trains and the Fire Brigade, and 'passengers', actually services volunteers, with horrific injuries lovingly faked by a team from the St John's Ambulance Brigade. Helping to ease these people from wreckage had seemed difficult, hazardous and very, very real.

Carrick's shout – he had directed a rescue team on that day at Cranmore – cut into everyone's shocked minds and

106

restored order. People made for phones, hose reels and extinguishers, those manning the desk shepherding several members of the public in the lobby to the rear of the building away from danger.

Carrick picked himself up, made sure that an ambulance was on its way for Woods, who was out cold, and the constable he had rescued, now conscious but in considerable pain, and that someone trained in first aid was looking after them in the interim, grabbed a fire extinguisher and ran outside. Two other parked cars were already ablaze and flames were licking greedily at the plastic guttering and down pipes at one end of the building.

There was a petrol station next door.

Without being told to a couple of probationers had stopped the traffic and were making those in vehicles close to the blaze leave them and retreat to a safe distance. A large lorry loaded with pallets and an oil tanker were slowly reversing away from the scene, utilising part of the wide pavement.

Another vehicle's fuel tank exploded, showering debris and burning fragments on the fire fighters, smouldering pieces clattering into the forecourt of the filling station. Two uniformed constables who had been manning a fire hose, too close, reeled away, one of them with his clothing alight. Others dashed to them and smothered the flames, some unwisely beating at them with bare hands.

A third car was well alight by the time the Fire Brigade arrived, even though it was only a matter of minutes. They immediately banished all amateurs from the area. Carrick threw a quick regretful glance over his shoulder in the direction of a blazing pale blue Ford Escort as he went indoors.

Joanna's car.

Lorna Templeton had forced herself to mount a set of rickety stepladders and go into her loft to sort out the things that Larry had left behind. There were a thousand and one reasons why she did not want to undertake the task, not least that looking at his possessions would make her very upset and feel even more guilty than she did already. She had phoned Elspeth about it, who had spoken to John, and

107

he said that their local Scouts would welcome the things that were only gathering dust in Lorna's loft.

The actual ropes and other climbing gear had belonged to the school, of course, and were being used by the games master who had taken over the outdoor activities when Larry had felt that he could no longer carry on. But there was a tent, with groundsheet, his boots, several different sets of outdoor clothing that would fit older boys, maps, survival gear and a box of things like compasses and emergency rations. Larry had bought the equipment out of his own pocket and had kept it so he could take his children camping. There were also, Lorna discovered, her grief overlaid by desperation to escape as soon as possible from this spider and – horrors – mouse playground, several wallets of photographs. She dropped everything but these down through the hatch on to the landing beneath, watched with a kind of terrible fascination as several enormous spiders ran out of the boots and went off, legs positively twinkling, in the direction of the bathroom, and then gingerly descended.

She had not known about the photographs, Larry had never shown them to her. It was easy to see why though; they were rather poor quality and might well have been taken by the children. Nearly all of them were either over-exposed, fuzzy, or both. Why had Larry kept them? For sentimental reasons probably.

It was really dreadful to have to think of him in the past tense like this; had, had been, used to . . . Her eyes overflowed with tears. Not one of the photographs was even a good clear one of him. Nothing she could keep and cherish.

She had gathered the bundle of wallets and they were in the kitchen bin before she remembered Carrick. She fished them out again, wiping off a tomato sauce smear from a baked bean can before putting them by the phone in the living room. She would ring him before she threw them away.

Later, drawn to the poignant reminder of happy times past, Lorna took them up again and spread them out over the dining-room table, keeping the contents of the four wallets separate. Yes, they had definitely been taken by children, or rather by two children on two different trips.

108

One had been more of a budding photographer than the other, two sets of pictures being clearer and better composed. But it was mostly a case of children without heads posing beside a waterfall, children riding ponies without heads *or* feet, one of Larry out of focus abseiling down a viaduct, a group picture where no one had been quite ready . . . The last wallet was a little better with scenes of hills, trees, a shot of Larry talking to a man by the school minibus, the same man scowling at the camera from the driver's seat of a Land Rover, another man at his side. The last was of a sad-looking little church on a very grey day.

Lorna went quickly away from the table. She did not want to look at them anymore.

Carrick's shout had roused Strong from his faint. There were a few totally confusing moments while there was upheaval generally and then he found himself lying on a cold, tiled floor. Very soon a blanket mitigated some of the chill and what felt like someone's pullover – it was still warm – was placed beneath his head. He ceased to shiver, almost. The pain in his leg was something else though but he put up with it stoically until the ambulance arrived, quite unaware that a young WPC had been holding his hand for a while telling him about her Siamese cat – her stunned brain utterly unable to come up with anything else.

Pete was dead. He knew it. Pete whose dad grew such wonderful carnations and won prizes with them at local shows. The news would kill the kind old man. It seemed strange that the IRA should pick on a provincial police station.

Life became disjointed for a while.

Strong knew, instinctively, when he woke up in hospital, a large tunnel thing keeping the weight of the bedclothes off his leg, that the man sitting by the bed was the one he had landed on. There was a large bruise on his temple. Worse, he was almost certainly fairly senior CID.

Carrick saw where the patient's gaze had been directed and guessed the conclusion that had been reached. 'No, you didn't do that one – just the ones on my backside.' He chuckled and then said. 'DCI Carrick. How are you feeling?'

'Not too bad, sir, thank you,' Strong whispered. This was more friendly than he had expected.

'Your family has been informed and I understand your parents are on their way down.'

Strong hardly heard, a truly dreadful thought having struck him as he looked at the mound on the bed and he actually felt the blood drain from his face.

'Sure you're okay?' Carrick asked urgently.

'They haven't . . . I mean, I haven't had my leg . . .' He simply could not utter the word.

'Amputated? No, by no means, Kevin. But I understand that you were hit by two bullets and both your tibia and fibula are badly broken.' 'Smashed' was the word used by the doctor Carrick had spoken to earlier. 'They have had to be pinned. It'll be a long haul, I'm afraid, but you're young and fit so—'

Strong was sufficiently upset to interrupt. 'A chum of mine did just the same in a car accident. He played football for our relief and for the town. Now he's got such a bad limp he can hardly get about and . . .' He had been about to add that his friend's mind had gone a bit haywire as a result of the injuries as well and he had seen a psychiatrist but sudden tears took him unawares and he was forced to hide his face in both hands.

'No two people are the same,' Carrick said, patting a somewhat thin shoulder and feeling inadequate. When the other had succeeded in conquering his moment of weakness he went on, 'As you've probably guessed I'm here to ask you to tell me everything you can remember about the shooting.'

Strong scrubbed at his face with both palms. 'It all happened so quickly, sir. I'd braked out front and Pete – that is Constable Peter Hepplewhite – said . . .'

'Shall I come back later?' Carrick asked kindly.

Strong shook his head. 'He *is* dead, isn't he?'

'I'm afraid he is.'

'Burnt to death,' Strong choked.

'No, a shot killed him instantly. And Lee.'

'That little *shit*. If it hadn't been for him . . .' Here Strong abandoned himself to his grief and sobbed his heart out. A little later he heard the door to the small side ward – of which he was the only occupant – open and then close and assumed that Carrick had felt he had no choice but to leave. What a fool I've made of myself, he thought miserably. How bloody unprofessional could you get. Then Carrick suddenly spoke very softly. But not to him, it soon became clear.

'I have an idea you're brilliant at this kind of thing. His chum's dead and his leg's been shot to bits and he's going through hell.'

'There's shock too, of course,' said someone else, a dry voice full of quiet authority. 'It's a bit soon to pump the young lad full of questions.'

The words were sympathetically uttered but nevertheless 'young lad' rankled more than slightly. Strong dried his eyes on the sheet and beheld his second visitor with open curiosity. Here, surely, was even more senior Bill. Or was he?

Carrick introduced Gillard by his christian name; there was no need for Strong to know anything more about him. Then he said, 'Incidentally, what the hell have you done with my car?'

'It's outside – in the car park,' Gillard said, sounding surprised.

Strong could tell that there was a lot more that Carrick wanted to say on that subject and that only his own presence was preventing it. The man called Patrick knew it too, his eyes glittering with amusement. When he spoke next though he was very grave.

'I'm really sorry about your colleague.'

'Thank you, sir.'

'And speaking as one who was rather messily blown up by a grenade and whose legs were a kind of soup of the day until the medics got to work on them, I can *assure* you that full recovery is perfectly possible. A lot of it depends on you though. It *will* be hell for a while. If you want full mobility you'll have to learn everything all over again – learn to walk for a start. Then, when you've done that, learn to dance, go rock climbing, ride a bike, ride a horse. If you sit at home feeling sorry for yourself, you're finished.' He smiled ruefully. 'Try not to do as I did and drink too much. It affects the coordination something cruel.'

There was a short silence while Strong assimilated this advice and then he said, 'I didn't see the bastards who did it. I'd bent down to pick something up off the floor.'

'Did you get a good look at the van beforehand?' Carrick asked. Woods, none the worse from his heavy collision with a door frame, had been too intent on rescue to make a note of the registration number.

'I only saw that it was red, sir. There was nothing written on it. It had pulled right across my bows and that's why I reversed into a spare parking slot.'

'You can't have noticed the number plate then if it was sideways on to you?'

'I'm afraid not, sir.'

'It's disappeared into thin air. It was spotted by quite a few witnesses but none of them quite managed to get the number. No red vans have been reported stolen and teams are trawling round used vehicle dealers to see if one changed hands recently.'

'Could it have been resprayed?' Gillard asked.

'There was plenty of rust on it,' Strong recollected.

'Unlikely, in that case.'

'Was it terrorists then?' the constable asked.

Before Carrick could comment Gillard said, 'No, we don't think it was.'

'No?' Carrick echoed.

Gillard shook his head. 'I'll explain later.'

'Unless it was someone out to get Lee,' Strong said, not completely seriously. 'He said someone had seen him in the flat he burgled.'

'He *admitted* it?' Gillard wanted to know.

'I haven't had time to bring you up to date,' Carrick told him. 'Some of the jewellery was found at his house.' Speaking to Strong he said, 'Tell me everything that you can remember he said.'

After a little thought Strong said, 'He didn't come straight out with it. He was sounding us out to see if he'd be treated lightly if he told the truth. He said things along the lines of "Suppose this bloke just wandered in and picked up a few

112

bits and pieces and the door wasn't locked". He said that there was someone else there already, in a room he hadn't gone in, and this man ran out when he saw him. We didn't take Lee very seriously, I'm afraid, sir. He had a record as long as your arm and was always trying to wriggle out of what we'd nabbed him for. Oh, and he mumbled something about "that bloody woman".'

'Shirley, no doubt,' Carrick said. 'I'm sure it was her who grassed on him. Tell us all he said about the man in the flat.'

Strong was getting very tired.

'And then we'll go away and leave you alone,' Gillard said with a grin.

'He said he'd only seen a dark shape out of the corner of his eye as this man went out of the front door. He thought he might have been wearing a long mac.'

'No other details?'

'Nothing else, sir.'

'Faith, the boy can hardly keep his eyes open,' said Gillard with an Irish lilt to his voice. 'In case you remember anything else, I'm sure the good Chief Inspector here will give you his phone number. I shall come and see you again soon – when you're feeling better. Just to see how you're getting on.'

Strong thanked him wanly, wondering if the promise would be kept.

Carrick wrote his number on a piece of paper, handed it over, and they took their leave, both, though neither mentioned it, feeling deeply sorry for Strong.

Gillard was the first to speak. 'I owe you a fairly grovelling apology. I sometimes have in my possession a pager that makes no sound which you wear in a special harness next to your skin. It produces a pulse that you can feel when someone wants to make contact. When it happens I never tell *anyone* where I'm going. I forgot to leave you a note saying we'd have to delay making a start and it would be ungracious of me to blame your questioning for rattling me sufficiently to make it slip my mind.'

'But it did.'

'Probably.'

Carrick halted. 'So where do we stand then?'

Gillard also stopped. 'I'm getting used to the idea.' He held out his right hand. 'A few home truths never hurt anyone and I should have been straight with you from the start. Looked at like that the aggro was my fault.'

Carrick warmly grasped the hand and nothing else was said until they were outside. There, Gillard gave him the keys to his car.

'Would you mind fetching the motor? I'm trying not to spend too much time out in the open.'

This had the effect of making Carrick feel naked and vulnerable as he walked across the large hospital car park but it would take more than hoodlums driving red vans to stop him. And he was damned if he was going to let Patrick Gillard out of his sight from now on. Carrick was sure he was innocent of murder but there was no doubt he was the key to solving this case, not least because he had at his disposal personnel and facilities that were simply not available to a policeman. The most important thing was that he had returned.

These musings were borne out when they were in the car and heading back into the city.

Gillard said, 'The call was from Daws himself. To prevent any risk of what he had to say being overheard by anyone else we met up at a safe house belonging to the department in Dorset. What he told me was this. Yesterday four foreign criminals, one of whom is wanted for terrorist offences, were allowed into the country. They were posing as tourists and all had forged passports. All four were met at Heathrow and taken by minibus to what appears to be a perfectly genuine adventure centre.'

Carrick whistled. 'It goes without saying that the source of this information is twenty-four carat?'

'We've had a man inside Customs and Excise for years.'

'So in other words they were permitted to enter the country by the Home Office?'

'Yes, just like last time.'

'I presume you have orders to close this place down?'

'That's a mild way of putting it. He's mad enough to want it nuked.'

'So in other words the PM wants it nuked because it's been set up in defiance of his orders.'

'Daws let you in on more than I'd thought. Yes, there was a directive from Number 10 after the last fiasco to the effect that the plan was never to be tried again. The Home Secretary must be naive enough to think that the PM won't find out. It's all bloody political, of course. The man's ambitious and there's a very secret but serious leadership crisis going on at the moment. The Anti-terrorist Branch is being used to test an idea of his; an undercover unit that cuts corners, bends the law in order to beat serious crime. Daws has told the PM – who's going to smash it as messily as possible.'

'The PM *wants* a huge scandal?'

'There have been more public splits in the party lately, as I'm sure you know. He wants to be seen as a man all-knowing and ready to crack the whip if people step out of line.'

'And so your brother was murdered as a direct result of political in-fighting?'

'It makes you want to throw up, doesn't it?'

'Where is this adventure centre?'

'You're in for a shock. It's right on your doorstep. There's a house and farm buildings within a Country Park on Mendip. The buildings had been semi-derelict for years, apparently, and then someone modernised the house and converted a barn into an equipment store. Daws said that there was intelligence still coming in but it would appear that it only started functioning recently.'

'I'm sure I've heard about this place,' Carrick murmured. 'I've an idea that some people from the nick went there for some kind of training in an old quarry.'

'It would figure. What better way to give the place respect-ability with the local police? They won't be telling their latest guests about it, though.'

'Suppose I just raid the centre on suspicion?'

'You'd grab all the crooks and then your senior people would come down on you like a ton of bricks and want to know all about your motives. Those behind it would simply vanish back into the woodwork.'

115

'But they wouldn't try it again.'

'No, they'd merely get away with it. What Daws wants is evidence.'

Carrick knew that he had no choice but to go along with the wishes of a powerful man in MI5 if he wanted to discover the full details of Lawrence Gillard's death.

'Do you think this new venue represents any kind of danger to the public?' Patrick asked.

'I seem to remember that there's a boarding school for boys not very far away and there used to be a riding school for disabled children within the park itself.'

'They deserve a medal for sheer stupidity already,' Gillard said in disgust.

Carrick had decided to go home and find the pair of them something to eat before they did anything else. 'Let me get this straight. There is a bona fide operation by your department to expose these people and get the place closed down. You're in charge of it.'

'Correct.'

'Well, you obviously know that I went to see Daws. Did he tell you that he knows you arranged to have a boat overturned and that the man who did it died in Bosnia fighting for the Croats?'

'No, but it was only a matter of time.'

'On both counts?' Carrick persisted, not perceiving surprise.

'Tristram was a sort of champion of the underdog.'

'But you're hardly able to be described as that!'

'I see you still have a huge bee in your bonnet over this. No, of course I can't. The driving factor was that Commander X had been responsible for the deaths of two children.'

'It's still not ethical though, is it? Your friend Tristram ... I mean, it wasn't his war!'

'I agree. And he was just a little bit different from most people in the head. He was also a brigadier retired from the Tank Regiment.'

Carrick remained silent.

'So you can set your heart at rest about me pulling rank and ...' Gillard smiled peaceably. 'I can still get into a lot

116

of trouble over it and it's the reason I'm going to be very careful this time. I shall only fire if they fire first.'

Carrick knew that he was only speaking figuratively, but an assassin already had.

Chapter 10

The shootings at Manvers Street caused public outrage and intense media interest and speculation, the latter one of the reasons Carrick needed a little breathing space at home. He had given a press conference that afternoon and also responded to countless questions from reporters who were endeavouring to ambush his every move. So when he heard his phone ringing as he opened the front door he could not suppress a groan.

'Shall I answer it and make out I'm your daft butler?' Gillard asked.

'Better not,' Carrick replied, although the offer held great appeal just then.

He did not usually give witnesses, and those he had cause to talk to in his professional capacity, his private phone number but in the case of Lorna Templeton had broken his own rule. The reason for this was that Larry Gillard's murder was somehow so personal. When he replaced the receiver after talking to her and had checked on the provisions he had in the house, he found his guest full-length on the sofa, half-asleep.

'Lorna Templeton's coming round with some photos she's found of the Brecon Beacon trips. They were among some things Larry left behind in her loft.'

'I hardly see how they could be helpful,' Gillard said, his eyes closed.

'No, nor do I. But I'd asked her to look out the stuff and she's offered to bring them specially. So I invited her to supper. My only real concern right now is how I'm going

118

to make three people a meal out of frozen chicken joints, two tomatoes, a tablespoonful of rice and a chunk of stale cheese.'

A little more interest was displayed. 'Do you have a microwave?'

Carrick replied in the affirmative.

'A tin of condensed soup?'

'Probably.'

'A bottle or two of wine?'

'Those too.'

Gillard levered himself upright. 'Then we have a feast. Where's the galley?'

Earlier that year, just after they were married, Carrick and Joanna had sold the flats that they had each owned, together with Joanna's private investigation business, and bought an old farmhouse on the outskirts of the village of Framwell, some eight miles east of Bath. Much work had needed to be done and the house was in the process of careful restoration after the neglect of many years. There were four bedrooms upstairs, one of which, originally a maid's room, was being made into a second bathroom. On the ground floor there was a large living room, that had at one time been dining room and parlour, a study, downstairs cloakroom and a long airy kitchen. Modern blockboard panelling in the latter had been ripped down to reveal warm red brick walls and a 'secret' window, and, best of all, a large recess that had once housed a range complete with bread oven and hooks in the chimney upon which to hang cooking pots. A four-oven dark green Aga now resided in this space but the bread oven had been retained and small lights placed inside, illuminating Joanna's collection of copper measures and a couple of dried flower arrangements.

'You open the wine,' Patrick said, donning Joanna's cook's apron. 'A glass or two gives me inspiration and I kid myself I'm just like the chefs on TV.'

The chicken joints, six in number, were thawed in the microwave and then tossed in a little seasoned flour. They were then browned in a mixture of olive oil and butter in a large iron casserole and a sauce made from condensed mushroom soup thinned with a little white wine and poured

119

over. Gillard added the skinned, chopped tomatoes for luck and put the casserole in the oven to cook. The rice turned out to be just about enough for three. This was simmering in a pan and the cheese being grated to sprinkle over the casserole before it was put under the grill to finish when Lorna arrived.

'That smells wonderful,' she enthused in the manner of one who is really hungry.

Carrick had wondered how she would react when she saw Patrick – he had forewarned her that Lawrence's brother would be present – and tactfully stayed away from the kitchen when she went to see how the chef was getting on. They both emerged very shortly afterwards, Gillard with a consoling arm around her shoulders, Lorna's eyes bright with tears.

'I still feel awful about Larry,' she said when they were drinking coffee after a surprisingly tasty meal. 'I mean, it was partly because of me that he took over the trips for the kids in the first place.'

'But he enjoyed it,' Patrick said. 'It actually made a new man of him. He lost weight and for probably the first time in his life had a real interest. You mustn't blame yourself. The only pity is that he gave it up. And you, of course.'

'If he'd been with me at the cottage that night he wouldn't have—' She broke off and coloured.

'Driven out to the lake? I still might have contacted him and asked him to get the car fixed. And you might have been with him. You might be dead too. We could carry on with this kind of conjecture all night. It's a waste of time, Lorna. All we can do is concentrate on catching the bastard who killed him.'

She dug in her handbag and produced the photographs. Gillard signed to her that she should give them to Carrick.

'No,' Carrick said. 'Brecon was your war.'

With the air of one who is doing something for politeness' sake Gillard quickly flipped through the two children's records of what had probably been the most exciting thing that had happened to them. Sometimes he paused and a smile twitched at the corners of his mouth, no doubt when he came to the headless, hoofless ponies. Then, when he was looking at the third wallet of pictures his body stilled as though it had been turned to ice.

'Christ,' he whispered, the word uttered as an evocation, not blasphemy. Quickly he turned to the picture beneath, which was also given a searching stare. The rest were glanced through without further reaction and placed on one side. The fourth set were then dealt with and likewise discarded.

Lorna said, 'I wonder if you're looking at the pictures of the two men and the Land Rover and the other with one of them talking to Larry. I have no idea who they are – they're certainly not members of staff from the school.'

Without confirming her suspicions, Gillard said, 'And I suppose you haven't a clue who took them?'

'No, but I can find out.'

'Any idea which trips they represent?'

'It must have been just before Larry asked you for help. I can only guess from the sweater he's wearing. I bought it for him and not long afterwards he chucked it in the washing machine with everything else and it shrank. So he gave it to Matthew.'

'He didn't mention these people to me,' Gillard said worriedly, tapping one of the pictures with a forefinger.

'Perhaps he thought they were forestry workers. Or men out shooting deer.'

Gillard smiled at her. 'Many, many thanks. You've brought us a very significant piece of evidence. If you make any enquiries at the school, please make them extremely low-profile. I can't explain further, I'm afraid, and even if I did give you their names they wouldn't mean anything to you.' He returned the rest of the photographs to her.

Lorna gathered up her bag. 'I'm sure you both want to discuss this in private.' And despite their genuine protests and offers of more coffee, departed, thanking them for the meal.

'She's lonely,' Carrick said when he returned from seeing her out. 'An attractive girl like that shouldn't be.'

Studying the photos Gillard said, 'I'll ask my mother to have her over to see the children. It would do them all good.'

'So what have we got then?'

Gillard handed them over. 'The man talking to Larry and behind the wheel of the Land Rover is Christopher Ladd. Sitting at his side is Lyndberne – or, if you prefer, Commander X. This is more than I could have hoped for – Ladd's involved all right.'

Ladd was probably a good-looking man but at the moment when an unknown child had pressed the shutter release had been scowling ferociously at the camera. He had thick, wavy fair fair and very dark brown eyes, and from the way he was sitting in the driving cab, his broad shoulders seeming to fill all available space, Carrick deduced that he was a very big man indeed. His passenger was peering over his left shoulder and looked quite insignificant by comparison; thinning sandy-coloured hair and pale blue eyes, a pasty complexion.

'A contrasting duo,' Carrick commented. 'The late Commander hardly looks a force to be reckoned with.'

Gillard smiled grimly. 'Don't forget that he was in possession of not only a bent mind but several heavily armed henchmen.'

'Who were?'

'Genuine hoodlums. Make no mistake about it – the guy's cover was almost one hundred percent perfect. What made him so dangerous was that he'd lost all track of right and wrong. He *lived* the part so well that he actually got a kick out of not only taking people apart but killing them too.'

'Is Ladd likely to be as dangerous from that point of view?'

'Perhaps not. But he was always ambitious. I can easily see him in a situation where the desire for power – say promotion to the head of the entire Anti-terrorist Branch – would blur any moral principles he might still be in possession of.'

'He might be in command of this unit.'

'Yes, it's very likely. So he'd want to hang on to it – prove himself.'

'We'll have to talk to the child who took these pictures.'

'We'll have to be careful. There's every chance that Ladd has remembered the small boy or girl he tried to frighten off snapping him in a forest. The man who attacked you in

122

Larry's flat might have been snooping around looking for the photos, and if Lee's tale is true it might have been the same man: Ladd. If he failed to find the pictures on the night Larry died it's possible he went back for another look and ran into you.'

'Don't you think he'd have others to do his dirty work?'

'And admit there's a flaw in his perfection? I doubt it.'

'Lee said that the front door of the flat was unlocked. Whoever shot your brother might have taken his keys and then put them back in his pocket afterwards. But that leads one to think that Larry wasn't shot at the lake. For surely his killer wouldn't have disposed of the body in the water, having removed the keys from Larry's pocket, and then returned, waded out and replaced them. That would have been terribly risky.'

'There was no sign of the lock having been forced?'

'None. They could have used skeleton keys, I suppose.'

'Easily.'

'If there was an accomplice and another vehicle they might have put the body in that while someone went back to search the flat. But surely that would only have made life difficult for them and it would have been far easier to have entered the flat when Larry was out and made it look like a common-or-garden burglary.'

'But these are *cops*, James,' Gillard said with biting sarcasm.

'God, yes,' Carrick muttered. 'One does tend to forget that.'

The phone rang a while later and it was Lorna.

'I did a little detective work,' she began diffidently. 'You know how it is when someone has a camera and takes pictures on a trip and how they usually only appear in a group photo when someone else is asked to press the button . . . It wasn't too difficult to find a face that only appeared the once like that and it was made easy for me because the girl in question has bright red hair and is a terrible show-off. She's pulling a face in a group picture with Larry and stands out a mile, so to speak. I happen to know Sarah as I take her for English. Her parents run the garage

123

where I buy petrol. So I rang her and asked her about the men she photographed. It took a moment for her to remember as it happened quite a while ago when she was in the first year. But she did remember in the end, and remarkably clearly. They were playing hare and hounds in the forest – Larry was the hare and laying a trail of sawdust – and ran across a track, causing some men in a Land Rover to brake hard to avoid hitting them. He, the driver, swore at them. And Sarah, being Sarah, took a picture of him. She thought at the time they were carrying guns but—'

'Guns!' Carrick exclaimed.

'Rifles. In those surroundings it would not have been too unusual, would it? I mean, there are forest rangers and people like that.'

'And the other picture? The one with Larry?'

'Oh, the man came to complain. He told them they shouldn't have been there. Which was nonsense, of course. He *said* he was the forest ranger.'

'I still find it a little odd that Sarah took the pictures. She doesn't seem to have snapped any other people they met during the weekend – and they must have seen others surely?'

'She wants to be a press photographer when she leaves school – she shoots what she calls "situations".'

'She might have the scoop of her career already. But please ask her not to tell all her friends about the interest you've shown. It's for her own safety.'

'Oh, dear. That sounds rather worrying.'

'No, there's nothing for you to worry about. I'm just being rather cautious until I know more.' Carrick rang off, hoping he had put her mind at rest.

Carrick relayed the information to Gillard who said, 'No, I don't suppose Larry would have mentioned a bloke calling himself a forest ranger. And for all we know they might have strayed into a restricted area.'

'So Ladd *was* there keeping an eye on things. Could he have been in the area when you were there?'

'If he was he didn't show himself.'

'Not even in disguise?'

124

'There was nobody that big. He's six foot four and weighs around fourteen stone.'

'A good prop forward then.'

'Yes, he did play rugby.'

Carrick decided to air what was on his mind. 'Look, it seems that most people are blaming the IRA for the shootings at the nick. You said earlier that it probably wasn't. Does that mean you think that Lee was the real target?'

'It's a bit far-fetched, isn't it? But according to various and reliable sources those responsible are not from the other side of the Irish Sea, nor are a terrorist cell connected with them resident in this country. I can't believe such bloody mayhem would be perpetrated merely to remove a witness who could have been dealt with at another time and in another way. I've no doubt there's a method in such wicked madness – we shall have to wait and see.'

Chapter 11

The Country Park was an area of several hundred acres that had originally been part of an estate belonging to an eccentric Victorian quarry owner known as 'The Stone Baron'. On his death the mansion, formal gardens and a large area of parkland had been retained by the family but a huge area of worked-out quarries, woodland and open moorland had been bequeathed to the nation on condition that it was turned into a park for ordinary people to enjoy. There was also a farmhouse, barn and byres which, even at the turn of the century, had been ruinous and beyond the purse of the local authority – in receipt of the gift – to restore. With the permission of the trustees the buildings had been boarded up with a view to undertaking the work when it could be afforded. This day had never arrived. Recently, within the past year, the property had been leased, again with the permission of the trustees, at a peppercorn rent with the proviso that complete restoration be carried out.

This much Carrick had been able to glean from records at the local council offices. Helpful staff had been unable to tell him the identity of those in residence now or even if the property had been sub-let to another party. Eventually, the plan was that the house and out-buildings would be used as a visitor centre, the former a museum on the theme of the history of the Mendip region.

Sitting in a tall beech tree growing only a matter of five hundred yards from the house, Carrick and Gillard had a panoramic view of a large area of the park. To the north there was thick woodland, to the east and west rolling moor-

126

land, and to the south, behind them as they sat dressed in camouflage clothing on a thick branch of the tree, fields with the approach road winding between them. West again, on the other side of a high beech hedge, lay the lush lawns dotted with silver firs and Monterey pines of the adjoining property, the one-time 'Stone Baron's' home. One or two chimneys could be glimpsed above the trees.

They had arrived before dawn, the faint glow in the eastern sky giving them just sufficient light to see by. They had not been alone, their observation point having been chosen for them by a member of Gillard's team who had been keeping the house and park under close surveillance. This man, simply introduced by Gillard as Nathan, had stepped from the gloom at the meeting place carrying ropes and other climbing gear.

'Still nothing going on?' Gillard had asked in an undertone.

'Nothing, sir. There are people living in the house all right, a man and woman – plus of course the lot they met at the airport and brought here. You can see them moving around indoors but no one's stuck their nose outside yet.'

'What does the man look like?'

'Short, dark and ugly just about sums him up.'

'Thank you.'

After assisting them to climb into the tree, Nathan had disappeared as quietly as he had come, melting into the shadows.

'This is quite a different set-up from what they had at Brecon,' Gillard said now. They had built themselves a 'hide', bending small branches so as to be undetectable from both the ground and the house they had under surveillance. Patrick had fashioned for himself a hat of leafy twigs, decking out the binoculars in similar manner.

'But they must have realised that they'd gone right over the top on that occasion,' Gillard continued. 'Nevertheless I shall have to keep reminding myself that just because we can't see armed patrols it doesn't mean those indoors are not well-protected. If this *is* being run by some kind of secret off-shoot of the Anti-terrorist Branch then we mustn't underestimate them. It worries me though that nothing

127

seems to have happened. Nothing has occurred after dark either according to a pal of Nathan and that's when you'd expect activity – night exercises and so forth.' He gave the binoculars to Carrick and made himself more comfortable.

The farmhouse was built of local stone and was a low, squat building with a cow byre to one side. A large stone barn with a sagging thatched roof faced them across a cobbled yard. From where Carrick was sitting he could see right into the kitchen window, on the other end of the house from the byre, and he had a good view of the yard. The minibus must have been hired and returned for there was no sign of it; the only vehicles parked in view were an elderly tractor hitched to a flat trailer and a Sierra Estate. Nathan had reported that the buildings contained some farm machinery, bales of straw, a few canoes and mountain bikes, and miscellaneous other outdoor pursuits equipment.

Carrick said, 'I'm staggered that they were so successful in luring criminals to this country before. Was that solely on the strength of Lyndberne's reputation?'

'Presumably. And one must give him his due for the overseas organisation.'

'So who's the draw now – who's running the masterclass in crime this time?'

'You've hit the nail right on the head. I'm afraid the answer is: God knows. Last time, I think, Lyndberne knew the set-up was a bit thin so used me – when he got hold of us – to enhance his reputation. He almost literally crowed, "Look at the big MI5 fish I've landed". Without wishing to sound as though I'm crowing too he did forget that big fish in MI5 have to earn their status. His making me the so-called students' servant left me with every opportunity to lick them into shape, my way. Some of the younger ones soon came to see me as a kind of father-figure. It got to the stage where none of them actually believed that Lyndberne was in charge and that it was part of the test to spot this. The course, you see, was all about subversion. So I subverted them.' He grinned. 'I'm only mentioning this because I doubt very much whether they'll do *that* one again.'

'Are the takers on this course known to you?'

'Three are.'

128

'Were you responsible for putting any of them away?'

'Only one. Frodheim, the one wanted for terrorism offences. Some years ago in my undercover army days, he went on what I can only describe as an exchange visit to Northern Ireland and blew up a few soldiers and innocent bystanders to keep his hand in. I'd been lurking in a bedsitter in the house next-door to the one they were using as a bomb factory and when Frodheim and the local terrorist cell had an AGM we nabbed the lot. He was sent home to stand trial for killing four security guards during a bank raid the previous year in exchange for Germany deporting several dubious Irishmen suspected of plotting to bomb British army bases. The reason he didn't get life imprisonment was that he helped the police with several of their inquiries, grassing on most of his chums. I'm actually surprised he's still alive. Now he's wanted in Holland for blowing up a bus full of Israeli tourists and killing or maiming most of them. I gather he was in the pay of an obscure Islamic group.'

'One might applaud the aims of this plan then.'

'Indeed. But you don't go after terrorists in English national parks and places like that.'

'Is it remotely possible that you're the carrot this time?'

'What, come and lop off one of Patrick Gillard's ears as a superb postscript to your holiday in the sun? I wouldn't have thought so.'

'This guy Ladd would appear to have an axe to grind so far as you're concerned. Okay, what else could be the draw? What could be so special here that couldn't be had in, say, Libya?'

Gillard held out his hand for the glasses. 'Expertise. We're not talking about training freedom fighters in a remote African country to handle rifles – these customers are hardened criminals.'

'So Ladd himself is what's on offer then – his experience?'

'What, *openly*? A senior cop prepared to sell a lifetime's training and inside knowledge for big money? It's certainly different. But if I were a prospective customer I'd smell a very large, dead rat.'

'Perhaps they're concealing his true identity.'

'James, the punters just wouldn't be so gullible. That's

why such endless lengths were gone to for Lyndberne. It took years to build him a criminal reputation.' He broke off for a moment, thinking. 'I suppose it would be possible to pass this place off as Ladd's own house and make it look as though he was in business privately. As I said just now, it would certainly be different.'

'And enhance the reputation of British police abroad no end,' Carrick observed sarcastically. 'I'm beginning to wonder if the man's real aim is to catch these people or merely make himself a pile of heavily laundered money.'

Gillard stared at him but his eyes were unfocussed, reflective. Then he said, 'They were in no hurry to arrest them at Brecon. The reason was given that it was hoped to discover as much from them as possible – other names, plans afoot, etc – before they were detained.'

'How long was the course?'

'Two weeks. And they still hadn't called for the Black Marias on the last day. Lyndberne – Commander X – said at his debriefing that the plan had been to arrest them all when they were being taken by private launch across the Irish Sea before transportation to the airport. We shall never know now, of course.'

'Catch the bastards and keep the money? No, surely not. *Someone* must be keeping an eye on all this.'

'As you say, we mustn't indulge in flights of fancy.'

The day wore on. A postman came and went and, fleetingly, so did a British Telecom Land Rover, the driver probably lost and stopping at the house to ask the way. During the afternoon a woman came out of the house, got into the Sierra and drove off. They watched and she went in the direction of Shepton Mallet. Half an hour later five men emerged. Two of them entered the byre and loaded several bales of straw on to the flat trailer. Then four climbed aboard, using the bales as seats. The fifth, the shortest of them, got into the driving seat of the tractor, started it up and the dilapidated equipage chugged away in a cloud of blue smoke.

Gillard, who was in possession of the binoculars, avidly gazed at what was happening below. The tractor and trailer followed the rough track that ran around the side of the barn and then turned through a gateway, the gate having rotted and fallen off its hinges to lie in the grass many years previously, putting on speed on the unmade lane beyond. About a hundred yards farther on it turned left, disappearing behind high hedges. But the puffs of exhaust issuing from the vehicle were still visible and it was possible to observe its progress for half a mile or so. It then turned left again – or merely followed a sharp bend in the lane – and came into view as it progressed steadily between two fenced pastures. Another curve, to the right this time, and it was going away from them into the woodland on the far side of the fields.

'A recce?' Gillard wondered aloud. 'To show them where school starts tomorrow? And d'you know what?'

'What?' Carrick asked obediently.

'Frodheim was sitting right at the back. He hasn't changed at all.'

'So we wait to see if they come back and then go and have a look for ourselves?'

'When it's dark.'

They waited, consuming army emergency rations that Gillard had conjured up from somewhere and each in turn trying to doze while the other watched, despite the discomfort of the safety harnesses they were wearing and a 'bed' of wood.

An hour and a half had passed before they heard the tractor returning. When it came into view nothing seemed to have changed; the men on the trailer were sitting in roughly the same positions and, as on the outward journey, did not appear to be talking amongst themselves. Four distinct individuals, silent and dour.

Dusk, or dimity as it is known in the West Country, did not fall until just after ten and it was still not quite dark at eleven. A thin crescent moon rode in the clear sky giving them just enough light to see by to make the hazardous descent. Carrick, who had climbed up first and fixed ropes to assist Gillard – at a huge disadvantage with his right foot having no sensation – was the last to leave the tree, having to rely again on fingers and toes, his heart in his mouth as he slithered on mosses and lichens growing on the bark. He could not remember climbing a tree since he was about six years old.

It was a long walk back to the car, parked far enough away to avoid making anyone suspicious, where they stowed the climbing gear. Gillard suggested that they move the vehicle, just to be on the safe side, and it was concealed in a narrow track that led to a gate into a field. They could now approach the farmhouse from a slightly different direction.

Before they had set off again Gillard said, 'At the risk of repeating myself, I must stress that just because we haven't seen any armed bods patrolling the place doesn't mean that it's safe. It isn't. If Christopher Ladd is involved with the running of this project any security arrangements will be sophisticated and deadly.' He had consulted an OS map spread on the bonnet of the car with the aid of a torch with a beam so fine it was no thicker than a pencil. 'We can climb over the gate and walk round the boundary of this field.'

In single file, Gillard leading, they walked for quite a way in the cover of the tall hedge growing round the field. Carrick concentrated on not tripping or treading on any dry sticks that might snap and make a loud noise. This was very difficult in the dark.

After what seemed like hours, for they were walking only slowly, they left the comparative safety of the hedge and crawled for a short distance along a shallow ditch, Carrick biting back an exclamation as a stinging nettle brushed his face with almost vicious intent. Then Gillard paused without warning and Carrick almost cannoned into him.

'This is where we crawl through the fence into the lane the tractor used,' Gillard whispered. 'I suggest we cross it an angle and go beneath the fence on the other side. It's best to play safe and use all the cover we can find.'

This they did, pausing only for a moment or two before making their way, on all fours – Carrick glad that they were wearing gloves as there were plenty of thistles – towards a clump of trees, large bushes actually, that grew about twenty feet away. Gillard did not go through the hawthorns, for that was what they proved to be, but kept to the side with

132

deeper shade. There, once more, he stopped to whisper instructions.

'I think the moon might go behind that small cloud soon. When it does, make a dash for the other boundary. Take care you don't go full tilt into the wire – it should be roughly where that low clump of briars are. Keep down. If your head and your backside are near the ground the rest won't matter.'

There was hardly any wind and the cloud was very slow-moving. Carrick left all the questions he had on the tip of his tongue unasked – they were best left unsaid and he did not want Gillard to think him nervous. He had been surprised how aware he had become of his surroundings even in the near-darkness, all five senses pouring information into his brain. There was the scent of bruised vegetation, the soft sound of the plants brushing against his clothing as he moved, the warmth of a tree trunk he had touched in passing.

An owl hooted and in the next moment Gillard had roughly slammed him down into the grass. Carrick carefully drew breath, hoping that his companion could not hear his heart beating like a trip-hammer.

'It sounded like a real one,' Gillard breathed in his ear. 'But they're usually in pairs.'

Nothing much happened for what seemed a very long time.

Then, right over their heads: 'TOO-WIT!... TOO-WIT!... TOO-WIT!'

And, in the distance, another 'Too-wooooo . . .'

Like a large moth, the bird swooped from its perch on a thorn tree overhead and flew silently away.

'Here endeth the first lesson,' Gillard murmured. 'Owls are usually found in pairs but not necessarily singing the same tune in the same county.'

The moon went behind the cloud and without further urging Carrick set off. Mindful of what Gillard had said he slowed when he got to the briars and went forward on all fours. Almost straight away he glimpsed a fence post. Gillard was right on his heels and they held the barbed wire strands as wide as possible for each other so they could go through.

133

The thick woodland that the tractor and trailer had disappeared into grew almost right up to the fence. There was only an area of ground rutted with wheel tracks to cross and then they were among the trees. Carrick had an idea that they would be going nowhere near the track that meandered through the woodland which was represented on the map by a thin dotted line. When Gillard struck off at an angle opposite to it he saw he'd been correct.

They continued with their stealthy progress. Soon the ground became damper as they went down a slope. A small stream trickled at the bottom, which they crossed, Gillard pausing to tell Carrick to tread on stones as much as possible and avoid leaving footprints in the mud. They even walked upstream in the water for a while. It was very shallow, not even reaching the laces of their boots.

'Verily, I might rust away,' Gillard was heard to mutter.

His navigation was excellent and soon, after leaving the stream behind and taking the left bank, they were on good ground some ten yards from the main woodland track, this easily visible between the trunks of young silver birch. Also visible was a high wire fence and a white-painted gate spanning the track. A notice read, DANGER. KEEP OUT. QUARRY. BLASTING OFTEN IN PROGRESS.

'Did you have time to check up on where the people at the nick did their training?' Gillard asked softly.

'Yes, it was on a rockface near the entrance. It's a climb open to the public.'

'Thank you. It wasn't here then. Don't touch the fence.'

Carrick's cheek was still on fire from where he had brushed against the nettle and he had no desire to get a worse shock from touching anything else. His gaze followed the tiny beam from the torch up the metal stanchions and barbed wire to where, on the top, there was a single smooth strand of wire. Was it electrified or just connected to an alarm system? Gillard grunted as if in in satisfaction and then led the way back into the trees, away from the gate.

They followed the fence downhill for a short distance then came to a thick stand of spruce, the lower branches dead and brittle, having lost the battle for life through lack of light. Forcing a way through them – it was pitch dark here

134

– was unpleasant and made more noise than Carrick would have liked but he reasoned that Gillard knew what he was doing and kept going. Thousands of dead spruce needles that they were dislodging were finding their way down his neck and through the fabric of his gloves.

'There you are,' Gillard said under his breath. 'I thought it might be just to keep out the casual trespasser and poacher.'

The fence came to a sudden end. The thin strand of wire on the top did not, however, Gillard's torch picking out the glint of copper as the wire descended from the top of the end post to a small metal box on the ground secured with a padlock. He did not touch it.

'We can't carry on blundering through the trees like this,' he whispered. 'If anything they look thicker than ever. We will get on the other side of this, though.'

Taking great care they circumnavigated the wire strand and walked back along the fence on the other side in the direction of the track. It was a great relief to be able to walk more easily and silently when they left the spruce behind. Gillard went very slowly now, checking every inch of the way and Carrick gave him plenty of room, dropping back a few paces; you do not crowd a man in such circumstances.

Almost immediately Gillard paused, examining something on the ground. When Carrick got to the spot he saw that it was another of the steel boxes.

'Stay here,' Gillard instructed.

He went from sight in the direction of the lane. Quite a long time elapsed. Carrick found himself wondering if his companion was armed and rather hoped that he was. If the worst happened and their presence was detected only he himself was authorised to make arrests. If those being taken into custody put up a fight ... He thought it utterly wrong that the man who had used the name Lyndberne had employed real criminals to help put his plan into operation. Such a ploy was hazardous enough without risking involving people who might suddenly refuse to obey orders.

'Come on, man,' he muttered, nerves jangling.

Then, 'This way,' Gillard hissed. 'Don't touch the wire – it's right across the track.'

They crossed the lane, keeping the strand of wire on their

left, traced it to another metal box and, again, carefully went round it. Very soon there was another check, Gillard crouching down to examine something else at ground level. It was yet another wire but thicker and covered with green plastic, practically invisible on the forest floor. Crawling, he traced it to a tree close by, where he stood up, slowly.

'Bastards,' Carrick heard him say.

Carrick held the torch while Gillard unloaded it; a primitive, even home-made device resembling a shotgun primed with a deadly selection of missiles that included broken glass, nails and large ball bearings.

'A pound to a penny it's the same one they had at Brecon,' Gillard said. He laid a hand urgently on Carrick's arm and they both froze, listening.

It was an engine of some kind, ticking over somewhere in the distance. To Carrick it sounded like a portable generator. Was it his imagination, or the moon, or was there a glow of light through the trees ahead?

Gillard set off again, back towards the track, indicating to Carrick that he should only walk in the wheelruts and not to either side or in the middle. Progress was painfully slow but the sound of the generator grew louder.

It was then that Carrick brushed a thick cobweb from his face and his hand encountered another wire. He tackled Gillard to the ground and for several seconds nothing happened.

Then the wail of a siren tore through the night air.

136

Chapter 12

'Stay still!' Gillard said urgently when Carrick moved to
shift his weight off him.

'It was my fault. I touched a wire.'

'I should have spotted it. On second thoughts, they might
know which sensor was triggered. Follow me. Crawl. We'll
have to pray that if there are any more surprises they're like
the other one and set at head height.'

The siren wailed on and on and then, ten seconds or so
later, moaned down the scale and became silent. The quietness after the eerie racket was like being struck deaf.

They were now lying in a shallow ditch somewhere just
inside the fence – there had not been time to check it out
fully beforehand. Covering themselves with leaves they lay
very still. Just when Carrick was beginning to think that they
were safe he heard a vehicle and a powerful searchlight was
switched on close by. Slowly, it scanned the woodland, the
beam passing literally inches above their heads.

We're still safe, Carrick thought. We're below ground level
here and if we don't move . . .

Raising his head the merest fraction he saw the lights of
a vehicle coming down the lane; a Land Rover pick-up
with a searchlight mounted on the roof of the cab. Peeping
through the leaves and twigs he had burrowed into, he could
make out a man standing in the back of the pick-up directing
the light. The vehicle stopped and two more men got out
of the driving cab. They had a dog with them.

'If they let it off the lead and it finds us, I shall knife it,'
Gillard said in Carrick's ear. 'I suggest we then resist

strongly whatever they have in mind for us – unless they merely want to hand us over to the local cops – with a view to taking the Land Rover.'

It was a bad moment for Carrick when he realised that his being a policeman right then would not do him a lot of good. He had to stay anonymous or he would jeopardise Gillard's entire assignment.

The men did not let the dog off but the lead was an extending one. The animal sniffed around for a while, Carrick guessing that it was crossing and re-crossing the track somewhere behind them. He could hear the footsteps of its handler being towed along in its wake. Then, suddenly, it was right upon them, digging Gillard out, barking. He did it no harm, probably because it was also excitedly licking his face, just shoved it to one side as he stood up. The light came to rest on him with unmerciful intensity.

Carrick went for the dog-handler, hurling himself sideways and bringing the man down with a tackle round the knees. Fortunately, the dog did not attack him but ran around, still barking, tripping everyone up with its leash. Carrick hit his man hard and jumped up just in time to grab the driver round the neck and pull him over backwards. Then he headed for the light, utterly blinded by it.

He was caught from behind with a thoroughness that was utterly shocking, several pairs of hands laid on him at once. What happened next haunted him for a very long time afterwards; the kind of experience the memory of which wakes you in the night in a cold sweat.

Not a word was spoken by those who had hold of him. He was slammed face down on to the ground and, in the pitiless glare of the light, stripped down to his underpants. Hands held his wrists and ankles and he was spreadeagled, ropes attached to pegs hammered into the ground holding him in that position. All this was carried out with expert attention to detail.

Carrick said nothing. There was no point in shouting out or doing something crass such as pretending he had been going for a walk in the woods. There was no point. He had an idea they knew very well who he was and they ensured his continued silence by gagging him.

138

Nothing moved, no one so much as coughed, and he was aware of nothing but the silence and the brilliant light. They were waiting for someone or something.

The waiting went on for a long time and Carrick, shivering, had plenty of time to wonder what was in store for him. Then, after what may have been half an hour, perhaps three-quarters, he heard footsteps approaching. They seemed very loud because he had one ear pressed to the ground.

The footfalls ceased right by him, the toe of a boot actually nudging him in the ribs. But kicking was not part of the plan, there was to be nothing so crude as that. He assumed, when first touched by a pair of strong hands, that he was being examined for injury. A thumb and forefinger almost stroked up his left arm from wrist to elbow and then gripped, clamping the tendons and nerves near the thick end of the muscle.

The cry of pain rose in Carrick's throat and was choked off by the gag. The grip had been fleeting but agonising, like being grasped by red hot pincers. It happened again, only on the other arm this time. And again, back on the right.

After this there was no pattern, no warning touch first, and his entire body became prey to every whim of this man, to sudden and utterly insupportable agony. Soon, the ropes on his wrists and ankles had cut into his skin as he writhed, helpless. After a while he fainted.

He was not revived in any way, there was just a patient wait for him to come round. Then it began all over again.

A while later the gag was removed when he started to choke. It was left off but a cloth bag of some sort was pulled over his head through which he could hardly breathe. Desperately, Carrick tried not to scream out his pain. He could feel the blood trickling from his wrists by now, a kind of warmth-seeping-into-the-ground sensation. Perhaps because they did not want him to bleed to death the ropes were removed shortly afterwards and he was heaved over on to his back. This presented fresh fields to his enterprising tormentor.

By now he was at the stage where he wanted to crawl away and hide; there was no pride left. He would have said

139

anything and done anything to stop it. Sometimes, in a lull, he thought it was all over and relaxed but that was what the man wanted him to think. Once, he managed to turn over again and started to crawl away. He was permitted to wriggle away for a short distance, his limbs feeling oddly weak and heavy and then was brought back again, back into the light, always the blinding light.

Sometime before he blacked out for the third time he flailed an arm in desperate retaliation and his fist cracked into the side of someone's jaw. There was a short period of revenge.

Birdsong; a thrush trilling gloriously only two or three feet away. Carrick lay quite still for a while unwilling to move and break the spell that was bringing him this miracle of daylight, life and the cessation of pain. The miracle had its way with him after a while and he wept into the torn ground, the scene of a battle not only lost but ... He could not put into words his sense of loss, as if he had somehow forfeited his own identity. Why hadn't they killed him?

He had to find Patrick.

He had assumed all along that Gillard was receiving similar treatment nearby. When he was able to move, initially crabwise and after sitting for a long time endeavouring to rub some life into his racked muscles, he could see no sign of anyone. His own clothes were in a pile on the ground close by but everything else – ropes, gag, the pegs that had been used to fasten him down – had been taken away.

Slowly and clumsily he dressed himself, aghast that every now and then he felt tears running down his cheeks. Walking was a real problem and it was about an hour before he had even moderate control of his legs. (He could not know just then that such scientifically applied torment had crippled people less fit for weeks.)

Where to go?

Deep down, he did not want to go anywhere. 'They' might be waiting for him, another variation of the game of cat and mouse.

Without thinking he set off to look for Gillard but was

140

brought up short by the realisation that although the booby traps and so forth must have been deactivated when the siren went off they had almost certainly been switched on again. To blunder around was asking to be killed or maimed. He sat on the ground, his legs having given away again, and tried to think straight.

The first certainty was that his ordeal had left him mentally confused and disorientated, he would be no help to Gillard even if he found him. The best thing to do was to find his way to the car and go and report what had happened.

But whom could he tell?

It was no use raising the hue and cry at the nick because, in theory, the police were not involved with this. He could hardly explain that the night's escapade had been in connection with solving Lawrence Gillard's murder because he would then have to list his reasons. The powers-that-be would also send every man to comb the country park from end to end, ruining MI5's investigation.

Carrick sat and shivered.

His car was at least a mile and a half away. In the end, he walked, setting a course by the rising sun. He felt like a zombie and his journey was forever a mystery to him. But he must have safely avoided the fence and other hazards, either that or they had been deliberately left switched off to enable him to escape. He remembered encountering nothing and nobody and reached the car in a state of almost complete exhaustion.

It was six-thirty in the morning.

Again, where should he go? Where *could* he go? Not home. 'He' might be there. His brain refused to think of anything else. Yes, there was something else: the memory of the way he himself had cringed and whimpered . . .

By another miracle his keys were still in his pocket.

There was one place he could go. Where he would be safe. Where 'they' would not expect him to be.

Oddly, driving the car was easy and brought to mind the advanced course he had taken at Hendon. But concentrating on taking the correct route was another matter and he kept getting lost, unable to remember roads that he knew must

141

be familiar to him. He was shivering again; shock, he vaguely supposed.

He nearly drove right past his chosen destination – was it such a good idea after all? – but was feeling so ill now, stabbing pains in his head from the previous injury, that he knew he was fit to drive no further.

No one answered his ring at the bell.

He had parked his car out of sight from the road, tucking it by the old stable door in the small courtyard. Fear assailed him as he stood out in the open and he found that he was running – running! – through the garden and then the small gate in the boundary wall. The tombstones in the churchyard seemed to move as he made his way towards the door of the building, a kind of slow, crazy swaying to and fro in time to the sound of his shoes crunching on the gravelled path.

This door, blessedly, was slightly ajar but it took all of his strength to open it wide enough to enable him to enter. Within, all was at peace, nothing defiled this place; motes of dust shining like specks of gold in the shafts of sunlight streaming through the stained glass windows.

'They' still might find him.

'No, no,' he moaned to himself, sinking on to the nearest pew. 'Pull yourself together, you idiot. It's broad daylight in the middle of Hinton Littlemoor.' He looked at his watch but the church clock beat him to it, striking nine. Nine! Had it taken him two and a half hours to drive about twenty miles? No, it couldn't have done. He must have gone to sleep in the car before he set off.

His sight was blurred now but he could see someone moving about near the altar.

Fear was a physical sensation, choking him.

No, he was all right, the someone was wearing robes. It was John and he was coming closer.

'James! My dear fellow . . .'

Carrick had the most bizarre surge of mental clarity. 'I think I've been doped,' he managed to say.

The rector and his wife took over completely. Carrick supposed he must have returned to the rectory under his own steam for surely John could not have carried him? It tran-

142

spired that Elspeth had been in the shower when he had rung the doorbell and had wondered if it had been John – who had gone to the church to say Matins – returning having forgotten his key.

Carrick was aware of his outer garments being removed, the mud sponged from his body, and then of being tucked up in a blanket on the sofa in the living room. He could hear Elspeth speaking on the phone in the hall.

'Anne? Thank the Lord you're in. You know how we sometimes ring you with odd emergencies...? No, it's a friend of Patrick's this time. Something dreadful's happened to him... I don't know – he can't talk about it yet. John said that he mumbled something about being doped... Can you? Bless you. I'll leave the door off the latch.'

'I think it's serious,' John said when she came in. 'We might need an ambulance.'

'Have you ever known Patrick want an ambulance?' she countered. 'We'll see what Anne says when she comes.'

Anne Walker, the Gillards' GP, was a friend who lived nearby. She arrived shortly afterwards; a no-nonsense woman whose hospital experience had been called on by this family on more than one occasion. She entered the living room of the rectory prepared for anything. Whipping the blanket off Carrick she beheld an enigma.

'Shall I go away?' Elspeth asked a trifle nervously, knowing that the woman was fully capable of removing the patient's underpants without so much as a by-your-leave. Any niceties involving churchmen's wives and naked male visitors would elude her.

'Don't touch me,' Carrick said, eyes closed. 'If you do I shall scream.'

Anne bent over him. 'Where do you hurt?'

'All over.'

'You mean it's actually painful to lie there?'

'Yes.'

'You don't look as though you've been beaten up.'

'I haven't been. I think it's something to do with pressure points.'

'Open your eyes.'

Carrick had intended to ask John to phone the Colonel.

'Well, you've certainly been dosed with something. Your pupils are dilated. I'll have to take a blood sample so we can find out what it was. Until I know for sure I'm afraid you'll have to make do with a couple of ordinary painkillers.'

'Tea,' Elspeth decided. 'He'll need a drink to take the pills with.'

'Yes, please,' Anne said, rummaging in her bag for bandages.

'I wouldn't mind one too,' John said. 'Really, this is extremely worrying . . .'

'*Four* teas.'

Despite her gruff manner Anne was very gentle as she bandaged the torn skin on wrists and ankles. Pressure points, she mused. But not in the sense of places on the body where one pressed to control bleeding. To hurt, and to cause these small but livid marks, strong fingers or pincers of some kind had gripped areas where there were nerve centres. He would feel quite ill for several days.

'He's suffering mostly from exhaustion,' she said after she had quickly drunk her tea and was leaving. 'I'm guessing but I should say he was subjected to severe pain while restrained, hence the skinned wrists and ankles. Leave him to sleep. If you're still worried about him when he wakes or if he suffers from nausea then let me know right away. I'll get back to you with the results of the blood test.' In the doorway she paused. 'Are you going to inform the police?'

'He is a policeman,' Elspeth told her smoothly. 'I think we'll have to leave it up to him.' When she had closed the door she marched purposefully to the phone. 'John, I intend to ring Colonel Daws. Would you give me the number?'

'Is that wise, my dear?' Countered the rector.

'I don't care if it's pure madness,' she responded tartly. 'The pair of them went somewhere the night before last. Where's Patrick?'

'He never discusses his missions with us. You can have no idea what he or James intended to do.'

Worry drove her to uncharacteristic ire. 'No, I'm probably a deluded old woman. What I do know is that Patrick sorted out two piles of camouflage clothing which he left on the kitchen floor for a while. James was wearing one lot and I

144

know that for sure too because I mended a tear in the sleeve of that particular battledress top. So, I repeat, where *is* Patrick while James is arriving here alone – *here* of all places – in such a perfectly dreadful state?'

Faced with such terrifying logic John could only hurry away to find the telephone number.

Daws was not particularly helpful. When she had replaced the receiver Elspeth went into the garden and dug the dandelions out of the lawn with ferocious stabs, using an old chisel.

'By all means get Carrick to ring me when he wakes,' the Colonel had said. 'I shall, of course, be most interested in what has to tell me. But I've learned over the years to let Patrick get on with things in his own way. I'm sure you have nothing to worry about.'

She would speak to James before she rang the Bath police to tell them where he was. You do not always tell the servants what the master is up to.

DS Bob Ingrams was feeling cautiously pleased. The progress that had been made was not remarkable but he felt that anything achieved after the hell of the shootings was a good thing. He had been off-duty when the attack had been made, for which good fortune his wife – not the most self-reliant of women – was still prone to become weepy. In thanksgiving she was cooking him all his favourite meals; steak, fried eggs and chips and other delicacies of that ilk, and as he was usually languishing under the subtle cruelties of a strict diet this was paradise indeed.

York CID was still reeling under the shock of losing a promising young officer and having another with serious, possibly crippling, leg injuries. Nevertheless, they had found the rest of the jewellery. Ingrams gathered, reading as it were between the lines, that the task had not been a particularly drawn-out or onerous one, a couple of Peter Hepplewhite's friends having merely taken it into their heads to paste the living daylights out of a man known to handle stolen property. In official jargon, a fence was now helping them with their enquiries. Among all kinds of goods several boxes of jewellery had been found and pieces that

145

matched the descriptions already in their possession had come to light. Inter-force co-operation had extended to their being sent by courier to Bath and at this moment Ingrams had them spread out on his desk before him.

The watch was magnificent and it did not take a horologist to tell him that it was valuable. Even the jewellery, described dismissively as 'Victorian', was quite exquisite to Ingrams's untrained but appreciative eye – he had seen a lot of expensive stolen jewellery in his time, much of it, in his view, overpriced baubles.

Carrick had noted in the case file what Constable Strong had said concerning the remarks Lee had made on the journey down. It was to be assumed that he had previously travelled to Bristol, and Lawrence Gillard's home, for the sole purpose of theft. York CID was emphatic that the man had never been known to resort to violence, the only weapon ever found in his possession a crowbar. There was nothing to connect him with the murder. Ingrams had suggested that Shirley be questioned in an effort to discover if she also had been present. He personally was not keen to write off Lee altogether as far as the killing was concerned; it had crossed his mind that the woman might even have paid him to kill her ex-husband. She still appeared to want custody of the children.

These latest developments now meant that Sadie Bartlett, or Sapphire, was no longer under suspicion so far as the stolen jewellery was concerned. Her wrestler boyfriend had been interviewed by two of the beefiest CID personnel that Bristol could muster – stepping in with a little help in the aftermath of the shootings – who had declared themselves fairly satisfied that he had not been involved with the crime. That night he had been involved in a wrestling bout with one Extra Heavy Metal, incurring severely bruised ribs, and had been taken to hospital for an X-ray.

Where the hell was Carrick?

Ingrams had tried phoning his flat but there was no reply. The Chief Inspector usually left messages as to where he might be contacted but apparently not this time. Reluctantly, Ingrams decided to ask Hobbs if he knew where he was.

'Seen the boss?'

146

Hobbs, who had been walking away down the corridor when Ingrams stuck his head out of the door and bellowed, stopped and turned round. He came back.

'If you want to address me, Ingrams, kindly don't hail me as though I was a bloody taxi.'

'Sorry, sir.'

'Why, have you lost him?'

This had been the previous DCI's stock-in-trade response to queries as to people's whereabouts. You're both birds of a feather, Ingrams thought. Both complete fools.

'As far as I know, sir, he hasn't come in this morning and I don't remember seeing him yesterday. He's not at home either.'

'Perhaps he's meeting that wife of his at the airport or wherever. Isn't she away somewhere?'

'Yes, I believe she is – something to do with a university course.'

'There you are then. What are you working on at the moment?'

'Well, now we've just about tied up the muggings cases, I'm collating evidence on the Gillard—'

'Leave it,' Hobbs interrupted. 'It isn't a crime that this force is going to solve and the sooner MI5 realises it the better. In my view his death can definitely be laid at the door of someone his brother had banged up who planned revenge and got the wrong man. Whoever it is is probably in Bolivia by now. I think you'd be much better employed giving me a hand with this computer store scam.' He looked at his watch. 'But right now I've a meeting to attend at HQ. If Carrick doesn't turn up at least there'll be *someone* in authority from here to fly the flag.'

Head held high, Hobbs stalked off.

When Ingrams had first worked with Carrick, in the days before the latter had been promoted, there had been difficulties. The Sergeant, who had resented his move from Filton and the easy-going, chummy even, Inspector in Charge, had collided heavily with the meticulous regime that the frosty Carrick ruled over. Ingrams had known that the man had recently, and tragically, lost his wife, a situation that obviously made matters worse. There had been the now famous black eye episode when Ingrams had painfully realised that Joanna, Carrick's one-time Sergeant and on-going friend, was not to be trifled with. The struggle between him and his new superior had gone on for several months and resulted in a resounding victory for Carrick.

This was not to say that there had been any brow-beating and as time had gone by Carrick had definitely mellowed. Ingrams had soon discovered that Carrick had a sense of humour. He was intensely hard-working too and not apt to leave his staff in the lurch at night so he could disappear for a dinner date. He did not ensure that those under him got the blame when things went wrong, and when a long-drawn-out case was safely concluded he usually bought everyone a drink at the local pub.

All this was going through Ingrams's mind as he went back to his desk. In some respects he agreed with Hobbs even though there was something about this man, who kept coming back like the smell of bad drains, that the Sergeant could not put a name to but which filled him with unease.

Carrick had noted down the finding of the St Christopher medal in Patrick Gillard's car and had actually stuck it inside the cover of the case dossier by its self-adhesive back. Ingrams went quickly to it now, pulled it off the file, put it in the plastic holder with his warrant card and went out.

148

Chapter 13

When Carrick awoke after sleeping for almost twenty-four hours he could not think where he was for a moment. Sitting up in slight alarm he beheld the family photographs on the mantelpiece then subsided back into the warmth again. Of course, the rectory.

He felt alarmingly weak and ached all over as though he had been stretched on the rack but otherwise . . .

The memory rose like a spectre; the light, the pain, the humiliation. It had been like lying on a stage, an audience watching his every twitch of pain, every cringe, hearing every moan and whimper. He had snivelled. He wanted to snivel now, shed tears of pure self-pity.

Elspeth had not closed the sitting-room door tightly and had left a small lamp on in the hall all night so that her guest could find his way, if necessary, to the downstairs toilet. She had heard no nocturnal movement – actually not sleeping a wink herself – and at first light tip-toed down to the kitchen, leaving John snoring in bed. She peeped round the door at Carrick and, hearing even breathing, retired to her domain and the Rayburn to make herself some tea. This done, the house as quiet and still as only a country dwelling can be at six in the morning but for the twitter of birds in the garden, she heard a sound. Tactfully, not quite sure whether what she had heard was only a muted sneeze, she rattled crockery for a moment or so and then walked down the hall.

'Are you awake, James?' she called softly without going into the room.

There was a muttered affirmative.

'I'll fetch the dressing gown that Patrick uses when he's here and get you some tea.'

When she returned, drawing the curtains in a small side window so that the sun, glimmering through the trees on the garden boundary, banished the gloom from the room, she knew she had been quite correct. His eyes were very bright, his expression that of someone bereaved.

'I don't know where Patrick is,' he whispered. 'I'm so sorry.'

She drew up a stool and sat down. 'You don't have to *apologise*. Please drink your tea before it gets cold.'

His eyes never left her face. 'I couldn't go and look for him. I was too scared.'

Elspeth picked up the mug of tea that she had placed within his reach and held it out. 'I shall talk to you like a Dutch aunt. Sit up and drink your tea.'

Meekly, he obeyed.

'You are not to blame yourself,' she continued, speaking more quietly. 'And I want you to be aware that Patrick too has lain on that sofa when he's been hurt and also cried on my shoulder when life simply couldn't be borne for one moment longer. You've been brutally treated and are suffering from shock. You were also drugged in some way. People who have been drugged often get the horrors afterwards.'

'I ought to phone the Colonel,' Carrick said a while later.

'I did – yesterday. He was his usual stone-wall self but said that if you want to tell him what happened then contact him as soon as possible.' Elspeth rose to her feet. 'I advise a small breakfast, but not if you're feeling queasy.'

'A *small* breakfast,' he replied with a smile.

'I'll put a chair by the phone in the hall for you.'

'Isn't it a bit early?'

'Calls are re-routed to his home when he's not in his office. Yes, get him out of bed.'

Daws answered the phone immediately and was not delighted at what Carrick had no choice but to impart over an open line.

'I've put some very low-key surveillance into place since

150

Mrs Gillard rang,' the Colonel said. 'The last thing we want is for hundreds of police to invade the area.'

'I realise that,' Carrick replied. 'But you must give me some kind of undertaking that you'll treat the matter with the utmost urgency.'

'I assure you I have no intention of forgetting about it,' Daws retorted tartly. 'Have you any idea who these people are?'

'No names were mentioned. I can only assume that they are the outfit the Lieutenant-colonel expected to find there. The star of the show was someone who must be able to wring a chicken's neck one-handed. Thanks to him I can hardly move this morning.'

'Umm,' Daws said, thanked him and rang off.

'I don't suppose he even asked you how you were,' Elspeth said when Carrick had journeyed slowly into the kitchen. She surveyed him sadly. 'I closed the door while you were speaking but I'm desperate to know a bit more – about Patrick, I mean.'

Carrick said, 'I can't tell you much because I simply don't know what happened to him. All I can say is that we were probably apprehended by what I'll describe as the Metropolitan Police's version of D12. They're running an enterprise and didn't want us to interfere.'

She brightened a little. 'It's all perfectly legal then?'

'That's the trouble. It is.'

Bob Ingrams's quest with the St Christopher medal had not been wholly engendered by his hatred of Hobbs or even any particular loyalty to Carrick. What drove him to go from shop to shop that morning – while unbeknown to him Carrick slept the sleep of the dead – was this. If the killer of Lawrence Gillard had placed the medallion in a car belonging to his brother as a threat or warning, aware that he would know the identity of the person who had put it there, it represented the most arrogant, self-congratulatory and downright wicked gesture Ingrams had ever come across. And whatever it was supposed to convey to Patrick Gillard, it was as good as a two-finger salute to the police investigating the case. In short, Ingrams was taking it very personally.

It puzzled him that no one else seemed to think of the clue – and it *was* a clue – in this light. There was every chance though that if Gillard was aware of this person's identity he was not saying for personal reasons, not least to protect other members of his family. Did the DCI know who this person might be and had not entered it in the dossier because Gillard had asked him not to? Ingrams determined to ask him when Carrick showed up; he hated working blind, whatever the reason for it.

The medallion was not a cheap one and looked new. It appeared to be gold-plated and the figure of the saint carrying the child was carefully enamelled in red. On the reverse was a white sticky pad but it was the edge that caught Ingrams's eye; marks that resembled the milling on a coin. He took it into a good light. It was an engraved maker's name: KEPLER – VIENNA.

First of all Ingrams went to all the filling stations and garages he could think of, starting with the one next-door. He could use his car for this and it did not take him very long. They had plastic trinkets on key rings among the Mars Bars, warning cones, tow ropes and replacement windscreens but nothing that approached the medal for quality. Next, he transferred his attention to jewellers' shops. For this he had to leave his car behind, Bath's congested traffic system and lack of on-street parking leaving him with no choice but to walk. He had not realised that the city boasted so many jewellers and by the middle of the afternoon had aching feet and a dreadful thirst.

Most of the shops he had visited carried extremely high quality merchandise, the staff viewing his little piece of evidence with disdain. Someone had even suggested that it might have come out of an expensive Christmas cracker. This was perfectly possible, Ingrams realised miserably, dropping into a seat outside a pavement cafe. It might not have been purchased within a thousand miles of Somerset either.

After a Sally Lunn and a large pot of tea he felt sufficiently refreshed to carry on with his plod around the shops. He completed all the jewellers that he knew of, including small ones in side streets, and then started on the kind of establishment that sold gifts, leather goods and key rings. First of all he went into the largest department store, Jolly's.

The opulent smell of leather assailed his nostrils as he entered the luggage department. The prospective customers looked as though they earned ten times more than he did. All of a sudden his little shiny disc was no more than a tawdry trinket.

'Kepler, Kepler,' murmured the youthful assistant whom Ingrams approached. He seemed quite taken with the idea of helping the police solve a mystery and bent over the medallion, the light of the chase gleaming in his eyes. 'You know, I'm pretty sure, Sergeant, that they make umbrellas.' He turned the medal this way and that in his hand. 'I've seen something like this in a catalogue.' He considered. 'Yes, I know – or, at least, I think I know. I think Kepler mount these on the handles of their umbrellas. You know, like some car manufacturers put logos on the gear levers of expensive models.' He gestured to a wall-mounted phone. 'Shall I ask our buyer for you?'

Ingrams said he would be very grateful.

The answer came back straight away. Yes, indeed, Kepler made umbrellas. Very good quality ones. And their latest range was decorated with St Christopher medals on the handles. Perhaps if the Detective Sergeant would care to take the lift to the third floor he would be able to compare . . .

Ingrams rarely felt the desire to hug complete strangers but his thanks were profuse before he hurried away.

Ten minutes later, having waited until a customer was served, he had his answer. The medallion was definitely off an umbrella and he held in his hand one of Kepler's wares to prove it. It seemed unlikely though that someone would buy such an item in order to prise something off it. Surely, the umbrella had already been in the possession of whoever had left it in the BMW. But it was his duty to explore every possibility.

'Have you sold many of these umbrellas lately?' he asked the woman assistant.

153

'Well, I know that ten came in a few weeks ago and we have only three left. Some of them went that day of the bad thunderstorm.'

'Do you know if many other shops in Bath sell them?'

'Only Cavendish's in Stall Street. They're rather expensive.'

Ingrams glanced at the price tag on the one he was holding. 'Ninety-two pounds fifty!'

'It's a lot just to keep the rain off, isn't it?'

'And they all have the same red and gold medal?'

'Oh, no. It's co-ordinated. The British racing green ones have green and gold, navy blue have blue and gold—'

'So how many dark red ones like this have you sold?'

'Maroon's not too popular. One, I think. I'll check.' She went away.

Ingrams collapsed into a fancy gold chair with a blue satin seat and wiped the perspiration from his forehead with his handkerchief. It looked as though he might have an upper-class murderer.

The woman came back. 'We've actually sold two like that recently.'

'Were they account customers? Do you keep a record of names?'

'One was, Lady Amelia Heythropp-Lamerton. She bought it for his lordship. I only know because I served her. The other one must have been sold on my day off. But when I was in the stock room I remembered something. A gentleman came in the other day asking if I could get him a replacement medallion, just like the one you have there. He said he'd lost it. I must admit I was a bit surprised – they look well and truly stuck on.'

'Can you describe this man?'

'No, I'm terribly sorry. We were really busy – it was one of those days when you never stop.'

'Did he place an order for one?'

'Not in a manner of speaking. I just said I'd get him one and he said he'd pop in now and again to see if it had arrived. He didn't leave a name.'

Ingrams took another close look at the medallion. There

154

seemed to be tiny grooves on it. He then examined the umbrella. Experimentally, he twisted the end of the handle.

'Well, I didn't know that!' the woman exclaimed, seeing the unscrewed medallion in Ingrams's hand and the hollow handle he had revealed. 'Let's have a look at the leaflet that comes in the box. Yes, here we are,' she went on triumphantly. 'It's for putting keys or loose change in so you don't lose them.'

The Detective Sergeant screwed it up again, dug in his pocket and found his newly acquired penknife. It wasn't a Swiss Army knife like Carrick's but had proved its worth already. Seconds later another question had been answered; the sticky disc on the reverse of the medallion was no more than a tiny circle of double-sided tape, cut to size.

'If I leave you my phone number, please let me know if and when this man returns,' he entreated. 'Memorise everything about him. But for God's sake, don't even hint that the police were asking about him.'

She promised that she would.

To make doubly sure Ingrams called in at Cavendish's, but they did not stock the maroon umbrellas at all, just the navy blue and British racing green ones.

'I think it can be summed up neatly by saying that you were sent on an acid trip,' Anne Walker said briskly to Carrick once his blood test result was known. 'Not to worry – you're over that now. As to the rest, you can thank being so fit for being able to move at all. It'll take a while though, before you've completely recovered. I've brought you some fairly strong painkillers.'

The GP, who had literally stuck her head in the door to impart this information on her way to the first of her calls, waved cheerily in response to Carrick's thanks and left.

'How are the horrors?' Elspeth asked sympathetically.

Carrick had to smile. 'I'm at the stage when I can't really tell the drug-induced ones from my own sense of self-preservation that urges me to take the first plane to Australia.' He had rung the nick and reported his whereabouts: there seemed no urgent need for his presence there.

Matthew and Katie were still staying with their grandparents and partly because of this – Carrick had no wish to bring them into any kind of danger – he had decided to leave and go home. He would face any problems when they arose, there was no point in brooding about them.

'You're always welcome here,' Elspeth said at the door. 'Please take care.'

There was nothing at the old farmhouse that was now home to imbue him with any kind of dread or misgivings, rather the familiar surroundings soothed and calmed shattered nerves. Half an hour later, he took two of the painkillers and drove into the city.

There were far more vehicles parked than normal in front of the nick, a large Jaguar occupying his space. He had no choice but to park at the rear, finding a space, finally, about as far as it was possible to be from the rear entrance and walk there. Once inside, he grabbed Woods by the arm as he hurried past, looking worried.

'Who the hell *are* these people?' asked Carrick, having to raise his voice above the babble of conversation from the unknown men in uniform.

'Sorry, sir, I didn't see you,' Woods said. 'A deputation from the Met, no less. Worse, the Super's not here and Hobbs is bursting at the seams being nice to them. I should go home if I were you.'

The advice seemed highly sensible but Carrick wanted access to his office. There were things he urgently needed to read up.

But it was too late; he had been spotted.

'Thank God you're here!' Hobbs said. 'It's all to do with the shootings. The West Country's been chosen first in an initiative to promote greater awareness ... The team's visiting towns and cities in the region to—'

'A greater awareness of what?' Carrick interrupted.

'The risk of terrorism,' Hobbs replied. 'They're in the Super's office.'

'And this lot?' Carrick wanted to know with a wave of his arm.

Hobbs shrugged. 'Bumwipers, probably.' Importantly, he led the way.

Everyone – and there were about eight men in uniform

in the Superintendent's office – stood aside politely to make a pathway to the desk. But someone was seated at it. He rose as they entered.

'Commander Christopher, this is Detective Chief Inspector Carrick, sir.'

They shook hands.

Here was the man photographed sitting in the Land Rover with Lyndberne at his side. Patrick's description was perfect: big, blond, good-looking and couldn't put a foot wrong. He also had a jaw like a gin trap and the smile he was bestowing on Carrick had something disturbingly robotic about it. Carrick's vision blurred and he thought for a moment that he might faint.

That handshake . . .

The same grip.

Those same hands.

The hands under which he had wept like a girl.

'He's working with MI5, sir,' Hobbs was burbling. 'Chief Inspector Carrick has a contact and is investigating the death of the man's brother. The body was found at a local beauty spot.'

'*Really*?' Christopher said. 'Have you any leads so far, Chief Inspector?'

'Not really, sir,' Carrick found himself saying while looking at the faint bruise on the man's cheekbone that he himself had inflicted. 'We've recovered a few items of jewellery, part of a haul missing from the deceased's flat. The self-confessed burglar died in the attack here last week but he wasn't a murder suspect. I'm afraid the trail's gone cold.'

'Are you looking into the possibility of the man's having been shot in error and that the real target was the brother?'

'Yes, that's why MI5 are involved and—'

'Give me a ring at HQ tomorrow. I might be able to give you a few pointers.'

'That's very kind of you, sir.'

'Are you all right? You don't look very well.'

Carrick mumbled something about having been assaulted, made his apologies and left the room. He just succeeded in reaching the gents' before he vomited and had to stay there for an hour, shaking, ill and utterly wretched.

157

Chapter 14

Joanna rang at nine that evening and upon hearing that her husband of almost a year was off work with a stomach bug was all for rushing home to look after him.

'You never used to fuss,' he growled, hating having to lie to her. 'No, thank you, I'll be fine. Besides, you've work to do.'

'It's a bit tedious really. Are you *sure* you're all right?'

'Right as rain,' he lied again. 'Just feeling a bit weak. I'll have an early night.'

'I'll be home in three days,' she reminded him before she rang off.

Normally, the thought of seeing her again would have made him feel very happy. But he did not want to see Joanna: right now he wanted to see no one. Determinedly, knowing precisely what he was going to do, he went to the drinks cupboard and took out a bottle of Famous Grouse whisky. It wasn't the answer, in the end it would make him feel worse, but in the meantime he knew it would make him feel a lot better.

'Alcohol is a depressant,' he told his reflection in the sitting-room mirror. 'Cheers, you bloody coward.'

There seemed to be no solution to the problem. It was a measure of Ladd's supreme confidence that he had come out into the open. Ingrams had rung Carrick earlier in the evening – having merely heard that the DCI had come in to work but been taken ill and gone home – to bring him up to date with the news of the rest of the jewellery's recovery and his own findings concerning the medallion.

158

The latter was interesting but not real evidence. The only way Ladd could be stopped was by hard evidence. Carrick was beginning to think that all he could do was to contact Complaints. His real source of information – and, it had to be admitted, inspiration – had obviously been abducted.

That was the worst part: not knowing how he could help Patrick.

'I couldn't go back to that quarry,' Carrick muttered into his third large tot of whisky. 'It would achieve nothing but get me done over again.'

He had to stay out of Ladd's way.

Which made him a coward.

The phone rang for the third time.

'Is that James Carrick?' asked a man's voice.

Carrick said that it was.

'Good evening. My name's Terry Meadows. I've been asked by a mutual acquaintance to look you up.'

'In the present circumstances I think I'd prefer some proof of your identity.'

'Certainly. My wife's name is Dawn and she used to work as a nanny before we were married. My hobbies are climbing and caving and I once went on an activity holiday with Dawn's boss and his wife to Brecon in South Wales.'

'Where are you speaking from?'

'A phone box near the bus station in Bath.'

'You have a car though?'

'Yes.'

'Head out of the city as though you were going to Hinton Littlemoor but instead of taking that turning stay on the main road until you come to the Fuller's Arms where there's a crossroads. Turn right for Framwell. Half a mile along the road to the village take the left fork. Go past the thatched cottage on the right and turn right into the narrow lane about twenty yards farther on. It's the first house you come to, Long Acre Farm.'

'Roger. See you in about half an hour then.'

It could still be a trick, Carrick thought as he replaced the reciver.

'No,' he sighed out loud. 'Ladd's got what he wants now.'

Twenty-five minutes later a car purred into the drive and

parked under the window near to which Carrick was sitting. He went to open the front door so that his visitor did not have to ring the doorbell.

Meadows was about his own age, Carrick supposed, not quite as tall but powerfully built. This was not to say that he moved like a weight-lifter; the strength was understated, unaffected. He had thick wavy brown hair, brown eyes and expressive features. It was an honest face, but Carrick felt slightly disappointed. Here was no second Holmes, which was what he had been hoping for: Meadows was definitely a young, albeit powerful, Watson.

'Daws asked me to come,' Meadows confirmed. 'I don't work for him now but he knows that as far as the governor's concerned I'm always ready to volunteer.'

'The governor being Patrick?'

Meadows grinned. 'Of course. Call me Terry.'

'James,' Carrick ushered him into the living room. 'What will you have to drink?'

The man's gaze took in Carrick's whisky glass and the opened bottle. 'It depends on whether I can stay the night.'

'You're welcome.'

'In that case I'll have a drop of that.'

When they were seated Carrick said, 'I understand you were Patrick's assistant.'

'Sort of.'

'Do you mind if I ask what you're doing now?'

'Not at all. I left D12 when I got married. Dawn had been too closely involved with some really hairy situations. I didn't like that so to keep the wolf from the door set up my own security consultancy. It's doing all right.' He smiled reflectively. 'But sometimes, when I'm asked . . .'

'I don't know where Patrick is.'

'That's nothing new. Disappearing's a speciality of his.'

'Did Daws brief you?'

'No. He called me at work so couldn't go into too many details. I already knew that Larry had been killed. Elspeth rang me and told me just after it happened. I could hardly believe it really – such a nice, ordinary bloke.'

Carrick told him the story right from the beginning. He had written practically every word of the case notes so it

160

was easy to fill in all the background of facts and evidence and intersperse it with his own thoughts and suspicions.

'I hope you have the negatives of those photos,' was the first thing Meadows said when he had finished.

'They're here – with the prints in the wall safe.'

'Thank God you didn't take them to the nick. Mind if I have a look?'

Carrick went to fetch them. 'I haven't mentioned anything about Brecon in the case notes,' he called. 'As far as I'm concerned, officially that is, it's a witness's private theory.'

'Yes, that's Lyndberne,' Meadows said, holding the rather dark print near to a table lamp in order to examine it more closely. 'Or Commander X as we had to call him. So the driver's Ladd, is he? Only he's now using the name Christopher. He looks a bit of a bastard.'

'Patrick taught him all he knows – back in his army days.'

'Back in Ladd's army days, you mean. Patrick's still a serving officer. So is Daws for that matter.'

'Yes, of course. I was forgetting. He still has to go for the annual assessment. I don't think I quite made that clear when I said he was in Cirencester.'

'It's actually the undercover operatives assessment. It's a farce really so far as Patrick's concerned. He always breaks all the rules. But seeing he set up the test *and* wrote the rules, I suppose he has every right to.'

The light tone with which this was uttered and the general air of detachment angered Carrick. 'Look, the man might be *dead* by now.'

There was a pause and then Meadows said, 'Yes, I know. I thought about it all the way down from London. I have an idea that Daws keeps me on because while all the intellectual, thinking bods are having nervous breakdowns after they've been taken apart, I tend to say "bugger everything" and go back and sort it out.'

Carrick discovered that he was speechless.

'Nothing personal,' the other went on. 'Patrick once flipped when some bikers tied him to a gate and thrashed him with their belts until he almost died. He went back and faced them but almost went out of his mind over it. In the

161

end Ingrid and I went in too. Call me an anchorman if you like.'

Moistening his dry lips Carrick said, 'Daws has sent you to be my anchorman.'

'In a way.'

'Ladd isn't a common criminal. He's a very senior police officer.'

'If he shot Larry Gillard he *is* a criminal.'

'Yes, you're right,' Carrick said despondently. 'And I was so glibly telling Patrick that Ladd's rank would make no difference – even Chief Constables have been arrested for driving while over the limit. But I'm still up against the system.'

'No, not even that. You're up against your own fear.'

'But I didn't say anything to Daws about ...'

'No, no. I rang Elspeth before I set off to find out if Patrick had contacted her. He does sometimes if he's otherwise off the map. She told me that she was very worried about you.' Meadows swirled the golden liquid that was in his glass, holding it up to the lamplight to admire the colour. 'Tell me what this guy did to you.'

'Very little in actual fact,' Carrick answered bitterly. 'Oh, I know I was tied face down on the ground after they'd taken most of my clothes off but that was nothing to what happened on a leadership course I attended when I was with the Met! The doc said I'd been doped. That only made it seem worse.'

'And?'

Carrick shook his head, the memories too harsh.

'It helps to talk about it,' Meadows said understandingly.

'I – I'd like to be able to say that I was kicked and beaten,' Carrick stammered. 'But it was nothing like that. It felt like ... as if someone knew where all the nerve centres were in your body and ... stuck hot needles in them.'

'Just with his fingers? Like bashing your funny bone only a million times worse?'

Carrick nodded.

'You've just convinced me that it *was* Ladd in the forest. Patrick must have taught him to do that.'

'*What?*'

162

'It's how he gets the truth out of people. Only if he has to – he hates doing it. It seems to me that Ladd was warning you off in a big way.'

'Where did this *art* originate?'

'Japan. It's not widely known about.'

'He was taught it during his special operations army days, I suppose?'

'No. Patrick went off on his own and learned all kinds of things before he worked undercover for the army. He doesn't talk about it, just refers to it as his survival package.'

'Decent of him to pass it on.'

'It's really a self-defence mechanism – useful in unarmed combat.'

Carrick took a deep breath. 'So what do we do now?'

'You're the investigating officer.'

'I just need a different angle on the case.'

'Is this quarry marked on the OS map of the area?' Meadows asked thoughtfully.

'It's just described as old workings.'

'Have you any idea if D12 has it under surveillance?'

'Daws said he'd put a watch on the place. Patrick and I met a bloke called Nathan who'd been watching the house.'

Meadows smiled. 'Nathan's the sort of guy who can hide in your front garden for a week and you wouldn't notice him. But Daws doesn't send him into any real hazards. If you let off a gun in his direction he dives down the nearest rabbit hole. No, I reckon hanging around in an area you say is bristling with security devices is a waste of time. We've no guarantee that's where Patrick's being held anyway. I think we ought to tail the big man himself – Ladd.'

'I just wish Daws would get some kind of permission and go in – with soldiers if necessary.'

'He will. But he needs evidence first. If, as you say, the PM wants to spray slurry all over the people responsible, he must have proof.'

Carrick suddenly remembered that he was the host. 'Have you eaten? Would you like some supper?'

'What about you?'

'I'm afraid I'm still not feeling too good. But I can fix something for you.'

163

'I wouldn't hear of it. Can I cook myself something like egg on toast? I came straight from work.'

'Raid the kitchen. There's fresh food that needs using.'

Expecting to hear the tin opener being used and smell bacon frying, Carrick was beguiled to detect that his guest was busy with chopping board and knife, whisking something with a fork in a basin, and then came the wonderful scent of garlic sizzling gently in hot butter. He followed his nose into the kitchen.

'Fresh herbs!' Meadows exclaimed. 'What a treat.'

'They're from the garden. I was going to put them in a salad.'

'Some of them, chives, parsley and a little thyme, are going in an omelette. It's my speciality. You put in a few very small nuggets of butter just as it's cooked and fold them inside so they're just melting when you eat it.' He deftly wielded the salt and black pepper mills and moments later the fluffy golden omelette had been tipped on to a warmed plate. 'Like a small taste?'

Carrick tasted and very shortly afterwards was carrying it away to find a knife and fork. Inside the omelette, as well as the herbs and butter and a hint of garlic, were tiny curls of fresh parmesan cheese. He suddenly realised that he had not consumed anything, other than cups of tea and biscuits, for about forty-eight hours.

Terry, smiling contentedly, made himself another one.

Shirley returned from seeing her solictor – she had started proceedings to apply for the custody of her children – to find two policemen on her doorstep. She complained loudly when they intimated that they wanted to talk to her, her somewhat deep voice becoming shrill with protest. Too many cops, she told them, had crossed her threshold recently. They insisted.

Inside, they gave her the news of Thomas Lee's death. They then went on to say that a quantity of stolen jewellery had been recovered from his home. More jewellery and a watch had been found at the house of someone known to deal in stolen goods. Lee had been on his way to Bath for further questioning when the attack had been made on the police car carrying him. The matter was still under investigation. All the recovered items exactly fitted descriptions of things stolen from her ex-husband's flat, probably on the night of his death.

'So he *had* broken in and taken it, the little bastard!' was Shirley's reaction to this.

'You already suspected that he had?' asked the shorter of the two members of York CID.

'Only after someone called Carrick came to question me. I got the idea that he suspected me over Larry's death so I put two and two together and asked myself why. Then I remembered the jewellery and how I'd mentioned it once to Tom. He was always broke – had a criminal record too.'

'Did you confront him with your suspicions?'

'Yes, I did.'

'And he admitted to stealing the jewellery?'

Shirley flared up again. 'Do you take me for a fool? Do you think I'd have let him get away with that? No, he denied it. But I didn't really believe him – I told him we were finished.' Her eyes became fierce slits. 'I'll have you know that it originally belonged to my parents. My mother gave it to Larry. She had no business to – it should have come to me. You see, it had been handed down from my father's parents, not hers.'

'And you didn't ask Lee to get it back for you?'

'Of course not!'

'I gathered from Detective Sergeant Ingrams at Bath that the jewellery was being held in trust by your husband for your children.'

She tossed her head. 'What of it? And why hadn't it been put in the bank?'

'Policemen ask themselves that all the time, madam.'

To her relief, they went then.

She flopped down into a chair. God, what a mess. But with Tom dead at least there was no proof of what she'd said to him in the heat of the moment. She always got a bit hot under the collar when she thought of the way her mother had calmly done her out of the stuff. The watch was worth a small fortune and at auction might fetch several thousand pounds. What would Matthew want with a thing like that?

He was only interested in motor racing. And what would happen to all of it now? Most likely it would be put into the care of a solicitor until the court made a decision about the kids' future.

Shirley put her feet up. She would do everything in her power to ensure that the kids came to *her*.

What made her maddest of all now she knew the whole story was that Tom *had* pinched the jewellery – which she'd taunted him he was too scared to take – and sold some of it for himself. He'd lied ... and after all those hot meals she'd cooked for him too!

But overall she felt vindicated: tipping off the police about him had paid off.

At first light Carrick was woken by sounds that proved to be Meadows in the kitchen making tea. He was dressed for the outdoors in thick cotton trousers and sweatshirt, both in a drab shade of green.

'I'm going to have a very low-profile look at the quarry,' he announced, passing over a mug of tea to Carrick. 'I'll try and approach it from the other side. Don't worry if I'm out all day.'

'Take care.'

'I intend to. I've been thinking. *If*, and it might be a big if because we don't know this guy Ladd at all, but if he's not treating the whole thing as the cop versus the crook scenario – and from what you've already told me it seems highly likely – then it's a duel.'

'I follow,' Carrick said. 'Go on.'

'I mean, Lyndberne – Commander X – had clearly ignored which side of the fence he was on, just played the bigger, better crook. The fact that the plan seems to have been to arrest all these foreign villains is neither here nor there. With Ladd, a bloke to whom Patrick taught all he knows, we might be involved with a scenario where the pupil is trying to outwit the tutor. It's all supposition but if he regards Patrick closing down Brecon as Round One, and Commander X falling out of his rowing boat – yes, Patrick did tell me about his involvement with that – as Round Two then Patrick won both of those. That was when Ladd

166

probably decided to wade into the fray. Thinking along those same lines, then Ladd shooting Larry was Round Three to him, pure revenge. He left the medallion in the car as a kind of declaration of war. He obviously has a big ego, this bloke, and it was a challenge. It can't be anything else. He threw down the gauntlet. Personally I think he's showing every sign of being as raving mad as his oppo was.'

'Round Four was picking up Patrick and me in the woods. But he has Patrick now so presumably that's the end of the contest.'

'Not necessarily. It's too quick and too easy. And even if he has Patrick nailed to a wall somewhere and dying by inches it's not clever. Any lout can do that. What he wants, at a guess, is the satisfaction of knowing that he's the best. And to do that he has to use the methods he was taught.'

Carrick was beginning to change his mind about the Holmes and Watson theory. 'You know him better than I. What would Patrick do now?'

'From his own point of view, he'd want to nail Ladd for Larry's death.'

'That's my objective too.'

'And Ladd will want to prove that Patrick had a hand in Commander X's death. He might also want to discredit MI5 – especially as he must realise that MI5 wants to close down his entire unit. Looked at like that, the guy's fighting for survival.'

'He could force Patrick to write a confession but there would be nothing to stop his retracting it later, saying it had been made under duress. No, it can't come to court. Lyndberne didn't play by the book and this man won't either.'

'I feel like lifting him and thumping the truth out of him.'

Carrick was recollecting an earlier theory. 'Let's go right back to the beginning. The idea might have been to take Patrick out in some way before the school opened, possibly temporarily. If he was followed from home – with a view to grabbing him when he was on his own – and they tailed him to Larry's flat, whoever was tailing him might not have realised that the brothers had swapped cars. They might have been told merely not to let the BMW out of their sight

167

and camped outside Larry's place thinking the driver was staying the night. Ladd had met Larry at Brecon but if the latter hadn't given him his surname he might not have known Patrick had a brother. Someone coming out of the main entrance to a block of flats and driving away an old banger might have been ignored. Who knows? Patrick could have changed his jacket or whatever he was wearing. Several days later the watchers followed the car, which presumably they knew had been in for repair, to the lake. They picked up the driver and got the wrong man.'

'And shot him when they realised they'd made a mistake?'

'We found no evidence to point to Larry's having been shot at the lakeside. If they took him to the farmhouse . . .'

Meadows's eyes were shining. 'They realised they'd got the wrong man when they arrived at the farmhouse and Ladd clapped eyes on him. God, given the way these people operate, he'd have had no choice but to shoot Larry. And knowing him, he wouldn't have helped himself – Larry always went off at the deep end.'

'Then a damage control exercise,' Carrick said slowly. 'They'd have taken the body back to the lake – but not in Patrick's car. Forensic could find no trace of that having happened. Unless, of course, they put it into a thick plastic bag of some kind. And then dumped it in the water.'

'Ladd then put the medallion in the BMW as a warning, or whatever, in an effort to milk some small advantage out of what had been a very bad bungle. Yes, it's a good theory. I like it.'

'All we have to do is find the murder weapon and the car they used to transport the body back to the lake,' Carrick observed dryly.

Chapter 15

Although leading the group from the Metropolitan Police, Commander Christopher had with him only two of his own unit. The initiative, a kind of roving 'think tank', visiting the regional forces in turn to help combat terrorism on the British mainland, had been the idea of the head of a divisional crime squad, another Commander by the name of Courtney du Lac. Du Lac, now retired to the Central Medoc wine-growing area of France and reputedly a count, had envisaged a Register of Terrorists and an international police force to fight terrorism long before the idea was actually adopted. It was doubtful whether he would have approved, had he known, of the manner in which some of the resources of the Met's own department were now being used ...

Christopher went to a meeting chaired by the Chief Constable of Avon and Somerset Police, but had news whispered in his ear that caused him to leave the gathering at the first opportunity. With his two subordinates, one of whom had given him the message, he left at once, using one of their own cars.

As instructed, Carrick rang Headquarters and asked if Christopher was free to speak with him. He was told that the Commander had left.

'What time was this?'

'Only about half an hour ago, sir. But he can't have gone for good, his car's still outside.'

'Are you sure?'

'Yes, I can see it from reception where I am now. I saw him arrive too.'

'Perhaps if he returns while you're around you'd be good enough to tell him that I rang.'

'Can I give him a message for you?'

'No, it's all right – I'll try to catch him later.'

Carrick was ashamed of the relief that he felt. He had been asked – no, ordered – to contact Christopher and had done so. Christopher would expect that of him: not just because of his rank but due to his belief that he had the DCI at Bath right under his thumb.

But had he?

Carrick was not sure if he could honestly answer that question yet.

He was positive that the treatment meted out to him had been for no other reason than to instil fear. The way Christopher had subsequently shaken hands with him – the careful placing of fingers a split second before the actual clasp, the very touch, the smile – had been done deliberately to remind Carrick of his humiliation. But Carrick had no proof that Christopher had assaulted him, no more than he had proof about anything else in connection with this case; he had not been able to see his captors. The entire episode had been insurance on Christopher's part that if Carrick had to handle any evidence that might connect him with the murder, he would not use it. And a single St Christopher medallion was not evidence.

This suspicion had been strengthened mid-morning when Ingrams had rung to say that the Commander had borrowed the case file, promising to return it the next day.

'Are you happy about that, sir?' he had asked carefully.

'No,' Carrick told him abruptly. 'I'd rather you didn't discuss the case with him either.'

'I get the feeling I'm being kept in the dark about some aspects of this.'

Ingrams didn't usually use words like 'aspects'.

'Because of the MI5 angle, Bob. That's also why I can't talk about it over the phone.'

The words had tripped readily off his lips as an excuse – how he hated lying to people like that – and then he had the disturbing thought that yes, indeed, his phone might be tapped. Christopher might know that Meadows had visited him. But it was unlikely that he would know who he was as Terry had entered the complex at Brecon right at the last after Lyndberne had left. (Unbeknown to Carrick at this time, Meadows had in fact diligently searched his whole house for snooping devices but found nothing.)

He had forgotten to mention to Terry that Patrick had recognised one of the men seated on the trailer.

'God, I'm a fool!' Carrick said out loud. 'Frodheim! It must have been him who shot up the police car. Who the hell else could it have been? Where else would Ladd – or Christopher or whatever his bloody name is – get someone to do that without batting an eyelid? He'd hardly risk incriminating himself or any of his personnel.'

Carrick couldn't believe that any serving officer would obey orders to do such a thing.

Also, if Christopher wanted to prove to Frodheim that the set-up wasn't a trap, what better way than to give him that kind of job to do? Another puzzle was that if Frodheim and the others were due to be arrested, why hadn't they been so far? What was the Commander waiting for?

The scheme *had* to involve money, fees for the 'tuition', probably sent by bankers' draft from abroad. No self-respecting criminal would arrive in a country carrying large amounts of cash, it would be too risky.

Lyndberne, or Commander X, had used the capture of Gillard as proof of his skill, to enhance his own reputation. Now it looked as though his successor had provided authenticity to his operation by commissioning one of his 'pupils' to murder a man who might have seen him in Lawrence Gillard's flat. What could Christopher have been doing there, though? Looking for the photos? How would he know about Lee? The answer to that question had to be that he had someone inside, a 'mole' who was giving him information, probably in the mistaken idea that he or she was assisting in an important internal investigation.

'No proof, no bloody proof,' Carrick groaned.

He was trying to avoid thinking about it; what would happen when he and Christopher next came face to face?

171

He was quite likely one of those sad cases who needed counselling and for someone to hold his hand and tell him he was suffering from Post Traumatic Stress Disorder.

Almost choking with self-disgust Carrick wandered restlessly from room to room, quite unable to face going in to work. Call yourself a Scot, he berated himself. Wallace must be revolving in his grave. Two hours later he was no nearer reaching any kind of decision and had reached the stage where he was contemplating resignation. There was no point in going on like this.

The phone rang and it was Ingrams again.

'If you're well enough, sir, I think you ought to come in.'

'Why, what's happened?'

'There's been an armed raid on a building society branch in Milsom Street just as they were closing, and they got away with a quarter of a million pounds. An ex-Marine who tried to have a go was shot dead. The getaway vehicle was a red van and Woods reckons it was the same one that was used when the lads from York were shot up. He was literally passing at the time. He's insisting that the exhaust was held on with wire in exactly the same way and a patch of rust on the near-side wing looked the same.'

Carrick had never known Woods be wrong on a matter of observation. 'Did he get the number this time?'

'Yes, but it was false. The car with that registration was scrapped two years ago.'

'Find out who it belonged to. I'm on my way.' Somehow, anger had replaced his state of nerves.

To hell with MI5.

He went straight to the scene of the crime. Hobbs was already there, talking to the shaken staff. The evidence was stark and simple. At just after five-twenty, when there were only three customers waiting to be attended to, two masked men had burst in, one of whom had fired several rounds from a semi-automatic weapon of some kind into the ceiling. Everyone, including the staff, had been made to lie on the floor and one of the clerks had been singled out, the weapon pointed directly at him, to unlock a security door, thus giving the raiders entry to the area behind the counters. They had made straight for the manager's office

172

and he had been forced to hand over all the money in the tills. The safe could not be opened; it had a time lock and could not be accessed until six pm.

When the pair had been making their escape they were challenged by a member of the public. The man had tackled the leader and actually brought him to the ground but a second robber had kicked him semi-conscious and he had been shot dead where he lay disabled on the pavement.

'Just the two of them, sir,' said Woods, approaching.

Carrick said, 'You mean they left the van empty with the engine running outside while they carried out the raid?'

'Yes, unless there was another one hiding inside on the floor of the cab with orders to muster if things went wrong. I heard the shot and they were scrambling into the van and driving off before I could do anything about it. They were both of stocky build and wearing jeans and dark blue sweatshirts.'

'And masked?'

'Black balaclavas.'

'Which way did the van go?'

'Down towards the Post Office. We're still interviewing passers-by so we might get more info. I'd swear on everything holy it was the same vehicle. The patch of rust on the wing looked like a map of Africa.'

'Thanks.'

In his office the manager was seated, but not at his desk, being given a paper cup of water by a WPC.

'Sorry,' he was saying when Carrick entered. 'I suddenly felt rather strange. It's the shock, I suppose.'

The WPC said, 'Mr Nolan, this is Detective Chief Inspector Carrick.'

Carrick said to her, 'You might go and talk to that elderly woman sitting at the table in the far corner. She looks as though she could do with a little sympathy – older people often notice things that younger ones don't too.'

The manager shook himself as though emerging from a dream. 'He had a foreign accent – the one with the gun, I mean. European, but not French. It might have been German. I could only see their eyes, you understand, so I can't help you with descriptions. The only impression I have

173

is that they were dark – possibly with swarthy complexions but I'm not sure. As I said, it's just an impression. Everything happened so quickly.'

'Did you see what happened afterwards – when they ran outside?'

'Yes, I did. When they had the money and had lost interest in me, I immediately pressed an alarm button. I then thought that it was a stupid thing to do – it makes a fearful racket – and it might make them lose their nerve and start shooting indiscriminately. After that I suppose fear of what they might do to the staff overcame fear for my own safety. I'm not a brave man, I just didn't stop to think. I followed when they were leaving the building. I was in time to see that very courageous man throw himself on the one with the gun. They shot him.'

'How do we know he was an ex-Marine?'

'He was with a young woman so I suppose she must have told someone. I believe she was taken to hospital – presumably suffering from shock.'

Carrick went back into the street. Yes, to hell with MI5. He was going to raid that farmhouse.

Speed could be the only element of surprise: this was not a situation where people could lurk in undercover vans pretending to be gasfitters. So, with personnel borrowed from Bristol and after a delay while he had persuaded Buller to give him a search warrant, Carrick set off for Mendip, all blue lights flashing. He had armed support; three members of the TSG, a siege expert should affairs take that course, and dogs and their handlers in the event of anyone taking to the woods.

They achieved the capture of those in the farmhouse with no opposition. Carrick found that the front door was unlocked when he tried the handle. He did not pause of his stride until he reached a long, low sitting room where a couple were just in the act of leaping to their feet.

'Police,' he announced. 'I have a warrant to search this house and the outbuildings.'

They both started to protest but Carrick cut them short, asking their names.

174

The woman answered first. 'My name's Barbara Conway and this is my husband Jeff. What the hell is all this about?'

This was the woman he and Patrick had watched leave the house and drive off in the Sierra Estate. The man, the one whom Nathan had described as 'short, dark and ugly', had driven the tractor.

The sound of tramping feet rang through the house.

'I demand to know what you're looking for' Mrs Conway said.

'The men who are staying here,' Carrick replied.

'Men? Oh, you mean the students. They've gone home.'

'When?'

'Not long ago actually. About an hour. A taxi came for them and took them to the airport.'

'What, all of them?'

'There were only four.'

The husband spoke for the first time. 'We run a perfectly legal business here.'

Carrick ignored him, continuing to direct his questions at the woman. She appeared to be the more intelligent of the two and he had an idea that within this marriage her word was law.

'Where were they taken? Heathrow?'

She nodded. 'Yes.'

'That's a very expensive way of getting them there. Didn't you meet them in a minibus when they arrived?'

The two exchanged glances. Then the woman said, 'There was a mix-up with dates when they arrived and Jeff had to hire a minibus to collect them. We don't run these courses, just provide food and lodging. We made it clear that we were not prepared to ferry them around.'

'So transport is usually laid on by someone else?'

'That's correct.'

'I'd like a list of the names and addresses of your so-called students and also the name of the organisation that employs you.'

Ingrams entered the room, slightly out of breath. 'There's no one else here, sir, and no sign of the red van.'

'I want every room searched right down to and below the floorboards if necessary. Every wardrobe and cupboard

175

checked for false backs. Test all likely places in bedrooms, bathroom and living room for fingerprints. Every last square inch of the place, come to think of it. Look sharp, Bob, you don't need me to tell you what to do.'

'We don't have a red van,' said Jeff Conway.

'What about at the quarry?'

'We have no idea what goes on at the quarry,' Mrs Conway said. 'It's nothing to do with us.'

'But it's where your visitors went for their lessons, wasn't it?'

Conway remained silent, a dour look on his face.

'That list,' Carrick reminded the wife.

He was given the list and none of the names meant anything to him. Which was to be expected if the men had been travelling under false passports.

'Who does the quarry belong to?' he asked.

They both shrugged.

'You can take us there,' Carrick told Conway. 'When I get back. Stay right here.'

He went outside and radioed a request that a watch be mounted for the men at Heathrow and other airports. He knew he was wasting his time. It was highly unlikely that there were plans afoot for them to leave the country yet, if at all. At the back of his mind there was the nagging suspicion that Frodheim had either smelt a rat or become bored and simply walked out to create mayhem. The taxi story was almost certainly a lie.

On re-entering the house he first went upstairs. Everywhere there was the strong scent of cleaning materials, especially lavender polish, all the paintwork and mirrors gleaming, not a speck of dust anywhere. His heart sank within him.

'You drive,' he told Conway when they were outside. He got in the front of the Sierra, Ingrams in the back. Half a dozen others, including the members of the TSG, would follow in a police van.

Conway was told to take exactly the same route as he had done with his visitors and turned left out of the yard into a narrow lane. Carrick could see the tall tree from which he and Patrick had watched and in his mind's eye was picturing what he had seen. By this time it was well into the evening and getting dark, the sky heavily overcast, but Carrick was reasonably confident that he would know if Conway tried to take them somewhere else.

'You still haven't told me who runs these courses,' he said.

'Don't ask me,' came the mumbled response. 'Babs does all the arranging.'

'And you're quite happy about having a bunch of strange men in your home without knowing anything about them?'

'They're just young blokes on holiday as far as I'm concerned, and as long as the money rolls up that's all I worry about.'

From what Patrick had told him Frodheim must be at least forty-five.

They seemed to be taking the same route. By the time they turned left again and then followed the curve of the road in the direction of the wood Carrick's stomach was tying itself in knots. They came to the notice board and entered the deep gloom under the trees.

The gate and security fence had gone.

'Stop the car!' Carrick ordered. He got out, went to the van behind them and borrowed a powerful flash light.

The gate and fence had not only gone, the holes where the posts had been were now difficult to find, having been filled in with leaves and detrius from the forest floor. He did find one of the large gate post holes and there was earth in this too, moist and fresh. Turning aside he walked through the trees along the line of the missing fence and the same care had been taken here too, not a staple or single inch of wire to be seen.

'You know nothing about this, of course,' he said to Conway who had lit a cigarette and was leaning an elbow on the open driver's window in a bored manner.

'About what?'

'You must have driven through the gate that used to be here every day while your visitors were with you.'

'Nothing to do with me. It's not my property.'

'Was it usually open?'

'Most times. Once or twice I had to open it but it was

177

always unlocked. Stands to reason doesn't it?' He crashed the car into gear and they set off again.

They came to a clearing which the track meandered across and then re-entered the forest. A quarter of a mile farther on there was another clearing, larger, with piles of lengths of timber neatly stacked. Just around the corner from this the trees opened out once more, a single-storey hut visible in the dusk. Carrick was vaguely aware of a large tank of some kind on wooden supports looming above and to one side of it.

Conway pulled up. 'This is it. I don't know what you're going to see now but they did the rock climbing on the quarry face over there to your right and abseilled off the old railway viaduct about two hundred yards downhill to the left. The place used to have its own rail link. Ages ago. When it was steam. There was an incline that the wagons rolled down to join the line. That's in front of you. Be careful where you walk. There are some soddin' big drops down to where the railway track used to be and even bigger ones into the quarry itself.'

Ingrams, who on the journey had remained silent, said, 'We won't be able to see a thing, guv. It's too dark.'

Carrick was inclined to agree with him. Also stubborn. He had already decided against putting his team into the forest itself because of the risk of injury from any remaining booby traps – it went without saying that some kind of effort would have been made to remove those also but he wouldn't take the risk. Officially, his warrant did not cover searching this area but on the grounds that Patrick Gillard was missing he intended to have a good look round.

To Ingrams he said, 'Send the driver of the van back with it and get him to grab all spare people to drive all available vehicles over here so we can use the headlights to see by. We'll do what we can tonight, find out who this place belongs to and come back tomorrow.'

While he was waiting he went over to the hut and tried the door. It was open. Warily, he pushed the door wide and flashed the light from the torch around the interior. There was very little to see; several chairs of the stacking variety, a table and larger chair at one end, some bare shelves and an old-fashioned sink with a single tap over it.

'Who was here when you brought your charges?' he called to Conway, still slouched in the car.

'Just a couple of blokes. I don't know who they were, though.'

'Describe them.'

'I can't. They were all done up in sort of combat gear with balaclavas over their heads.'

'And everyone knows that's what outdoor activity instructors wear in high summer. You're lying!'

'I swear to you that's what they wore! I never saw their faces.'

'You're lying about being in the dark about what was going on here.' Carrick went back and spoke to him through the open window of the vehicle. 'They were wanted criminals, your students, weren't they? Real bad lads from overseas.'

Conway blinked in the bright light shining into his face. 'I don't know nothing about them . . . I told you!'

'The German one, the one who frightened you rigid. No one could tell him what to do, could they? When did he walk out?'

By this time Conway's face had gone a dirty white. 'I don't know what you mean,' he mumbled.

'He took someone else and the red van with him. Then he held up a building society office in Bath. A man who tried to stop him was shot dead. Make no mistake about it – you're in this up to your neck.'

Carrick returned to the hut, entering it this time. There was a light switch just inside the door but nothing happened when he clicked it down. Close to it on the wall was a small cupboard he had not noticed before of the kind that might hold electricity meters. So it proved to be but instead of the old-fashioned fuses he expected to find there were modern earth-leakage breakers, the wiring neatly and professionally done, everything comparatively new. Was this the power source for all those nasty surprises in the woods? It was all switched off and he left it that way.

179

He shone the light around the interior again. Yes, it was a school room.

'An apple for the teacher,' he said to himself, seeing a core and some sweet wrappers in a metal waste bin. Using his handkerchief to hold it, he picked it up.

'I wish I knew what to look for,' said Ingrams, wandering in.

'I'm sorry if I can't give you the full details yet,' Carrick said. 'But mostly we're looking for the guy who robbed the building society. He's done a runner. Either that, or someone's hiding him. He might be here.' He held out the waste bin. 'Put that in a bag, it's evidence.'

Ingrams peered at it dubiously in the light from the torch.

'There, on the rim. And don't touch anything in here. I intend to put a guard on it until we can do an official search. Well? Recognise it?'

'That little mark there? I can't say that I do.'

'It's the emblem of the Met.'

'So it is. We're nicking someone for stealing police property then?'

Carrick eyed him narrowly. 'Keep your trap shut but we might be involved with police corruption at a very high level.'

The vehicles that he had requested were arriving and for the next hour and a half as much of the quarry complex as possible was searched. Carrick climbed up on to the tank – it held water, he discovered – and still fearing that they would discover Gillard's body, had it drained. After several thousand gallons had gushed away out of sight down the hillside he clambered up again with his flashlight.

But for quite a lot of chunks of rock it was empty.

There was a tumbledown building at the top of the incline – the rails still in place – but it contained only large cogged wheels and coils of cable that had rusted into a solid mass. Pools of oily water covered the floor.

One of the dogs, Samson, a magnificent sable and tan German Shepherd, was then sent off into the darkness. He was a specialist; trained to locate human beings, alive or dead, in difficult terrain and empty, dangerous buildings.

After just over ten minutes they heard him barking some-where below.

Carrick and the handler slithered to a ledge some fifty feet down a steep slope, going well to one side so as not to send stones dislodged by their feet crashing down on the animal. Their only handholds were small bushes whose roots somehow had a grip in the shaley soil.

'He's taught to find anything that has a human scent too,' said the handler apologetically after an awkward silence.

The only findings on the raid then had been a wastepaper basket and a very old sock.

Chapter 16

Matthew could not sleep. He and Katie shared the spare bedroom with its brand new bunk beds and Laura Ashley wallpaper. He knew about this because their grandmother had taken them into to Bath with her a few days previously to help her choose it. Katie had chosen it. It was all right, Matthew supposed, tossing restlessly and not quite sure why he was thinking about it right now. He knew what would have been his choice, a paper with lions and tigers they had seen in another shop. But as grown-ups sometimes used the room they might not like that. So little pink and yellow roses it had to be.

He wished that they could stay here for ever and had lain awake for hours on several nights since their father had died, going over the possibilities in his mind. Katie could go to the village school, it was only about two hundred yards down the road. He himself was due to go to a new school in September and it would have been the one where his father had taught. But everything had changed now, they could not go back to the flat. That was the only good thing that had come out of the whole terrible business: not having to go back to that flat.

Their mother had written to Grandma, she had received the letter that morning. Grandma would only say that it was a request for them to go and live in York with Shirley. She had asked them again if they wanted to. Matthew and Katie had said no. Matthew knew that the letter had said more than that, unkind things that had brought tears to Grandma's eyes. Tears of unhappiness and anger.

'Stop fidgeting,' Katie said from the bunk underneath.

'Can't you sleep either?'

'No, it's too hot. And I'm hungry. And thirsty.'

'You *can't* be hungry. Not after that big dinner.'

'Well, I am. What time is it?'

Matthew pushed himself up on to one elbow and consulted his pride and joy hanging from its strap from the rail round the bed, the watch with the luminous figures that his uncle and aunt had given him for Christmas. It was waterproof to a depth of a hundred feet and could be used as a stopwatch.

'It's only half-past four.'

There was a rustle as his sister got out of bed. 'I'm going to get a drink of milk.'

'You'll wake Grandma up.' Their grandfather had gone off to London for a conference on something to do with the Church.

'I'll be quiet,' Katie promised. There was a fairly long silence and then she said, 'It's a bit spooky in the dark.'

'I knew you were going to say that,' Matthew said triumphantly. 'I suppose you want to borrow my torch.' This was another treasure, a gift from his father, and on the night he had found Katie using it to read under the bedclothes for *hours* there had been battle royal.

'We're only talking about batteries here,' his father had scolded him.

'No, I don't want your silly old torch. I'll put the light on.'

'You can't. You'll wake Grandma. I can see I'll have to come with you.'

'I hate you when you use that grown-up sort of voice,' she hissed at him in the dark. She had been reading an old-fashioned detective story that afternoon, one of Grandma's. 'Pompous ass!'

They both flopped down on their beds again, stifling their giggles in the pillows.

Matthew's hearing was acute. 'There's someone downstairs,' he whispered.

Katie groped for her dressing gown. 'I'm going to see.'

'I don't suppose it's a burglar.'

She froze. 'I hadn't thought of that.'

'You stay here. I'll go down and look.'

'It might not be anyone. Or something falling over. Or Grandma.'

Matthew took the torch from under his pillow and switched it on. Katie's eyes were rather round, her face a little pale. He opened the door and went towards the top of the stairs. He knew she would follow him but did not prevent her. He had an idea she would be useful with a poker if the need arose. She wasn't like other girls who were often silly and chicken-hearted.

They reached the bottom of the stairs and tip-toed towards the kitchen. The light was on in there, a long shaft of illumination along the carpeted hall.

He had heard their approach, of course, but was not reading any particular danger in those light footfalls and excited breaths.

'Don't be alarmed,' said their uncle when two heads appeared round the edge of the door. 'I've just grazed my face a bit, that's all.'

He had a bowl on the table before him and had been about to add a little disinfectant to the warm water it contained. Cotton wool was somewhere else, he had forgotten where so would have to use his rather dirty handkerchief.

'That's for *drains*!' Katie cried, rushing forward to stay his hand. 'I know where the TCP is.'

'Won't it do?' Patrick Gillard asked, too stunned with weariness really to care. 'Surely if I just use a little drop—'

'You'll burn yourself or something,' Katie said, firmly removing it from his grasp. 'Grandma said. She said it ages ago when we were little. Never touch the stuff in bottles in the cupboard under the sink.' Her bright gaze lit on the offending opened door. 'That's where you got it from, wasn't it?' she concluded accusingly.

'I do believe I did,' Gillard said, amused in spite of his headlong tumble halfway down into a quarry and long cross-country walk back to Hinton Littlemoor. You don't hitch lifts from strangers when unfriendly people might be looking for you. He knew he probably shouldn't have come here either but with any luck the whole dreadful business would be over soon. He needed to get hold of Carrick ...

184

'There's dirt in it,' Matthew said. 'You might have to go to hospital.'

Katie had found the first aid box. 'It'll come out if it's washed.'

Matthew was quite happy to leave things like nursing to his sister. He sat down at the table. 'How did you do it?'

'Well, you wouldn't believe me if I told you I was captured by pirates and I'm not the sort of person to tell you silly things like that so . . .' He broke off, smiling tiredly.

No, he shouldn't have asked, Matthew realised. According to Dad, Uncle Patrick was a soldier and had a dangerous job.

'Don't just sit there,' Katie said crossly. 'Make Uncle a hot drink with lots of sugar in it.'

For some reason Elspeth slept like a log throughout these ministrations but ever afterwards wished she could have been a fly on the wall while Katie bathed the mud and stone splinters from the lacerations on her uncle's face, soaking him thoroughly in the process. In between these wet and stinging, but surprisingly effective, assaults he sipped at the only beverage with which Matthew – not wishing to stray into the dangerous world of teapots – felt he could cope just then, a sickly chocolate concoction flavoured with orange out of a packet, one of Elspeth's favourites.

It came to Patrick that he did not know these young people very well. When they were small, and in the days when Larry and Shirley were still together, the nature of his own job had meant that he had rarely seen them. During school holidays they had stayed with friends or come here, to Hinton Littlemoor. Shirley had been a barrier, she had made her dislike of her husband's brother and his wife plain. And now here was this dark-haired young man regarding him gravely and sadly, obviously aching to tell him something.

'Want to talk about it?' he asked when Katie had finished cleaning him up. He had undone his collar and a couple of buttons on his shirt so that the material would dry more quickly in the warmth of the room. The appalling chocolate gloop was quite reviving.

185

'Mum wants us back. Grandma didn't say but I think she's going to court about it.'

Strangely, Gillard felt his heart turn over. 'How do you feel about that?'

'We *can't* go and live with her. It would be awful. She wanted us to go with her when she left Dad but I said we'd run away from wherever she took us. She said that Dad couldn't look after us properly, but she was the one who was always drunk.'

Katie sat down. 'I don't think we could stay here. It would cost Grandma and Grandad too much money. It wouldn't be fair on them.'

Gillard gazed at this child who was the mirror image of his mother as a girl. 'Wouldn't you be happier with your mum?'

'No, never. She was horrible to Daddy. I've never been able to forget that. And she'd stop us coming here, I know she would.'

'That would be the worst thing,' Matthew added. 'We'd never be able to go to the holiday cottage in Wales again either.'

'She'd stop us seeing you,' Katie piped up. 'And Auntie Ingrid. *And* Justin and Victoria. I don't want to go to York – it's a horrible cold place hundreds of miles from here.'

Gillard was aware of her vast, overwhelming wishfulness. And being but a child, she put it into words.

'I want to come and live with *you*.'

Three of them had taken him away, one of them armed with a Smith and Wesson revolver. Gillard had offered no resistance: there were too many of them and he had not wanted to risk Carrick's being hurt. Otherwise he had not been too worried about his companion, it was he himself they were really interested in. So he would co-operate for a while. Later, when they were away from the others and had relaxed a little ... He had adopted a non-aggressive stance: dejected, defeatist. You didn't look them in the eye. This was particularly important as the three of them were very nervous and jumpy, one in particular; Gillard had been able to smell him sweating.

Walking in the virtual darkness – the man in front, the nervous one, had a torch but the batteries were running out – Gillard had thought back to Brecon when Lyndberne had used violent criminals as his henchmen, the homegrown variety, not anyone from abroad. It was different this time, obviously an in-house operation. For these young men had to be Ladd's own. Gillard had wondered what they had been told. The truth probably, but with a lot left out.

Why *had* Ladd put that medallion in the car? One answer was that he was going to kill the other brother too. A bullet in the back of the neck right now?

They had carried on following the track, the chug of the generator quite loud now. It had become rougher with deep puddles. Gillard had decided to risk it and experimented by 'tripping' over a stone. He had been grabbed before he could fall, spun round, and one of them had slapped his face hard.

'Relax,' he had said peaceably. 'I have a tin leg.'

Disbelief, not spoken, just tangible.

'It's true. I'll show you if you like.'

'Just keep walking.'

'It's quite amazing the damage a grenade can do in a confined space. It made a hell of a mess of the hut too.'

The light from the torch was down to a mere glimmer by now.

'*What* hut?' said the nervous one.

'God knows *exactly* where it was. Not a million miles from Port Stanley anyway.'

Someone else said, 'No, you won't fool us like that. Anyway, we were told not to believe a word you said.'

Gillard was shoved on his way, but not violently.

Another fifty yards farther on the torch had finally gone out and the nervous man stopped dead.

'Suppose I walk in front?' Gillard suggested. 'Then your shadow won't fall across the path and I shall be able to see where I'm going. You all follow me.'

Silence.

'I can smell your fear,' he had whispered. 'This operation is getting a bit out of hand, isn't it?'

'Go in front then. Go on, walk!' A shove from the rear.

'What has the boss told you about me?'

Another shove.

'That I wrecked your last mission?'

One of them had come closer. 'If you don't shut up and get a move on, I shall—'

'Arrest me? I'm quite surprised you haven't already. You *are* cops, aren't you?'

Without waiting for an answer he had carried on walking, leading his little entourage across a clearing. When the trees had closed in around them again he said, 'And then there was that business of someone falling out of a boat and getting drowned. Scotland, wasn't it?'

He was immediately yanked to a standstill, hands gripping the material of his combat jacket.

'Going to crow about it now, are you?'

'Not at all. But spare a thought for the brigadier who did it and who died in Bosnia.'

Gillard had been released abruptly and turned to face them.

'Who was the guy you were with just now?' a strangled voice asked.

'He's a Detective Chief Inspector.'

Gillard set off again, aware of the consternation behind him. Soon they had entered an open area with a single bright light set on a gantry. It was a wasteland of greasy-looking mud and large puddles with a film of oil on the surface of the water. To one side was a large hut by a tank set on a framework of old railway sleepers. Next to this was the portable generator, belching out diesel fumes.

A lot of whispering had been going on behind him.

'Are we here?' Gillard enquired, turning to wait for them.

In the light he had observed that they were dressed in clothing similar to his own with balaclava helmets over their heads. Cold-bloodedly, he had assessed his chances of over-powering all three of them. Marginal but well worth a try.

One of them had pointed an accusing finger. 'You closed us down last time.'

'MI5 closed you down last time.'

He had received the impression that all the air then left their lungs.

188

'Two children were killed,' Gillard resumed sweetly. 'The bods your unit were planning to arrest were *dangerous*. Only they weren't arrested. Your one-time Commander was planning to shoot them all after they decided his set-up was crap. And, of course, having real hoodlums on the staff was a trifle risky too. This is all news to you, I'm sure. So, listen. The Commander who couldn't swim was a law unto himself and should have been shot like a mad dog years ago. But there was nothing wrong with my brother's sanity and *he* got a bullet. Did you pick him up thinking he was me?'

'He was released,' the nervous man said. 'At least, that's—'

'What the boss told you? Yes, I'm sure he did.'

Slowly, Gillard walked towards them, arms carefully at his sides, smiling.

'He's dead?' he was asked.

'Very.'

By then the gun was pointing towards the ground, its owner having forgotten all about it in his concern. Gillard had given him no chance to remember, first ramming a fist into his stomach then chopping him across the neck as he folded over. The other two had their heads knocked together.

He could run quite fast when the adrenaline was flowing and had crossed the wide open space in a surprisingly short time. He had not wanted to face Ladd under these circumstances. That confrontation would take place only when he himself chose.

All very heroic, he thought now, unaware that his face was wearing an ironic lop-sided grin. The trouble was he had plunged into the thick vegetation that surrounded the clearing and ended up slipping, sliding, and finally rolling down a steep slope. His head had come into violent contact with something, probably a rock, and he had stunned himself. A while later, his right arm seemingly hanging in empty space, he realised that he was lying on a narrow ledge – they had frisked him and taken away both his knife and slim torch – so had no choice but to lie quite still under a

189

curtain of matted vegetation until daybreak. Either they had not looked for him or the dog was elsewhere.

First light had revealed that the ledge was indeed very small and that his only company was an old sock. He had slid the rest of the way down and started walking. He had not come straight to the rectory.

Now his eyes focussed on the children, both gazing at him a little anxiously.

'How about you, Matthew?' he asked after Katie's declaration.

'It would be wonderful,' the boy breathed.

Enslaved, but treading carefully, Gillard said, 'It's not as easy as you two just packing your bags and coming down to Devon. There's the legal side of everything too and—'

He broke off mainly because Katie had flung her arms around his neck. If he survived his reunion with Ladd – and it would have to be faced or no one in the family would ever be safe – steps would certainly be taken to adopt the pair of them.

Would Ingrid want four children?

Matthew said, 'Your friend – the policeman – he was here.'

'Was he all right?' Gillard asked, keeping his tone light.

'Not really. Grandma said we mustn't bother him as he'd been hurt somehow.'

'I once saw Daddy cry,' Katie said in a faraway voice.

Chapter 17

The following morning there was a heavy shower over Bath. For a while the roads were awash and Ingrams arrived late for work because chaos had ensued after traffic-light failures. The reception area at Manvers Street was little better as far as water underfoot was concerned; rain had been driven beneath the entrance doors. He picked his way gingerly across the slippery surface and went into the general office. It was a shambles: overflowing wastepaper baskets and ash-trays, discarded coats and other personal items strewn about, a legacy of the abortive raid the night before. At midnight Carrick had conducted a very short debriefing and then gone home. Ingrams could not say that he blamed him, the DCI still looked ill.

There was a movement of air alongside him and an arm reached round him and dropped a file into the In-tray on his desk.

'Sorry, sir, I didn't hear you coming,' Ingrams said.

Commander Christopher, although wearing his long dark blue raincoat, was wet, water still dripping from his hair. He also looked very angry.

'Did you forget your umbrella, sir?' Ingrams asked, really for something to say.

The Commander had not intended to converse, he was already halfway out of the door. He turned.

'I think it's in my car,' he grated. 'Which has been stolen.'

'From HQ?' Ingrams gasped.

'From HQ,' was the reply. 'You might have a look round here for the umbrella as I'm not really sure where I left it.

It's dark red. Made by Kepler. That cost an arm and a leg too.'

The door slammed.

Ingrams sat down very slowly. Bloody hell, he thought. Bloody, bloody hell.

Carrick had slept through his alarm clock going off but was woken by the phone ringing at seven-thirty.

'It's me,' said Meadows's voice. 'Sorry I didn't contact you yesterday. The quarry was a bit of a dead loss, I'm afraid. The only thing I found that could possibly be of interest was an old red van. It was in a shed on what appears to be a disused railway line. It had no number plates on it.'

'It might be extremely important. What time did you see it?'

'It was pretty early. Just before nine, I suppose. No sign of life at the place at all.'

'Is there anywhere where people could hide out?'

'Impossible to tell without making a better search. Other than walking along the old line for a short distance towards the viaduct I could only observe from a distance. I didn't want to blow anything you might have had planned. There are all kinds of old workings and spoil heaps so there must be tunnels. It's all very overgrown – you'd need to clear some of that away first. I thought I heard a vehicle at one stage and hid myself fairly smartly. I think it was in the quarry area itself – I'd finished looking round there by then.'

'No sign of the boss?'

'Hasn't he turned up yet? No, I'm afraid not. Don't worry, the man has nine lives.'

'I should imagine he's used them all up now though, wouldn't you?'

'There's a point,' said Meadows blithely. 'Is there anything else you'd like me to do?'

'Thank you, no. But I've valued your support.'

'Feel free to contact me at any time,' were Meadows's parting words.

It was obvious that times had changed, Carrick reflected, replacing the receiver. For Terry life had moved on and he had new responsibilities. He would honour old loyalties and lend a hand if needed but there was no wish to involve himself deeply again with that demanding, if charismatic, leader to whom he had once given all. On the surface his help had been modest. In real terms . . .

'In real terms he did some snooping and gave me a good kick up the backside,' Carrick said to himself a few minutes later on his his way out. He could only hope that it would pay off.

Adjoining the house was a brick building with a corrugated iron roof that in the past had probably had various uses – chicken house, potting shed, tool store – and which was destined for demolition to make way for a conservatory. Carrick went in the direction of the garage unaware that in so doing he had broken a strand of black cotton, one end of which was being monitored. In other words, tied to someone's finger. A slight sound from the building though did reach his ears and he halted.

Feeling the tug, Patrick Gillard had woken instantly. He got up from his uncomfortable bed of folded compost bags and an old travel rug. Swearing soundlessly as he knocked over a trowel that had been leaning against the wall, he looked out through the open doorway. There was no one to be seen.

'James?' he said.

Carrick had been about to swing himself through the single unglazed window, feet first. Upon hearing his name he walked round to the front.

'Sorry if I caused a red alert,' said Gillard apologetically.

'Have you forgotten how to ring a door bell?' was Carrick's belligerent response.

'It was hellish late when I got here last night and there were no lights. I didn't want to disturb you.'

Carrick looked about him. 'Where's your car?'

'I didn't bring it. It's too obvious and I don't use it when I'm working. I took a taxi from the rectory and walked the last half mile.'

They gazed at one another for a few seconds in silence. It was broken by Carrick yelling, 'I'm sick to death of that bastard forcing us to creep about like mice in our own backyards!' He then astounded Gillard by launching into a tirade in Gaelic.

'I couldn't agree more,' Gillard said when he had finished.

'Where the hell have you been anyway? We turned as much of that quarry as we could inside out to find you.'

'That was yesterday?' he asked politely.

'Of course.'

'I wasn't there yesterday. After I got away from them I slipped down a slope on to a ledge and knocked myself silly for a while. When it was daylight I went back to the farmhouse. That night I walked to Hinton Littlemoor.' He perceived that Carrick was coming off the boil. 'What happened to you?'

'I'll tell you one day,' he said roughly. 'Meanwhile I've work to do. Terry located the van in a shed on the old railway line. I don't suppose for a moment that it's still there but I intend to take a look.'

'Van?' Gillard enquired, thinking Daws must be really worried if Meadows had been called in.

'One of my Sergeants witnessed a building society raid yesterday and he's convinced they used the same van that the mob had who shot up the nick. A member of the public was killed. At a guess your friend Frodheim pulled the trigger. Only, as usual, I've no evidence. We turned over the farmhouse but all the birds had flown. I shall really get it in the neck when the Super comes in.' He took a deep breath and let it go slowly. 'I'm sorry, I'm being abominably rude and you've a nasty graze on your face. I'll give you the key and you can let yourself in and have a shower and some breakfast.'

'Was it a red van?'

Carrick nodded.

'So that's where they went.'

Carrick looked at him blankly.

'You were so busy composing your no-doubt filthy Gaelic that you didn't listen. I spent the whole of yesterday watching the farmhouse with Nathan and his spy camera. A red van arrived at around ten-thirty. There just seemed to be the one bloke, the driver. Frodheim got in it and it drove off. Afterwards there was some coming and going around

194

the house; the man and woman you and I saw behaving like headless chickens. There was obviously some kind of panic on and I guessed that Frodheim and one of the others had gone AWOL. Later in the morning Ladd arrived with two of his cronies. They went straight indoors and nothing happened for a while. Then Ladd and four others emerged and they all squeezed in the same car and headed off in the direction of the quarry. None of the men with him were the ones we watched from the tree. So they must have all been from his own squad.'

'They dismantled everything,' Carrick told him. 'The security fence, the gate, everything. By the time I arrived the house had been cleaned from top to bottom. No prints, no traces, no nothing.'

'I wonder what happened to the other two? But we do have photos of the arrivals and departures. The van didn't come back though – not while I was there.'

'Were you there when we raided the place?'

'No. I started walking about four. Nathan was relieved by someone who stayed all night. He should be back on duty now, though.'

'We've got to find where Frodheim is hiding out – before he kills anyone else.'

'Ladd's been caught on the hop. But I'm sure he knows where they are. I think it's time we asked him.'

'How did you get on with your assessment this time?' Carrick asked grittily. 'I understand from Elspeth that the instructors try to outwit you. Terry told me you always break the rules.'

'I only give my mother an edited version of what goes on,' Gillard said with the ghost of a smile. 'We use live ammo and I usually try to demolish the entire set-up they've created before I'm captured – people sometimes end up in hospital.'

Carrick surveyed him. 'Rest first.'

'No, you don't understand me at all. The more I live on my nerves, the more stretched and tired I am, the more bloody-minded and dangerous I become.'

And he laughed.

Carrick discovered that the quarry was on part of the estate now belonging to the local authority and had no difficulty in obtaining official permission to search it. He learned that the area was a favourite place for car thieves to strip and burn stolen vehicles. He went to work fully intending to keep right out of Superintendent Buller's way but there was no difficulty as he did not appear to have arrived yet. Thankfully, there was no sign of Commander Christopher either. Not for the first time Carrick endeavoured to ignore his relief at not having either to meet the man again or speak to him. The very mention of Christopher's name still made him tense to the extent of causing cramping spasms in every muscle of his body. He was trying not to equate this phenomenon with the state of being frozen with terror.

The report on the wastepaper basket he had found in the hut at the quarry was on his desk. Amazingly, it ran to several pages. The gist of it was that in the opinion of the person who had conducted the tests it had been where it was found for a very long time. The reason for this conclusion was that it was engrained with soil similar to samples taken from the locality. (Carrick could thank an enterprising Ingrams for this.) There were many fingerprints but all smeared and useless for identification purposes. There were also traces of explosive substances of a kind used in mining, suggesting that it had been used at one time for carrying around sticks of dynamite. The emblem of the Metropolitan Police was interesting but the item was obsolescent and had probably reached its destination through Government Surplus sales. The apple core, the author concluded waggishly, still contained pips and was the remains of a Cox's Orange Pippin.

This time Carrick took a mining engineer to the quarry with him. It was damp and overcast and after the heavy rain the entire area was a sea of mud. They soon found the van, or what was left of it. It had been burnt out and pushed into a shaft near to the shed where it had been kept. It could be seen, about fifty feet down, wedged across the aperture, together with old beams and a quantity of scrap iron, perhaps the remains of the cover to the shaft. Carrick, peering through a curtain of brambles at it, knew that it would not be difficult to retrieve the vehicle with lifting gear. He was equally aware that the wreck would tell them nothing – all evidence would have been destroyed.

Where were the men though; Frodheim and his cronies? The mining engineer had a map and had taken most of Carrick's team with him to hunt for hiding places on the understanding that he would not place himself in danger if and when the fugitives were found.

A park ranger had promised to be on hand and now drew up in his Land Rover.

'Sorry to have been delayed, Chief,' he said cheerfully, jumping out of the cab. 'What's this I hear about you searching for vehicles involved in serious crime? The name's John Lane, by the way.' Lane was burly with a ruddy complexion and a beard.

'We've found it,' Carrick informed, indicating the large hole in the ground. 'It had been kept, I'm told, in that shed over there. Presumably this area's outside your patrol zone?'

Lane took a look. 'Yes, but it won't be for much longer. A company was leasing it until recently to quarry out a small but quite valuable form of limestone used to make fireplaces. All the rage now apparently, real stone fireplaces. I should imagine everything of value has been taken from the place over the centuries. The Romans started it all, mining for lead and silver. All the really old workings are over yonder. You seem to have some people over there already.'

'I brought an expert. So what's going to happen to it all now then?'

'It's going to be incorporated into the park – all the dangerous holes filled in and the quarry face made safe to give folk climbing experience. It's sad in a way but I suppose the place is a hazard.' He chuckled. 'It's where I used to run wild as a kid and we never fell down any of the holes in the ground. Kids these days spend so much time watching the telly they lose all their natural savvy. They can't knock down the viaduct though, thank God. It's listed. The line used to be a branch off the Somerset and Dorset and con-

197

nected Shepton Mallet to the outskirts of Bristol, I forget exactly where. It had closed long before old Beeching got his hands on our country railways. It never made any money.'

'Is there anywhere along the track bed where people could hide?'

'There are only a couple of plate-layers' huts but they're very small and the doors were off the last time I saw them. There's the remains of an engine house at the Shepton Mallet end – I certainly wouldn't hide in it and if anyone has they'd have had a good soaking this morning. The only other man-made construction is another viaduct where the line used to cross the River Wellow near the village of Fifely. I suppose it's conceivable that someone could have a hideaway down below by the river. It's a lonely sort of spot.'

'Could you take me there?'

'Jump in.'

'I'll need a few of the troops – just in case.'

A minute or so later Carrick had mustered the dog handler with Samson and two members of the TSG. Lane put the vehicle into four-wheel drive and set off down the incline, possibly the last thing that his passengers were expecting. They bumped down gently over the half-rotten sleepers and at the bottom turned right, in the opposite direction from the nearest viaduct.

The village of Fifely was only two miles away and they reached it very quickly. It sat tight on a narrow valley floor, the river to the left of it. From above the effect was not at all like a picture postcard; merely a few dingy cottages crammed into a sunless depression in the ground, the gloominess heightened by the tall evergreen oaks that grew on the slopes around it.

At one end of the village street was a small creamery – or 'milk works' as Lane smilingly put it – adding that it was threatened with closure. At the other the houses straggled towards marshy fields and there was a filling station with faded plastic bunting.

'What's that building there?' Carrick asked, pointing to what at one time might have been a church but was now boarded up.

'That's the old chapel,' Lane replied, slowing to a halt.

198

'Someone bought it after it closed and started to knock it about without planning permission. The local authority came down on him like a ton of bricks – they're very hot on housing development up here on Mendip – and the last I heard it was stalemate and he'd run out of money.'

'I think I'd like to take a look at it.'

'No problem. Just along here's the old station, Fifely Halt. We can get down to the road from there.'

Steep winding steps led down from the crumbling platform. Carrick paused halfway down, assessing the lie of the land, his mind already working on the possibility of having to cordon off the area, of getting in extra personnel, of surrounding the building. He had asked Lane to move the Land Rover out of sight of the village and to stay in it.

From below the viaduct loomed over all, increasing the forbidding aspect of the place. But for the occasional vehicle it was very quiet: lunchtime.

The chapel had the austere look of one in a Welsh mining town. Only some of the windows had been boarded up, those that fronted the road. The others were protected by metal grilles. A plaque on the wall by the main entrance proclaimed:

THIS HOUSE OF GOD IS DEDICATED TO THE
MEMORY OF
EZEKIEL HENRY MANNERING,
MISSIONARY TO THE POOR AND DESTITUTE OF
BRISTOL
1833–1875, SON OF THIS PARISH AND WHO
DEPARTED
THIS LIFE APRIL 22nd 1899
*BLESSED ARE THE MEEK: FOR THEY SHALL
INHERIT THE EARTH*

Some of the fine stone wall surrounding the chapel yard had been knocked down, seemingly for no other reason than to allow the entry of heavy vehicles. A pile of secondhand bricks had been dumped in one corner, close to it another of sand with grass growing in it. The side of the building had been defaced with graffiti.

199

The double doors on the front looked like those on a fortress and appeared not to have been opened for years, tall weeds growing in front of them. Carrick led the way round the back along a narrow path where they had to go in single file. Upon turning the corner of the building he came immediately to a set of steps leading down to a basement door, probably the entrance to a boiler house. Rubbish and more weeds filled the area at the bottom. The path carried on for another few yards and then led up to a rear door next to an outside lavatory, the door of which was wide open. It was full of rubble.

This part of the chapel was actually an extension with a flat roof and had the kind of exterior plumbing to suggest that it had been a kitchen or flower arranging area. The exterior door was not so substantial as those at the front but neither was it flimsy, fitted with a new-looking padlock. The securing fittings appeared to be new too.

Samson was uttering little whines of excitement and his handler placed a hand on his muzzle to silence him. In response to Carrick's silent query – raised eyebrows – the man nodded. Also in silence Carrick gestured the TSG members forward, signing to them what he wanted and that everyone else was to stand well out of the way.

The shots cut into the quietness, a flock of pigeons exploding skywards from their roosting places on the roof and gutters. Every dog in the village went into a frenzy of barking but was drowned out by Samson when he was unleashed and ran in.

The room was brighter and lighter inside than the exterior would lead one to expect but very plain, the walls whitewashed, the floor of dirty bare boards. Carrick walked through it, noticing that there was a sink under the window, a few shelves, and nothing else. Another door led into a passage with a very small room off to the left. That held only a stack of kneelers full of the moth, kapok spilling out on to the floor. A larger door straight ahead of him was open. It gave access to the chapel itself from which Samson was still barking, the sound echoing in the emptiness.

'Police!' Carrick shouted as the TSG men overtook him, storming through the door.

200

All Carrick noticed for a moment was the disarray, the *destruction*. The pews had been stacked in teetering rows, one on top of the other on the left-hand side of the main aisle. Leaning against them were sheets of chipboard, stained with damp where the roof had leaked on them. The carved rood screen had been partly dismantled and sawn into rough lengths for firewood, tossed into piles by the altar. This the erstwhile DIY enthusiast had used to stack old kitchen units on and there was a battered kettle and three chipped mugs.

Frodheim and the three others were lying together in a heap as though thrown down with the same abandon as the firewood, each killed with a single shot to the head.

'Blessed are the meek,' muttered one of the TSG men.

Carrick looked at him sharply but his expression was only of compassion.

Chapter 18

The bodies were still warm.

'Sir!' said the dog handler urgently.

Carrick went over to where man and dog were standing near a wall. There was no need for explanation: the blood-stains on the plaster and floor were evident. They were not fresh and Carrick had a vivid mental picture of another shooting, a man falling backwards and sliding down the wall.

This was probably where Lawrence Gillard had died.

Grimly, he issued orders that nothing was to be touched and that the two TSG men were to remain guarding the place while he put into operation a murder inquiry. He used his mobile phone to initiate this and then had himself driven back to the quarry. He took the police dog and his handler back with him and stood them down, ruffling the dog's ears before it was led away.

'Oh, Samson was probably right about that ledge,' he called after them.

Carrick had asked Ingrams to come out to the quarry as soon as he had finished what he was doing and the Detective Sergeant arrived to find himself put temporarily in charge. SOCO were directed straight to the chapel and Carrick wound down the search at the quarry area and went back to Manvers Street.

Hobbs was in the main corridor going in the direction of Carrick's office, a large buff envelope in his hand. 'From Forensic for you,' he said, holding it out.

Carrick took it and said, 'I'd like you to get yourself out to the village of Fifely and take over from Ingrams on a murder

202

enquiry. Four men have been found shot dead and I want all their descriptions and fingerprints sent to Interpol and checked with the International Register of Terrorists. Priority is to be given to finding the bullets that killed them and another person unknown who appears to have been shot at an earlier date where the wall and floor are stained with blood. Samples must be taken from those stains and sent to the lab for DNA testing and comparison with those taken from Lawrence Gillard. I want those results urgently. Have you got that?'

'Of course.' Hobbs hesitated and then said, 'Commander Christopher's car was stolen from HQ yesterday afternoon.'

Carrick stared at him.

'Not only that, it was driven back here and left in the car park at the side of the Path lab – that must have been very early this morning as it hadn't been there the night before – with the keys in it and a note requesting that it be thoroughly examined with regard to the Gillard case. The technicians, understandably, weren't sure what to do with it, especially when the registration was checked. Someone rang here and the only one in appears to have been Ingrams. For some reason known only to him, he gave the go-ahead. What the hell am I going to tell Christopher – that Ingrams has gone off his head?'

Carrick slit open the envelope, actually feeling a little light-headed. He scanned the four neatly typed pages of information and then sat down at his desk. Hobbs was still waiting for some kind of reaction from him.

'Tell the Commander nothing,' he murmured. 'If he asks you, refer him to me. Otherwise, keep quiet.'

Hobbs exploded. 'I have at least been trying to demonstrate that we have a grip on the job in hand.'

Carrick was still trying to assimilate the complex details contained in the report. 'So you've been co-operating fully with any little tasks he's given you to do, have you, Crispin?'

'That's what I'm for, damn you!'

Carrick rose to his feet. 'No, you're not. You're here to work for me, and if you're going to be blinded by gold braid every time someone like him walks in, and give away information behind my back, then as far as I'm concerned you'd be better employed digging holes in the road. Get out to Fifely and out of my sight.'

Carrick did not even notice the man go, having returned to the report. To sum up, the interior of the boot had been recently cleaned, there was still a smell of carpet shampoo and in places the carpet pile remained damp. Whoever had cleaned it had forgotten to wipe out the door seals and there was more than a slight trace of blood in the rubber near the boot lock. Samples had been taken and DNA-tested. There was no doubt that they matched those of the recent murder victim. There were also two human hairs that had been found on the upper surface of the boot lining and those too were identical to a sample taken from Lawrence Gillard's body. The carpet and rubber mat in the driving position also appeared to have been cleaned recently but samples of soil were taken from the rubber covers on the pedals and were found to be of an alluvial type found on river banks and lake shores. The same kind of soil was in samples taken from the shore at Chew Valley Lake but as the area was so extensive it was impossible to ascertain that both had come from exactly the same place.

'I've got him,' Carrick whispered.

He locked the report in a drawer of his desk, pocketing the key, and went into the general office. There was no one about, nearly everyone was dealing with the murder inquiry. All calls should have been intercepted by the control room but as he passed through the phone on Ingrams's desk rang. Carrick picked it up.

A woman asked to speak to the Detective Sergeant.

'I'm afraid Sergeant Ingrams isn't here right now. This is James Carrick, the DCI. Can I help you?'

'Oh, I hope I'm not being a nuisance, Chief Inspector,' said the lady in flustered fashion. 'This is Miss Sugden from Jolly's. Sergeant Ingrams asked me to let him know if and when a gentlemen called in for a medallion we ordered to replace the one he'd lost from his Kepler umbrella. He's just called in for it. It was a coincidence really as it had arrived this morning in the post and he popped in on the off-chance.'

'What did he look like?'

'Oh, a *very* nice gentleman. Tall and good-looking with fair hair.'

'Do you think you could pick him out if there was an identity parade?'

'Goodness! Oh, dear. Yes, I suppose so . . .'

'I'd like you to call into the police station here and make a short statement. It won't take long and I'll make sure that someone's here so you don't have to wait. It's extremely important.'

Miss Sugden assured him that she would.

The Superintendent's office door was ajar, no one within. He wasn't in the habit of visiting the canteen but Carrick checked anyway and drew another blank. Fervently hoping that there wouldn't be another major incident and reflecting that here he was with the hottest case in years and no one to report it to, he returned to his own room and rang HQ. After being shunted from one extension to another he ran to earth an Inspector who had been liaising with the visitors from the Met the previous day.

'They've gone on to Plymouth, sir.'

'I'm actually looking for the members of the Anti-terrorist Branch.'

'Commander Keeler?'

'No, Christopher.'

'Ah, well, Keeler's from what I gather is an above-ground unit – he tells people what he does. Christopher heads an undercover squad and keeps his head well down below the parapet. All I can tell you is that his car was stolen yesterday and he's gone right off the map.'

Someone else spoke in the background.

'Ah,' said the inspector. 'I've just been told that the two men who were here with Christopher have gone home – back to London.'

Carrick thanked him and rang off.

In the chapel there had been the remains of refreshments that had obviously been consumed by the murder victims; sandwich wrappings and a large Thermos flask that had contained coffee. If the coffee had been drugged it would have been comparatively easy for one man to shoot four others. Carrick simply could not believe that the personnel of Christopher's unit had become involved with the darker side of the operation. This conclusion was partly confirmed by what Gillard had told him of his somewhat stilted conversation with the men from whom he had escaped.

What would have been the outcome if he hadn't got away?

Had Christopher one more loose end to tie before he too returned to the shadowy life he led in London?

Carrick hurried to his car. He was not to know that Hobbs, who had indeed been carefully cultivated by the Commander and blinded by his rank, had not only told him about Thomas Lee but passed on the DCI's home address.

Patrick Gillard had decided to stay put for a few hours. He had accepted Carrick's offer of hospitality and showered, shaved, and renewed his acquaintance with the shirt that Carrick had borrowed from him, freshly washed and ironed in the airing cupboard. When dressed he consumed two slices of dry toast and a pint of strong, sweet black coffee. When the phone rang he answered it, just giving the number, but assumed his host's voice – very slightly deeper than his own with a mere trace of a Scottish accent. Fortunately it was Carrick himself.

'There have been developments,' he reported. 'I'll come back so we can discuss them – I've no idea if my phone's being tapped.'

Gillard hummed a little tune when the line went dead and replaced the receiver. Developments. That could mean several things. To be forewarned was to be prepared though and he rearranged the chairs in the living room slightly and moved one small ornament. Then he sat in a chair facing the door but well out of view of the window.

Listening.

The sound, when it came an indefinable while later, was very slight, the mere scrape of the sole of a shoe on the concrete path outside. Gillard had locked the back door but the kitchen window was slightly open. Upstairs, the landing and bathroom windows were open but he had closed a couple of others. His one-time pupil would decide on a silent entry, he was guessing, rather than burst through the front door. He would want to talk first.

There was a long silence. Gillard, holding his breath for a moment to listen again, could envisage the climb up the old wisteria that would give his visitor access to the landing window, an entry that was simplicity itself to a fit person. All he would then have to do was descend the stairs, which because of the interior alterations that the Carricks were having done, were still uncarpeted.

Again, a slight sound, a creak as wood bore weight.

'I'm in the living room,' Gillard called. 'The second door on the right.'

Slowly, the door opened and was given a little push so that it travelled back as far as it would go.

'You're taking a big risk,' said the man framed in the doorway. 'I might just shoot you right now.'

'Is your real name Christopher Ladd?' Gillard asked. 'Or is your surname Christopher?'

'You can call me what you like. As far as you're concerned it's immaterial now.'

'I'm unarmed,' Gillard said.

Ladd came farther into the room, showing no sign of lowering his silenced handgun. 'After all you taught us you expect me to believe that? While you're still in possession of your hands, feet and teeth you're lethal. Just sit quite still or else I'll forgo the chat.' He smiled broadly. 'Hobbs said you might be shacked up with Carrick. Who doesn't seem to have got very far with finding your brother's killer, incidentally.' He sat down.

'I don't suppose he wrote everything down, do you?'

Ladd shrugged. He did not appear to be particularly interested.

'So here you are,' Gillard said lightly. 'The ex-pupil coming back to show teacher how well you've done in the world. Well, I suppose congratulations are in order. You've reached Commander in the police force, heading an undercover anti-terrorist unit.'

Ladd nodded. His face was flushed, eyes over-bright. 'I'm at about the same age as you were when you were our tutor. But you were only major in those days. I think I've done rather better. God, my army stint seems like another lifetime!' He laughed outright and then the amusement fell from his face like the dropping of a mask.

'It seems I taught you too well,' Gillard observed.

'Too right, *Paddy*. I made Carrick really shout – just the way you instructed us. By the time I'd finished with him he was ready to lick my arse. He won't worry me from now on, I assure you.' He observed that Gillard had absorbed this information and then said, 'Your brother didn't like it either.'

'Larry?' Gillard said, displaying a small frown.

'The silly bastard refused to tell me where you were. I asked him several times but he told me to go to hell. If those fools hadn't brought in the wrong man—'

'Yes, it's a real loss of face when your men get an order wrong. It's also bad for morale when they witness you torturing a perfectly innocent member of the public.'

'What do you take me for? I sent them away, saying I wanted to talk to him in private.'

'And afterwards told them that you'd released him, no doubt.' From Gillard's tone it could have been assumed that they were discussing the ethics of fly-fishing.

'I could have hardly let him go,' Ladd said with another shrug. 'None of this would have happened if you hadn't interfered. You interfered last time too. MI5 has got to learn to keep its nose out of police matters.'

'And then there's ambition.'

'Of course I'm ambitious. Getting rid of filth like Frodheim ought to be rewarded.'

'And people who just happen to get in the way of such folk while they're let loose here?'

'You always get the odd hitch in every operation – you of all people should know that.'

'Frodheim robbed a building society and shot a man dead. You call that a hitch?'

'I was under the impression you arranged to have the previous head of my department drowned. Perhaps that makes us quits.'

Gillard shook his head. 'No, it doesn't. Two children were killed last time – or didn't you know about that?'

'They got in the way of a car, that's all. You can't plan for accidents.'

'You're not going to get away with that one either. The man driving the car was a well-known European maniac who knocked them down for no better reason than that they were walking on the same side of the road that he wanted to drive. You can move the goal posts all you like but it doesn't alter the rules of the game.'

Ladd stood up. 'You're out of touch.'

Gillard smiled upon him benignly. 'Sonny, the PM has issued orders that you and your God-forsaken unit are to be closed down.'

Ladd looked appalled. 'He can't! The Home Secretary told me that—'

'Put away the gun. You don't need it.'

'I shall dispose of it when I've disposed of you.'

'I'm offended. After all I've taught you, I get a bullet?'

Icily, the other said, 'What is it you want then? A cut throat? Shall I break your neck the way you showed me? What then? All the choices are out of your own stable.'

'You've overlooked something.'

'Which is?'

'Even though you have a gun in your hand, ever since you came into this room you've been on the defensive. That is the real difference between you and me. If you laid the gun aside, despite the fact that you're younger, bigger and probably fitter and that I lost the lower part of my right leg during the Falklands War, I could get the better of you in under a minute.'

Ladd thought back to the days several years before that war when he and others had sat in a classroom and listened to this man. Gillard was a bit of a chameleon, they had all known that; a ramrod-straight officer with the pointer in his hand one minute, the next on exercise goading them through obstacle courses with a mixture of mind-blowing obscenities and encouragement. He was also quite likely to look personally for lost sheep on the moors during survival training, suddenly a father-figure accompanying them to the finish and somehow turning their failure into triumph over exhaustion.

'Show me,' Ladd said.

Gillard rolled up the right leg of his trousers for a few inches to reveal stainless steel.

'I can't let that conceited remark go unanswered,' Ladd said. He gazed around the room and then walked over to an antique dresser and put the gun in one of the drawers.

Gillard stood up. 'I suppose I'm a bit like an elephant insofar as I never forget. I think I could still write reports on all the young men who went through my hands in my tutoring days. I remember you clearly. You were conceited, a bully, a show-off, and like quite a few men with those characteristics, shone at sport. When it came to the qualities that make a good soldier though you were surprisingly lacking. You never thought things through and were prone to acting rashly. Despite having a strong character you were easily open to suggestion, even when the proposals were not, in hindsight, in your own best interests. Being a bloke who tends not to bother with long words at such times, I just said that you were stupid. You were stupid and conceited, when you left the medallion in my car. You've just laid aside your gun, laddy. *Now* what are you going to do?'

Ladd winced, for the last two sentences Gillard had uttered were like whip cracks. He had forgotten how demoralising that voice could be. Other memories flooded back; of Gillard cracking walnuts with his fingers at a Christmas party, of him subduing a sixteen-stone private who had boxed for his unit and who got drunk and ran amok one night after hearing that his wife had left him for another man . . .

But, above all, nothing had changed. The man who faced him, wary but patiently waiting for him to act, to *do something*, was the same one who had heard out their sometimes inarticulate efforts to express themselves and helped them turn their often awkward bodies into the kind of graceful killing machine they knew him to be.

Ladd's nerve broke and he made a lunge for the dresser. Something small and heavy cracked into the knuckles of his outstretched hand and he halted, his whole hand white hot with agony. His yell when grabbed from behind was one of pure fright.

Gripping the front of his sweater Gillard drew him close. 'I taught you everything you know,' he said through taut lips. 'But I never teach people all *I* know – perhaps it's just as well for your sake that I didn't have to draw on skills I use only with great reluctance. I'm beginning to wish that I had. Something tells me that for all your supposed ideals this all boils down to one thing – money.'

A car that Gillard recognised drew into the drive.

A kind of madness came over him then and he manhandled Ladd into the hall, opened the front door and kicked him outside. Ladd looked for a moment as though he might try to steal the car of the man just getting out of it but did not, running off up the lane instead.

'Your man,' Gillard said, surprised when the words caught in his throat. 'He's confessed to killing Larry.' He watched with professional appraisal as Carrick sped off but was not unduly concerned. Carrick had to sort this one out for himself.

When he went back into the house he picked up and replaced the ornament with which he had struck Ladd, a small brass tortoise.

Carrick was not a stayer as far as running was concerned, wingers did not have to be. You went the length of the pitch like all Hell was after you and then tended to run out of steam. Until the next time. His man, he saw with joy, was no sprinter and the gap between them was closing uncannily quickly. Deliberately pushing to the back of his mind any personal complications that the chase might cause he just ran. They were close now. Don't slow down, he told himself. Get it right. Get balanced. Bring the bastard down.

This was achieved almost under the wheels of an approaching car, by a crashing tackle on to the tarmac. The driver of the vehicle decided not to get involved and swerved around them. Then they had the road to themselves.

Ladd twisted under Carrick and his hands came up to gouge and tear. Carrick hit him hard, twice, and then leaped out of the way as the heavier man prepared to throw him off. Swaying a little, Ladd got to his feet.

211

'You're under arrest,' Carrick said. 'For Lawrence Gillard's murder.'

'I'm warning you,' Ladd whispered, closing in. 'Touch me and you're finished. Just stand aside and let me get away and you'll hear no more from me.'

'It was you in Larry's flat, wasn't it?' Carrick countered. 'You're wearing the same aftershave now as you were on that occasion. I think you went there to look for the *other* brother. The one who you hadn't recently murdered.'

'So does that mean you have a good sense of smell or are a good detective?' Ladd sneered as he lunged forward.

Carrick's overstrung nerves caused him to shy like a horse, thus dodging whatever Ladd had been about to do to him. Then sheer self-preservation took over and he followed this with an uppercut with all his weight behind it.

'So he failed,' Gillard commented when Carrick returned carrying his prisoner. 'And when his conceit over-ruled any commensense he might possess and he ordered a replacement medallion for his umbrella not ten minutes walk from the nick . . .' He broke off with an expressive shrug.

'We have Bob Ingrams to thank for finding that out,' Carrick said.

212

Chapter 19

On the evening of the day that the political storm surrounding the resignation of the Home Secretary broke, Superintendent Buller took Carrick and Gillard out to dinner in the restaurant of his golf club. Carrick felt that this gesture was more to do with escaping from the throngs of journalists and television news teams hanging around outside the nick and following anyone in authority who emerged – even though a news conference had been held at ten-thirty that morning – than any particular generosity. For Buller wanted all the background information in order to be able to write his own report.

Gillard obliged with this, giving him an account, slightly edited, of what had occurred at Brecon a couple of years previously. Buller made notes. He then asked about Ladd, and Gillard told him as much as was relevant. The Superintendent then informed them that during interrogation by the Metropolitan Police's Complaints Department the Commander had spoken of a long-standing friendship with the previous head of his unit. They had decided to make money out of the proposed operation to ensnare wanted criminals by setting up a school for terrorists. The idea had actually been the brain-child of an Assistant Commissioner close to the Home Secretary. He also had resigned although quite innocent of planning any personal gain. It had been Ladd's own proposal to take 'fees' from those they were hoping to arrest. It had soon become apparent, talking to Ladd, that even at the scheme's inception he had planned that 'an accident' would befall his clients rather than arrest for fear of any mention being made of the money that had been handed over.

'You're not entirely blameless,' Buller finished by saying, addressing Gillard. 'If there was any firm evidence – and I have to admit that there seems to be none whatsoever – proceedings would be taken against you in connection with the death of a senior policeman.' He held up a finger in warning fashion. 'If I were you I'd say nothing and be thankful.'

Carrick regarded his superior with new respect.

Over coffee Buller said, 'It was a classic case of a crazy idea breeding its own kind of madness. Ladd insists that he only asked Frodheim to take out Lee but we all know that the man had no compunction about spraying the entire police car with bullets before making his getaway. What stupidity on Ladd's part! Did he think he could trust a terrorist to do as requested?'

'The Conways were more deeply involved than they'd made out when I first questioned them,' Carrick said to Gillard. 'Obviously, they had not been told the real identities of the men under their roof and Ladd could hardly tell them his real profession without risking security. Jeff Conway has previous convictions for petty crime, his wife's an unproven accessory. The rent on the farmhouse was being paid for them, plus all expenses, on the understanding that they obeyed orders and asked no awkward questions. I'm sure they thought they were working for crooks. In law, they've committed no offence as Ladd had official backing for what he was doing. You can't arrest someone for spring-cleaning their house. But it goes without saying that they knew something odd was going on – they must have known there were weapons in the house, for instance.'

'Has the building society money been recovered?' Gillard enquired.

'Not yet,' Buller replied. 'But it will be, I'm convinced of that. Ladd is still being questioned.'

Winking at Carrick Gillard said, 'Only James has to buy his wife a new car.'

Constable Strong had had a bad day. For a start the wrong

nurse had taken him into the grounds of the hospital in his wheelchair for fresh air, the married horse-faced one and not the pretty Malaysian girl who was so gentle when she changed the dressings on his leg, and smiled all the time. Then the consultant had looked in to give him news that had not cheered him up at all. Worse than this was not being regarded as well enough to attend Pete's funeral that morning. His parents had, bearing a wreath from all the family. They had then caught the train back home to York as his father could take no more time off.

'We'll get you in a hospital nearer home when you're better,' his mother had assured him just before they left. 'No point rushing things. The doctor here is one of the best in Britain for your kind of injuries.'

'He told you so himself, I suppose,' Strong had said sourly.

'Now then, lad,' his father had remonstrated. 'As a matter of fact it was the staff nurse.'

Another cause of misery then, that memory of behaving badly towards his parents.

Sitting in his wheelchair by the window in the patients' lounge, Strong had sunk into this retrospective gloom when he observed that he had two visitors. There was no choice now but to struggle to appear cheerful. He did not know it but he was wasting his time; both Carrick and Gillard were keen-sighted enough to have observed his wretchedness from a distance.

'Didn't think you'd want grapes,' Carrick said, handing over a four-pack of Tetley's beer after looking round furtively. 'Don't tell a soul.'

Strong thanked him warmly, stowing the gift out of sight beneath the blanket across his knees.

Their only company was an old lady due to go into a nursing home the following day who nodded and mumbled to herself in a corner. Gillard raised an eyebrow at Carrick and in a trice Strong found himself whisked outside into a small, enclosed rose garden.

'That's better,' Gillard said, stretching himself full-length on a seat and closing his eyes against the bright sunshine. 'James, I think *you* ought to bring Kevin up to date with events. I'll stop you if I think you have a point wrong.' He chuckled and gave every appearance of going to sleep.

'What I'd like to know,' Carrick said when he had given Strong a resumé, 'is who stole the Commander's car and delivered it to the Path lab?'

Gillard sat up and said, 'Well, it wasn't me and I can say that with my hand on my heart. I was at the farmhouse on Mendip for most of that day.'

'Terry?'

'No. I'm aware that you discussed with him the prime need to find the vehicle that was used to transport Larry's body – assuming that your guesses were correct – as I spoke to him at length by phone last night. He assured me that although the idea had crossed his mind he didn't do it. Questions will no doubt be asked in court but we might never know who it was. If I have to give evidence it will please me to be able to say that MI5 had absolutely nothing to do with it.'

'Who then? One of the Commander's men?'

'Who else? Someone who suspected that all wasn't as it should be.' He turned to Strong. 'So how's the leg?'

'I saw the consultant earlier,' he told them. 'He's going to operate again in a couple of days time to adjust one of the pins. It's not holding properly.'

'Better now than later when everything's healed,' Gillard told him. 'It means that your recovery will be in one go, so to speak, and you probably won't have to keep going back for more treatment. Believe me, I speak from experience. Do you play squash?'

'I used to, sir.'

'You'll beat me in twelve months' time.'

Strong shook his head emphatically. 'That's impossible.'

'I'll give you a thousand quid if you beat me at squash in twelve months' time.'

'That was very generous of you,' Carrick said when they were driving away.

'Too right,' Gillard said with a grimace. 'I'd better go and have some lessons – I should hate it if he got away with a walkover.'

'You've never played?' Carrick asked incredulously.

'No. But I'll give him a run for his money. The important thing is that, right now, he needs something to aim for.'

'It's a fine target.'

The children had been out on Dartmoor all afternoon and were tired, Justin especially. Bathed, he just about kept awake long enough to eat his tea and was then put to bed. Victoria, who had also had plenty of fresh air and excitement that day, had been asleep for an hour. Their nanny, Carrie, had been given the evening off and had gone into Plymouth with her boyfriend.

'Well?' Patrick Gillard said when his wife Ingrid came into the room and flopped down on the sofa beside him.

Katie had earlier helped her aunt clear away the younger children's tea things and was now lying on the floor, drawing, surrounded by felt-tipped pens in lurid colours. A fire-breathing dragon was taking shape on a large sheet of paper. Her brother had curled his long legs into an arm chair and was reading. Both of them looked up.

'Well, what?' Ingrid asked. She was slim, her black hair cut into a smart New York bob, and she was suffering slightly from jet-lag. It was hard to decide whether a five-mile walk directly after being collected from the airport, not to mention her husband's proposal, had improved the situation or not.

'If you want to talk about *us*, we'll . . .' Matthew began shyly.

His uncle smiled at him. 'No, I think Ingrid and I did all the discussing that's necessary this afternoon while you were exploring. I know it's early days but I want you both to realise that *we're* on trial so far as you're concerned. You might not like the situation of being left with Carrie when your aunt and I aren't here. Ingrid writes and won't want to be disturbed when she's working. I spend a lot of time in London. I'm not sure that we're the sort of parents you really need.'

Carefully colouring in the crimson flames gushing from the dragon's mouth that she had already outlined, Katie said, 'Grandma said you weren't like Daddy and we mustn't expect everything to be the same.'

'What else did Grandma say?' he asked, all innocence.

'She said we must work hard at school and learn to be a lot tidier as you were a soldier and everything had to be just so. But I said it would be all right as you didn't know about not putting drain stuff on your face so we could help each other like that.'

'Drain stuff?' Ingrid mouthed at him in puzzlement.

Katie had not finished. 'And next time you fall over and hurt yourself I shall put a towel round you so the water doesn't go through your shirt,' she said with a sunny smile.

Ingrid looked none the wiser.